Praise for
OUR HOMESICK SONGS
by Emma Hooper

"Lyrical . . . The town is filled with magic, and so is Hooper's writing. . . . *Our Homesick Songs* is a eulogy not just to a town but a lifestyle—one built on waves, and winds, and fish, and folklore."

—*THE NEW YORK TIMES BOOK REVIEW*

"Heartbreakingly beautiful."

—*NPR*

"[A] haunting fable about the transformative power of hope."

—*BOOKLIST* (starred review)

"With stark prose, Hooper captures the desperation and difficulty of life on the edge of civilization while maintaining the foundation of tenderness as her characters take care of one another in the face of near-insurmountable struggle. Heartbreaking and empathetic, Hooper's fine novel is a haunting evocation of changing times and the power of place."

—*PUBLISHERS WEEKLY*

"This delicate elegy for a dying way of life crescendos into a love song binding family members across the waters."

—*KIRKUS REVIEWS*

"Hooper has graced us readers once again with another beautifully moving story. . . . A lyrical, charming, and mystical story of a family on the edge of extinction, and the different way each of them fights to keep hope, memory, and love alive."

—*CHECK IT OUT, KWIT*

ALSO BY EMMA HOOPER

Etta and Otto and Russell and James

OUR
HOMESICK
SONGS

A Novel

Emma Hooper

Simon & Schuster Paperbacks

New York   London   Toronto   Sydney   New Delhi

Simon & Schuster Paperbacks
An Imprint of Simon & Schuster, Inc.
1230 Avenue of the Americas
New York, NY 10020

First Simon & Schuster trade paperback edition August 2019

SIMON & SCHUSTER PAPERBACKS and colophon are
registered trademarks of Simon & Schuster, Inc.

For information about special discounts for bulk purchases, please contact
Simon & Schuster Special Sales at 1-866-506-1949 or business@simonandschuster.com.

The Simon & Schuster Speakers Bureau can bring authors to your live event.
For more information or to book an event contact the Simon & Schuster Speakers Bureau
at 1-866-248-3049 or visit our website at www.simonspeakers.com.

Interior design by Ruth Lee-Mui

Manufactured in the United States of America

3   5   7   9   10   8   6   4   2

The Library of Congress has cataloged the hardcover edition as follows:
Names: Hooper, Emma, author.
Title: Our homesick songs : a novel / Emma Hooper.
Description: First Simon & Schuster hardcover edition. |
New York : Simon & Schuster, 2018.
Identifiers: LCCN 2017040900| ISBN 9781501124488 (hardcover) |
ISBN 9781501124501 (trade pbk.) | ISBN 9781501124525 (ebook)
Classification: LCC PR9199.4.H6495 O97 2018 | DDC 813/.6—dc23 LC record
available at https://lccn.loc.gov/2017040900

ISBN 978-1-5011-2448-8
ISBN 978-1-5011-2450-1 (pbk)
ISBN 978-1-5011-2452-5 (ebook)

For Aubrey, hope.

(1993)

There was a mermaid, said Finn.

Yes, said Cora. She pulled an old towel up over her, a blanket.

Out on the dark green night water, said Finn, there was a mermaid. And, because mermaids need to, it sang. Sad songs, homesick songs. Night after night, over a hundred thousand fish. And the only one who could hear it was a girl.

Lonely, said Cora.

Yes, a lonely girl, said Finn. Orphaned. But tying knots and listening to the mermaid sing made her feel a bit better. All through the night, she'd lie awake and knot and listen to the songs.

And then the storm, said Cora.

Yes, the storm, said Finn. There was a storm one night. And the girl couldn't think of anything but her parents not being there, and the knots weren't helping as much as they should, and the mermaid was singing and singing, not high and pretty, like you might think, but low and long, like she felt, so the girl got up, out of bed, and followed the song down to the water.

The sea.

Yes, to the sea. Where the storm was wild and it was probably too dangerous—

Definitely—

And it was definitely too dangerous, but she kept going anyway, the mermaid's singing washing up to her, calling out to her. She walked all the way to the edge of the sea and then, even though it was freezing cold, she took another step into the water. She should have sunk down, but she didn't. She stayed on the surface.

She what?

She stayed on the surface.

She did? I don't remember this part . . .

She did. Because the sea was so thick with cod, brought out by the singing, hundreds of thousands of them, she could walk on them, right across their backs, out and out and out toward the song . . .

Oh . . .

And it got louder and louder until it was louder than the wind, until—

．　．　．

Until she saw it wasn't a mermaid at all, said Cora.

Yes, said Finn. Until she saw it wasn't a mermaid. It was Dad. It was our dad. Singing.

Cora and Finn were on the ferry, going west. The sun had set and their parents were asleep, leaning against each other, surrounded by bags and boxes. There was no one else there. It was too foggy to see out the windows, to check for boat lights or anything else. Too quiet and late for music, too much pull of the sea for reading. There was nothing to do but tell stories. Tell this story.

And then? asked Cora.

And then everything, said Finn.

(1992)

The lichen on the rocks were orange and yellow and green. Ten-year-old Finn hopped from one patch to the next. He was wearing his sweater with two jumping fish on it and the zipper pull clicked up and down with every jump. Green, *click*. Green, *click*. Yellow, *click*. Green, *click*. The wind pushed his hair flat against his forehead.

Up ahead, fourteen-year-old Cora was in the same sweater, only bigger and with caribou instead of fish. They were on their way home from once-a-month school, where all the homeschooled kids in the region met to do some kind of activity or go on some kind of trip. It was funded by the government, as it was cheaper than running a real school for so few of them, and usually involved a trip to the fish plant or step-dancing lessons on someone's porch. The guides were always just someone's mom or dad. The government gave them seventy-five dollars to do it, so there were lots of volunteers.

We have to stop at the bakery, Cora called back over her shoulder.

How come?

Mom said.

To get pie?

Yeah.

But it's nobody's birthday, is it, or a special occasion?

Don't think so.

Do we get to choose what kind?

I do.

But I—

I do.

But nobody got to choose, because there was only one. In the whole bakery there was only one pie, with nothing around it and nobody there to sell it. Finn rang the bell and waited. Cora went and sat down at one of the tables in the shop's café. There was nobody at any of the others.

Eventually, Jack Penney, the baker, came in through the back door with a book under his arm. So sorry, he said. So sorry, so sorry. I've been trying to learn big machinery mechanics.

You have big machinery back there? For the bread? asked Finn.

No, it's a correspondence course, said Jack.

I bet big machinery doesn't smell as nice as bread, said Cora, from across the room.

No, I don't think it will, said Jack.

Are you leaving here? asked Finn.

Probably. Probably, yes, said Jack.

They got the only pie, dark berries and dark molasses crust, and continued on toward home.

Martha, their mother, was outside, fixing bits of board that had blown off the house in the night. Lassie tart, she said. Good choice.

You didn't give us any money, said Cora. We couldn't pay for it.

But Penney gave it to you anyway, didn't he? said Martha, in between hammer strikes.

He said it didn't matter because he's going to be rich soon, said Finn.

There you go, said Martha.

Still, said Cora. Still, Mom.

Aidan, their father, was inside, standing by the stove, stirring. Cora put the pie down on the counter beside him. Can I go next door to do my schoolwork? she asked.

Be home by six for dinner, said their father. And careful on the stairs, they might be rotted through by now.

Next door was abandoned. Cora liked to go there and pretend it was hers. What about you, Finn? asked Aidan. You got schoolwork?

No, said Finn.

Accordion practice?

No, said Finn.

You wanna chop carrots?

Sure. Dad?

Yeah?

Why are we having pie and boiled dinner? Is it somebody's birthday?

We can't just have nice food sometimes?

We don't. I mean, we never do, other times.

Well, maybe tonight we just are.

OK, said Finn. And then, It's nice, Dad. I'm glad we're doing it. He chopped perfectly round medallions of carrot, like pirate gold.

It will only be for a month at a time, said Martha.

On and off, said Aidan. One month each, one of us away and one of us back here, here with you.

And we'll both take some time off for holidays all together, once we've saved a bit, said Martha.

And, anyway, it will just be for a little while, said Aidan.

Until things here pick up again.

It's really no big thing.

No big thing.

Really.

If it's no big thing, said Cora, then take us with you.

No, said Aidan.

Yes, said Cora.

Not yet, said Martha.

Yes yet, said Cora.

No, said Aidan.

Why are you going? said Finn. He looked up from his plate, where he had arranged his food in piles according to color. Carrots and parsnips here, potatoes, pease pudding and bread pudding there, salt beef in the middle on its own.

Finn, you know why.

But you have jobs, you have jobs here.

We have vocations, said Martha. Not jobs anymore. Nobody needs fishermen when there are no fish to catch, nobody needs nets. You need to be needed to have a job.

To get paid, you mean, said Cora.

Well, said Aidan.

Yes, said Martha.

What will you do? said Finn.

What?

What will you do there that you can't do here?

We'll be helping power the whole country, Finn, said Aidan. We'll—

We'll be in a tool crib, said Martha. We'll be handing out tools. And taking them back.

Oil and gas, said Cora, toward the window, away from them. Like everybody else.

To who? said Finn.

To the whole country, the whole world, said Aidan.

To specialists, said Martha. To people who know how to use them.

You're not specialists?

Not at everything. Not at those things.

Oh, said Finn. He pushed a piece of meat into the carrots pile, into the parsnips. Apart from wind against windows, from forks against plates, it was quiet.

Will you go on a boat? he said.

It's too far, said Martha. We'll start on the boat, but then we'll have to fly.

Finn looked at Cora, then to the window where she was looking. He waited for a bird to pass, but none did. Oh, he said. Wow.

An adventure, right? said Aidan.

Not for us, said Cora.

I guess, said Finn.

Martha went first.

They drove her to the ferry, all of them in the car, Martha and Aidan in the front, Finn and Cora in the back.

It won't be for long, said Martha, once they had arrived, taking her bag out of the trunk, after kisses, after good-bye.

Sure, said Cora.

Really, said Aidan.

No big thing, said Martha.

Finn didn't say anything. Just watched as his mother walked onto the ferry. They'd all been on the ferry hundreds of times. Thousands of times. No Big Thing, he chanted in his head. NoBigThingNo-BigThing.

Martha turned around and waved one more time after crossing the heavy steel bridge onto the deck. Finn squinted his eyes and she blended with the boat's white-paint background, disappeared.

Before driving home, Aidan took a shining silver flask out of the glove box. There was a fish engraved across its front. He took a drink, held it in his mouth, then swallowed and started the car.

Cora stared fixedly out the window, away from her father and away from her brother. Finn tapped his finger against the seat's vinyl, NoBigThingNoBigThing.

That night, at home, the phone rang. Aidan picked it up downstairs, in the kitchen. Finn picked it up upstairs, in the hall, as quietly as he could, breathing sideways out the corner of his mouth.

Aidan, said Martha, everyone on the flight was from here, going there. Everyone.

The hotel line was fuzzy-quiet, far away.

And, she said, the plane was bumpy, less graceful, than I thought it would be.

And, she said, Aidan, when we arrived and all stepped out and down the airplane stairs and all looked around, looked up, there were no mountains.

Of course not, said Aidan, those are miles away. By Calgary.

I was hoping, said Martha. I thought maybe, in the distance.

I know, said Aidan. But no.

Finn listened until his father hung up the downstairs phone, until the gentle clatter as Aidan went back to putting away dishes, humming like he always did when he was alone. Finn quietly put down his phone and avoided the two creaky boards on the way back to his room.

Before bed, he ducked his head under his bedroom window's curtain to count boat lights out on the water. Finn had started doing this when he was three and scared because there were high winds and his father was out on-sea. Cora had come into his room to tell him to shut up because his crying was keeping her awake. She told him he should calm himself by counting boat lights on the water, that shining lights meant safe boats.

So Finn counted every night, no matter if his father was out or not, or if the wind was wild or small. Shining lights mean safe boats. They were like upside-down stars.

Sometimes, if she wasn't mad at him, Cora would stick her head into Finn's room and ask, How many?

That first year, Finn would say, Twelve, the highest number he could count to.

And then, two years later, Eight.

And then, Five.

And then, Three, all far away and slow.

Until, six years later, when Finn would squeeze and squint his eyes to try and see one, just one faraway fishing-boat light, and Cora would say, How many?

And Finn would say, One, at least one.

And she would say, Really? Still one?

And he'd say, Yes, I think so, still one.

Tonight Finn didn't see any. Not one. Since Cora was already in her room, had gone there as soon as they got back from the ferry and closed the door, there was no one to lie to. Zero, he said quietly to himself. Zero lights. He lay down, pulled up his quilt and, through the pillow and the bed and the floor, listened to the faraway song his father was humming. A familiar, old song. He closed his eyes and let it fill him up, let it spread out and over all his other thoughts, his own heavy heartbeat.

When Finn woke again it was full night. All dark, all quiet. He listened for Cora or for his father, for humming or breathing or snoring, for something, but there wasn't anything. He tried closing his eyes again, but the silence was too big, too full. He tried counting boat lights again, but there were none. There was nothing but the always-there wind and the always-there waves and him, just him. Miles from morning. Miles from his mother.

He got out of bed, went to the hallway phone and pulled it as far as it would reach toward his room. He dialed the number off by heart, stretched the curly cord around his door and, leaning on his bed, the farthest he could get without the cord breaking, Finn listened to it ring, one, two, three times. Mrs. Callaghan always answered on the fourth ring. Even if she was right there beside it, she would wait, she would count.

Good evening, Finn, she said. She had a satellite phone. It made everything sound underwater.

Hi, Mrs. Callaghan. Finn was whispering; he didn't want to wake anyone up. Mom left, he said.

I know, said Mrs. Callaghan.

She's gone, said Finn.

I know, said Mrs. Callaghan. But not for good.

Still, said Finn.

I know, said Mrs. Callaghan.

Will you tell me the story again?

Their story?

Yeah, said Finn.

OK, said Mrs. Callaghan. But don't worry if you fall asleep. I'll just keep going.

Until it's light?

Until it's light. I promise. Ready?

Ready.

(1969)

When Aidan Connor turned fourteen, his mother put a navy-blue toque on his head, looked him in the eye and said, Don't drown.

The boats left at night, just after sunset.

And then he was off, on the rocking, pulling water for eight or ten or twelve days at a time, more of his hours spent on boat than ground. Soon enough, Aidan couldn't find sleep on land, its rigid stony silence unnatural and unnerving.

One night, back at his mother's and unable to sleep, Aidan got up, pulled his fishing coat on over his pajamas and went out. Little Running was a small place, only six houses; if anything was happening he'd be able to tell. Five dark houses, and then the Dwyers', where the lights were still all on. Aidan walked over and tapped on the kitchen window until Joe Dwyer, big as an iceberg, noticed and opened it.

Evening, said Dwyer.

Evening, said Aidan.

Then Dwyer reached out and down and half helped, half pulled Aidan up and into the drink, the cards, the fire going within.

Three jacks, said Aidan.

Liar, said Dwyer's grandmom.

Look, said Aidan, turning his hand around, fanning it out. The cards had shamrocks instead of clubs.

Cheat, said Dwyer's grandmom. All Connors are cheats.

It was hot in the kitchen, the wood stove was going strong. Aidan wished he could take off his coat, but he only had pajamas on underneath, gray-white and thin.

Are you cheating my grandmom, Connor? said Dwyer. He stood up.

All Connors are cheats, repeated Dwyer's grandpa.

It felt like all the heat in the room was going straight to Aidan, straight to his head. All Connors are cheats. Everyone was looking at him, waiting. All Connors are cheats. He laid his cards faceup on the table and stood.

Look, he said. Let's take our money back and start the hand over.

Dwyer chuckled a little under his breath and sat down.

Aidan played as poorly as he could, lost five dollars and went home.

The next night he was assigned to the furthest downwind boat, the SC, *Solitary Confinement*, because if you were in it you could shout all you wanted but none of the others would ever hear you. Dwyer, who was in charge of allocations, patted the back of Aidan's coat, making a hand-sized divot in the down. He handed the boy a small flask with a jumping codfish etched on one side, streaked from years of whiskey drippings. And then we'll call it even, he said.

HELLO! shouted Aidan.

And, AHHHHH!

And, HELP HELP!

And, AHH! AHH! AHH!

No response from the boats in front. Just their stern lights bobbing calm and regular, from small to smaller. Aidan pulled his jacket sleeves up over his hands and blew warm air into them. The wind pushed against his neck, back toward the Runnings. No one could hear him and, apart from his boat's two lights, bow and stern, no one could see him. He took a deep breath. The air was cold and fresh as drinking water.

The water is wide

he sang,

I can't cross o'er

and the wind blew his voice away from him,

Nor have I wings,

still high and young like a boy's

With which to fly,

he sang,
and sang, and sang, until the sun was up and the nets were down

and the golden morning warmth cut through the mist and wind and let him sleep.

And, because Running Bay's prevailing winds had a bit of tilt to them, a bit of westward swagger, his voice was pulled across the water and away from Little Running, where his mother and Widow Callaghan and Mrs. Dwyer would have known it to be his, and, instead, landed in the stranger front rooms and bedrooms of Big Running, coaxing the wood fire at the MacDowells', unnerving the cats picking fish guts on the shore and catching the ear of thirteen-year-old Martha Murphy, who sat up in bed, was still awake, tying and untying knots in a length of rope twine while her sisters slept around her. Oh, she whispered under her breath. Mermaids.

One month earlier, both of Martha's parents drowned. Or so everyone said. When a body, or two, go out with the boats and don't come back again after a storm, people say they drowned, even though there are, really, any number of ways they could have lost life. Certainly there are lots of situations where a body, or bodies, end up breathing water instead of air; hurried, panicked lungs sucking it in, spitting it out, sucking it in, spitting it out, until the water makes the body heavy and there's no power left for spitting. But also, a body can, for example, be tossed up in a big wind and smashed back down again, broken on the wood of her own boat, or maybe something even harder, like a bucket or a mast or an anchor. Or a gust can bring to life something otherwise dead, like a pole or a tool, and it can fly into a skull, crashing and shattering, and that's that. Or a boat can get pounded into bits by the waves and a body can die of thirst or hunger or loneliness while clutching a bit of floating debris, floating further and further and further out for days and days and days. There are any number of ways a body, or bodies, can die at sea, so people just say drowned to simplify things. Martha Murphy was thirteen years old and had three sisters, two older, one younger, when both her parents drowned.

She was wearing itchy black tights that, as she had grown an inch already this month, were too small for her and pulled down with every step. Over these she wore a black dress that had been her sister's up until that morning, when she had gone to put on her own and found it indecently short.

Wear mine, said Meredith, her sister, throwing it over her bed onto Martha's. But don't give it back. You'll probably stretch it weird.

What will you wear? said Martha. You don't have another black one.

I'll wear Minnie's. It pretty much fits already.

What will she wear?

Mom's.

Oh.

And you can give yours to Molly.

What if Minnie doesn't want to wear Mom's?

She'll be fine.

What? said Minnie, coming into their shared room. She was still in her nightgown. It had to pass through three more of them and already had holes along the bottom.

You'll be fine, said Meredith.

So Martha wore her sister's black dress, now hers, and her too-small black tights, with her yellow rain jacket over both and her almost-black hair in a braid that bumped awkwardly over the jacket's hood. She walked in line with her sisters, first Minnie, then Meredith, then her, then Molly, down Big Running Main Street to the church that looked like the wind should have got it down years ago, where her grandparents were waiting, along with the rest of the town, to start her parents' funeral. Since there were no bodies there were no caskets, either, and when the time came for throwing earth, they all took turns throwing handfuls into an empty hole.

That evening, after the wake, Martha's grandparents from her now-dead mother's side gathered all the Murphy sisters into their front room: Minnie, Meredith and Martha side by side on the small sofa, and Molly on the floor leaning against their legs, her feet tucked away so as not to touch the wood stove and burn. Outside it was raining and raining and raining.

Leaving them there, their grandparents went upstairs; Martha could tell by where the wood was creaking overhead that they were in her parents' bedroom. They were walking back and forth, speaking softly to each other. Downstairs, Martha listened, Molly sniffled rhythmically every five seconds or so, Minnie smoothed her littlest sister's hair in even strokes and Meredith stared straight ahead, into the fire.

After half an hour, their grandfather called for Minnie to come up. She went and stayed for about ten minutes, then came back down and told Meredith to go up. Then Martha, then Molly. Downstairs, they didn't talk. They just listened and sniffled and stroked and stared. Then, after it was all done and their grandparents had left to catch an overnight boat back to St. John's, Molly said,

I got a fiddle.

But you already have a fiddle, said Martha.

I got a better one, and a bow with hairs. And rosin.

I got a splitting knife, said Meredith.

I got a quilt, said Minnie.

I got twine, said Martha. A needle, a card and twine.

They took a few minutes to look at each other's things, then quieted the fire, went upstairs to their room, took off their black clothes and went to bed, Martha sharing with Molly, Meredith and Minnie not sharing, but with their beds pulled up close to one another. Martha could hear them whispering.

. . . but you don't actually believe in them.

I don't know. Maybe I do. Maybe tonight I do.

What are they saying? whispered Molly into Martha's back. Warm breath.

Mermaids, said Martha.

Oh, said Molly. Do you?

Of course. Yes I do, of course.

Because everyone did. Everyone believed, everyone knew, that mermaids were the sea-dead, singing their love back to you. If it wasn't too loud with rain or waves, you could hear them in the wind, most nights.

(1992)

A month went by and Finn's mother came home and his father left.

A few days later, the word went around that Jack Penney, the baker, had gone too, gone west to be a big machinery mechanic, and that, before he did, he used up every ingredient he had making dozens and dozens of pies and tarts and muffins and breads and buns and had left them all out in his shop with a note on the door that said:

Please Help Yourselves.

Pretty much everyone on the island came to the bakery after that. It was like a party; people came from miles away, mostly on foot, boats or trucks, but some even on horses. There were more voices and people in the same space than Finn could ever remember. Martha carried home two dark loaves, one big and one small, a partridgeberry tart and a bag of crescent rolls; Cora carried six oat-and-cranberry cookies, three white baguettes and a box of cinnamon buns; and Finn carried a blueberry pie, six dinner buns and one of each of the four kinds of cookies. After everyone had gone, they left the bakery door open so animals and birds could come in and finish the leftovers.

• • •

Cora spent most of her time in their neighbors' empty house, reading travel books from the library boat or making up slow songs on her violin. Finn wasn't allowed in, but he liked to sit on the front step and listen. Usually Cora left the sitting-room window open a little bit so he could talk to her through it. Sometimes he brought his accordion too, if it wasn't raining, in case she wanted to play together, but she never played songs he knew.

What are you reading about today? Finn hooked his fingers over the windowsill's lip; there was just enough space for them.

Mexico, said Cora. She pressed the book up to the glass so Finn could see.

Happy Backpacker Guides Presents:

MEXICO!
1967 EDITION

There were some laughing people in old-fashioned clothes dancing on a sand beach on the cover.

They sometimes eat chocolate on chicken there, she said.

Wow, said Finn.

Yep, said Cora. It's way better than here.

Is it?

Yep. I hate it here, said Cora.

You do?

Yep.

Not everything. Not all of it, said Finn. You like the empty houses.

I like them better than ours. That doesn't mean I really like them.

You like rock jumping. And copying pans. And summer swimming, and—

I only like doing those things with people, said Cora. With friends.

But I— said Finn, then stopped. Anyway, he said, they'll be back.

They won't.

They will.

I bet you they won't.

I bet they will.

They put five dollars on it, even though neither of them had five dollars.

How long till they're back? asked Cora.

A year, said Finn.

Hm, said Cora.

They shook hands through the open window, then Cora went back to the neighbors' sofa and opened her book.

Want to play "The Fish of the Sea"? asked Finn.

Not right now.

OK.

Finn sat on the step, watching the road to see if anyone would come by. He decided he'd stay there until after ten blue cars had passed. But only one did, and it was white.

Well, I guess I'm going to look for caribou.

OK. She didn't look up from her book. She had her fingers holding several places in the pages.

You want to come?

No thanks.

Finn wore rubber boots so he could walk right through the bogs, but he still had to be careful not to get sucked down or stuck. There was a cairn about two miles out that he was aiming for. He had constructed it the last time he was there, carefully balanced on a raised plateau of red rock, and he wanted to see if it was still intact. The southern half of the island had trees, clumps of dark, skinny tamaracks and firs, but the northern half, where they lived, was too windy, so it was just rocks and lichen and bog and more rocks. If Finn stood up beside his cairn he could see out for miles. Miles and miles of bumpy orange and gray. And sometimes caribou, too, in heavy brown clusters, or less often just one at a time. As long as he didn't get too close, they would pay him no attention, just carry on eating or, if it was autumn, calling or, most often, just standing. They could stand perfectly still for minutes and minutes, like cairns. Finn would watch them while picking and piling rocks, counting out their stillness in seconds under his breath.

On his way back he watched the ground for any early cranberries, anything to add to one more family dinner of just-starting-to-get-stale bread and soup. Cora joined him halfway and they walked home together.

They'll be back, said Finn.

They won't.

They will.

Their time was mostly their own now. The Canadian Maritimes Distance Communities Homeschool work they had to do was easy; they'd do their week's worth on Sunday between lunch and supper and then Finn and Cora were free to do what they wanted for the rest of the week, so long as they did some music practice and didn't drown. This meant that Cora would go to the neighbors, where she'd started to keep the blinds closed so Finn couldn't look in. I'm making you a surprise, she said, that's why. Even so, Finn stopped to check each time he passed, just in case she'd left them open that day.

After checking, Finn would go south to build cairns with the caribou, or north to the shore, where he'd take his shoes and socks off and practice standing in the freezing water for as long as he could, or row himself east, across to accordion lessons with Mrs. Callaghan.

Martha would work nets. Nobody needed them for fish anymore, but sometimes she'd sell one as something to throw over garbage to keep it from blowing away on collection day.

Two weeks and one day before Aidan came home and Martha left again, it was Finn's eleventh birthday. Martha made bunting and hung it over his bed in the night while he was sleeping and Cora played "Happy Birthday" on her fiddle as an alarm clock. Because they were all sick of bread and sweet things, they had birthday crab cakes, with one of their emergency power-outage candles stuck in Finn's. Did you make a wish? asked his father over the phone, which they had hooked onto a bowl on the table with the cable stretching between them.

Cora gave Finn a small rectangular package wrapped in last month's *Island Happenings and Shipping Forecast*, on which she had drawn a picture of him with his accordion and a dog.

We don't have a dog, said Finn.

I know, but it looked lonely without it.

The dog was the black-and-white collie-type. It was very well drawn.

It's great, said Finn.

Thanks, said Cora. Open it.

Finn was careful not to tear the picture as he unwrapped. Inside was a slim book with a plasticky cover: *A Collection of Local Jigs, Reels and Airs Based on the Flora and Fauna of the Region*. It was dark red.

Wow, thanks, said Finn.

I thought maybe we could learn some together, said Cora.

Yeah? said Finn.

He flipped it open to a random page. "The Northern Long-Eared Bat Reel."

Sure, said Cora.

That's really lovely, said Martha. Did you steal it from the library boat?

Yeah.

Still, it's really lovely.

Don't forget, there's one more gift, said Aidan-on-the-phone.

Yes, yes, I'll go get it, said Martha.

She came back with something awkwardly long covered in the quilt from their bed. She handed it to Finn.

Does he have it? asked phone-Aidan.

Almost, said Martha.

Finn struggled a little, then managed to pull the quilt off to one side. Underneath was a fishing rod. Old-fashioned.

Wow, he said.

It was mine! said phone-Aidan. My first one!

Happy birthday, said Martha.

Do you like it? asked Aidan.

I love it, said Finn.

Really?

Really.

The next day Cora went back to the neighbors', and Finn, in his rubber boots and fish sweater, dragged their old dory down to the water with the new-old fishing rod rolling back and forth in it. Cora's picture of him, the accordion and the dog, was in his corduroy trousers' front right pocket. He waded through the shallows, pushing the boat out, and then, when the water was almost at the tops of his boots, he crawled up and in, rocking it a bit, but managing not to tip. He pushed off and paddled into the deeper middle water. Then he hooked and strung and weighted and baited the rod and then, with the leaded pull of water's soft gravity, let the hook sink down and down. And then Finn waited.

Even though nobody had seen a fish off their shore all year. Although nobody had caught a fish since the year he turned nine. Finn sat, and waited. There were no other boats out. Nothing but wind and water for miles.

He went out every morning, as the days grew rainier and the daylight pulled back and the mists and fogs rose up around him. Every day. Sometimes he would bring *A Collection of Local Jigs, Reels and Airs Based on the Flora and Fauna of the Region* to read and sometimes he wouldn't. The plastic library cover made it more rainproof than most books. Sometimes he brought his accordion and tried to sight-read with one hand while holding the pole in the other. Sometimes he would take a break to go to Mrs. Callaghan's and get her help playing one of the new songs.

Have you played this one with Cora yet? she would ask.

And Finn would say, No, not yet.

It was almost the end of September and, as he always did, Finn stopped by their neighbors' window on his way home from no-fish fishing to check on Cora through the cracks in the blinds for thirty-three seconds, but this time, he only got to eleven when Cora looked up and said, Finn?

Yeah?

You should come in, I want to show you something.

OK.

Finn waited for Cora to go unlock the front door, but she didn't. Instead, she ducked under the blinds so she was between them and the pane, and pulled the window the rest of the way open. This way, she said. Then she ducked back down under the blinds and away.

Finn left his fishing rod leaning against the house and crawled up and over the sill, the unsanded wooden frame scratching along his chest and legs through his clothes. He dropped down the other side and ducked under the blinds into what should have looked like the Ryans' front room. But it didn't. Not anymore.

Well? said Cora. What do you think?

Everything was bright yellow and pink and blue and green and red. The walls were covered in cutout skulls, all sizes and colors, all grinning. Some of them had flowers for eyes. There were big pieces of green card cut and pasted together into cactus shapes all up the sides of the sofa and fireplace. There were bright balls and animals and skeletons hanging down off the ceiling, and a giant, fierce-looking paper eagle clutching a terrified-looking paper snake over the top of the front door. The door itself had a bunch of bright red and orange and yellow pepper shapes and green lime-slice shapes on it.

Wow, said Finn.

It's Mexico, said Cora.

It's amazing, said Finn. And it's really hot.

I turned the radiators all the way up. For Mexico.

Oh yeah, of course. Wow. Finn unzipped his sweater. Where'd you get all the colored paper?

Kids' books from the library.

Oh, smart.

Thanks. You wanna hit the piñata? We can use the fire-poker, and one of the kitchen towels for a blindfold.

Sure. Just let me take off my sweater . . . it's really, really hot.

The average daytime temperature in Cancún in September is twenty-eight degrees Celsius.

Wow. So this is what it's like.

This is just what it's like.

They took turns hitting at a blue donkey piñata until Cora finally got it, on her third turn. She smashed it open at the belly and a cascade of cutout words and photos from the *Mexico!* book cascaded out all over them.

The next day the blinds were closed again, so Finn went back to no-fish fishing.

And the day after that.

And the day after that.

And then, the day after that, after he had been out for just over three hours and was in the middle of right-hand-only playing one of his favorite new songs, "The Ballad of the Newfoundland Black Bear," Finn felt the smallest bit of shake shudder through his left hand, just for a second before, all at once, the fishing pole pulled fast and sharp and away from him.

He mashed the accordion's keys as he lunged across the dory to grab it back, catching it just before it was pulled out over the side of the boat. As he did, he accidentally knocked *A Collection of Local Jigs*,

Reels and Airs Based on the Flora and Fauna of the Region out into the water and had to stretch and grasp to get it back with one hand while holding tight to the rod with the other. The accordion on his front made him top- and front-heavy and almost pulled him over. Once the book was back in-boat, he turned back to the pulling fishing rod in his left hand. Maybe, he whispered to himself. Maybe, maybe, maybe, as he lifted, dropped, reeled the line. Maybe. Lift, drop, reel. Maybe, lift, maybe, drop, reel. Until the sun passed across a gap in the clouds and lit the water so it was clear, and, just for a moment, Finn could see what he had: not a tire or a mess of seaweed or an old lawn chair, but a back-and-forth weaving, beautiful green-gray-silver codfish, mouth opening and closing, gasping and trying and alive.

Nobody could believe it. The word spread like rain, drenching Big Running first, then out with the wind south, east and west, across the whole island. A fish? A fish! A codfish. Nobody could believe it with their ears so they had to come around, come on foot, trucks, boats and horses, to see Finn or the dory or the picture Cora had drawn of Finn with his dog and the fish, or touch the bones that Aidan had kept after they ate it, all washed and clear-white on a plate on the kitchen counter, or the guts they kept in a jar in the freezer for proof. They do look fresh, said a barely-there, thin old woman from a southeast outport.

Can we smell them? said a man who had brought his kids. You can tell age best by smell.

I can't believe it, said his wife, her hands cupping the jar like a baby bird. I just can't, while her husband went back outside. For a cough, he said, though his hands were to his eyes and not his mouth.

What did you use?

How deep?

What time?

Was there rain?

Was it big?

Was it old?

And, most of all, Was it alone?

Were there more?

Was it alone?

Finn, whispered the thin woman, it could be you saved us.

Finn! shouted the kids. Finn! Finn!

And their parents joined in: Finn! Finn! Finn!

It could be, said the thin woman. It could be.

Their mantel filled with cards and gifts, and the cove filled with boats. Many of them had been dry for years and were barely functional anymore, and lots of people ended up doing emergency patching with gum or socks or ended up swimming and cold. Some went out in the day, because Finn had been out in the day, because he wasn't allowed out after dark or seven p.m., whichever came first, and some went out at night, because that's how it had always been, before. And some just stayed, day and night and day and night and day, there in the cove. They went with rods and with nets and with lights and with binoculars, with radios or with books or with nothing at all but hope and time, too much time. Finn navigated past them all as he rowed out in the morning, and back past again as he made his way home under the orange lichen sky.

Finn knocked on Cora's bedroom door. It was late, but she was still awake; she pretty much always was. She was reading:

Happy Backpacker Guides Presents:

ENGLAND!
1965 EDITION

Yeah come in, she said.

So, said Finn, pushing her door open enough that he could share in the light of her bedside lamp, I guess this means people will be coming back, hey?

What does?

The fish I caught.

If there are more.

Yeah, if there are more. But if there are, it means everyone will come back and you'll owe me five dollars, right?

I guess so.

OK, just checking. He stepped away, started to go back to his room.

Hey, Finn?

Yeah?

You want to count boat lights? Want me to come with you to count? She swung her legs across and off her bed.

OK, said Finn. Yeah. They walked to his room, climbed up on his bed and rubbed their sleeves across the window's condensation to get a clear view.

Wow, said Cora.

More than twelve, said Finn.

More than twelve, she said. There must be hundreds. Like upside-down stars.

(1969)

Almost every night young Martha would go down to the shore, down to the singing. In bed, eyes closed, she would wait for Meredith and Minnie's quiet talk to decrescendo into regular breathing and for the tension to fall out of Molly's thin body next to her, and then she would ease her weight as evenly as possible off the mattress, pull on a dressing gown and pick up her needle, card, twine and boots to carry downstairs. She'd pull her boots on once she got outside so her heavy footsteps wouldn't wake anyone. If it was raining or sleeting or cold she'd wear her father's old rain jacket too. It still hung where he'd last left it, on a jut of board that stuck out near their front door. Then Martha would walk down through the night to the water.

There was an old beached-up dory that she would sit in, legs curled under her for warmth. Sometimes it would be half or totally full of rainwater and she'd have to tip it up to drain first. Then, with her needle and card and twine, she would listen and knot nets, and the mermaid's voice would cut across the water and through the mist to her, right to her.

It wasn't always there, but usually it was.

She's like the swallow.
She's like the river.
She's like the sunshine.

And even if it was tight with fog or pouring with rain, this was warm and safe and hers. It wasn't always there, but usually it was.

They were all right, of course. People checked in on the Murphy girls, more at first, and now and again after that. The oldest of them was nineteen, and the youngest already twelve, so, They'll be all right, they'll be all right, the baker whispered to the boat-pitch man, who whispered to the priest, who whispered to the ferry woman, who whispered to her son, who whispered to the kittens he lured to his back door with fish eyes and tails while he tried as hard as he could to let their mewling blanket over the sound of the thought of the sea, the boats, both parents at once.

After a while Martha's net got too big to carry back and forth with her every night and morning, so she found a little canyon between two shore boulders where she could stuff it for safekeeping during the day when she wasn't there. She marked it with a cairn made of white stones that would catch the moon in the dark of night.

Meanwhile, one evening, while putting on his layers before going out with the boats, Aidan found a soft black feather in his coat pocket, too big and too dark to be from the down. He studied it for a while, then put it back in his pocket, careful not to break the rib. His mother was sterilizing jars in the kitchen; he walked down to say good-bye and then went out to the water.

Storm petrel, said Dwyer. Small but strong. Barely ever on land, those. How that got in your pocket I do not know. He handed the feather back to Aidan. It from a girl? he asked. Some kind of special girl . . . ?

No, said Aidan. No, no. It's just something I found on the beach. It's nothing.

He was in the SC boat again. He asked for it. Once they were out on the big water and he was safely on his own, he took the feather out again, one hand to hold it and the other to shield so the wind couldn't take it. A girl. There were a few girls in Little Running. Some his age, some a bit older. The McKinleys had dark hair, like the feather color. Sophie McKinley was just one year older than him and had been the faster runner in school, back when he had gone to school. In summer she would run people's big black pots out to Skipper Bay, where the water was cleanest, then bring them back full of salt water for crab steaming. She charged fifty cents a pot. Aidan had watched her many times, the way her legs were hard with muscle but still soft girl's legs. She was always nice to him. Always waved if she saw him. And, Aidan remembered with a drop in his stomach, she had given him some of her coins once. Not even very long ago. Bringing back his mother's crab pot, heavy with sloshing Skipper Bay water, she had refused payment, tossing the money over to Aidan instead. Sophie McKinley. The realization made him feel sick; he put the feather away and held on to the side of his boat to steady.

From the time he was seven years old, from the time when he learned how to tuck himself into bed and to sing himself to sleep, Aidan Connor had sworn to himself never to fall in love. Never, never. He closed his eyes so they wouldn't look back over toward Little Running, toward Skipper Bay.

She's like the swallow,

he sang. The longest song he knew, with all the verses.

That flies on high.

He sang it slow.

She's like the river, that never runs dry,

pulling his coat close, remembering his father's father singing at their table, after dinner, before drink, years and years ago.

Sophie McKinley knew nothing about the feather.

And how would I have got it in his pocket? she asked Patrick Darcy, who lived three houses down from Aidan and was often out with the boats on the same trips.

I don't know, said Patrick.

Aidan watched from across the beach, pretending to wipe buckets.

And anyway, why would I? Some kind of weird thing? I'm too busy for that. I'm going to be in the Olympics, said Sophie.

In Germany?

Yep. Probably. Or I'm trying at least. I'm hoping.

You still gonna come to the beach party tonight, though?

Oh yeah.

See you there, then.

Yep, see you there.

Aidan watched until Sophie had picked up her crab pot again and run off toward Skipper Bay. Then he walked over to Patrick.

It wasn't her, said Patrick. I think she likes me, actually.

OK, said Aidan, thanks.

Do you think whoever it was will be at the beach tonight? I bet they will. I bet you could have a good night tonight, boy.

I don't know. Maybe? We'll see, I guess. You done with your buckets? Yep. You can take them. I'll see you tonight? said Patrick.

I'll see you tonight, said Aidan.

There was a note on the door when Aidan got home that afternoon:

Working late, stew on back step.
Have fun tonight.
Rain certain. (Wear your coat.)

He opened the back door and got the orange casserole dish off the step. There was a cat watching it. He took the lid off, picked out a bit of salt beef and threw it to her. She ran away first, then back toward it. Then Aidan went inside and put the dish on the stove to reheat, stirring to stop clumps from burn-sticking to the bottom, standing with his face right over it; the steam warm and welcome and the scent making him hungrier than he had been. He thought about kissing a girl, if it would be like the steam. Wet and warm and hungry. Never, never, never, never, he reminded himself in time with the swirling vegetables, never, never.

Aidan was seven when his father left. Too young not to be surprised. Even though no one else was. Even his mother, feeding her husband's things to the fire one by one by one, almost everything except the one dark red wool sweater, the one pair of dark blue corduroy trousers and the one gray-green raincoat, the same kind and color as all the other men's, that he had walked away in. She fed almost everything else into the fire one item at a time, first underwear, then socks, then mittens and gloves, then hats. Books lasted one whole morning, scraps of razors and combs discolored and melted and hid among the ashes. Jackets and shoes were last. In order to be able to consume all those things, the fire had to stay full and hot for a very long time, so they couldn't let it die down at all for those weeks. His mother would sleep downstairs beside it, with the door open. If the fire got too low the cold would get to her and she'd wake up and stoke it and feed it again. But even she wasn't surprised. All Connors are cheats, her brother said when he visited, throwing a watch in among the embers and waiting for the glass face to cloud and crack.

I know, I know, she said back.

All Connors are cheats, the postwoman said, slipping in letters and bills; they burned faster than anything.

I know, I know, she said back.

Often, Aidan would sleep down there with her, because he wanted to and because, usually, she was too tired to carry him back upstairs to his room, where he belonged. Instead she would open up a gap for him to slip into between her back and the sofa, and, still in his daytime clothes, his seven-year-old body would cover as much of her, or her back at least, as it could, from the back of her knees to the place where her shoulders turned to neck, while, instead of the normal breath of sleep, she would breathe,

I knew, I knew.

It was raining on the beach, but not too hard. A group of kids were blowing on scrunched-up bits of beer boxes, trying to get them to light; they'd hollowed out a sort of shelter for it in a circle of beach stones. There were girls, quite a few of them. Sophie McKinley was there with her sister. And off to the side, sitting on an overturned boat, were Clemmie Begg and Rebecca Ryan. Some girls from further out, Nessa Doyle and Iona Quinn and Kerry Brown, were standing in a cluster by the water. And Dwyer's cousin Siobhan sat on a rock off to the side, with a wet guitar. Aidan stood a bit up the beach and tried to make a plan. He wished that once, just once, he could go to a party without his coat on. He had chosen a nice shirt to wear tonight. A newish shirt. Blue and red plaid. But no one would see it. No one ever got to see much of what anyone had under their coats. Unless . . . his stomach tightened. He scanned the party again. He kind of knew Siobhan, she'd been at a couple funerals he'd attended, but they didn't know each other well enough to be embarrassed or awkward. Maybe she had remembered him and asked Dwyer to put the feather on him. Some kind of special girl . . . Dwyer had said. She was strumming her guitar casually, watching the party. It was beautiful. She probably didn't really know anyone there. She was probably lonely. Sad and lonely and beautiful. Despite the fact that he was already cold with it still on, Aidan took off his coat and slung it over his arm as naturally as he could and started to walk down toward her.

Aren't you freezing? It was Sophie. She had snuck up behind him.

No, said Aidan, I'm fine. Although he wasn't, he was freezing. The back of his shirt caught the angle of the rain and pressed cold into his back.

'Cause I'm freezing and I've got my coat on, said Sophie. That's why we're trying to make the fire.

I guess I just don't feel it. He glanced back toward Siobhan. Patrick Darcy had wandered over to her and was offering her a beer. She had stopped playing.

Well, if you don't need it, how about you let me wear your coat over mine? I'd take the extra layer. Trying to keep my muscles warm, you know.

He passed it to her in a bunch so she wouldn't see his shivering hands. Patrick Darcy was now sitting beside Siobhan, trying to teach her some guitar thing. He doesn't even know how to play, said Aidan.

Neither does she, said Sophie, pulling his coat on over hers. And that thing's totally out of tune anyway. Sounds terrible. Here, you want a drink? She lifted a flask toward him.

OK, said Aidan. It was whiskey. Sharp and cheap and warming. He took another deep drink.

Want to go for a walk?

OK.

It kept raining as Aidan and Sophie made their way along the shore, less walking than climbing, stumbling over the wet rocks. It kept raining when they finally stopped after half a mile, taking shelter in an overhung cove. It rained when Sophie took the flask from her pocket again and pressed it to Aidan's mouth, rained as she purposefully spilled some onto his lips, cold and burning at once, and rained as she took the flask away and replaced it with her own mouth, her warm double-jacketed arm around his back, her hand warm through the thin, soaked cotton of his shirt. She tasted like whiskey and fire-smoke. She tasted amazing. And for one moment, one brilliant moment, even though it was still raining, Aidan felt hot. He leaned heavily, fully, into it, into her.

And then the cold metal of the flask pressed through her pocket into his rib and the whiskey around his brain cleared and he pushed away, sudden, abrupt.

No, he said.

What?

No, no, he said.

What? Why? she said.

I'm sorry, he said, now fully awake, back. He sat down.

What? she said again, standing over him.

I promised, he said.

Who?

Myself.

What?

I promised myself, he continued, never to fall in love.

Sophie started to laugh but stopped herself, and instead sat down next to him. Yeah? she said.

Yeah, said Aidan.

Why?

Because all Connors are cheats.

You have a point. But, I think we can kiss without falling in love.

I don't know . . .

I do. Trust me. I won't even talk to you tomorrow. I'll be horrible.

Promise?

Promise.

And the day after that?

And the day after that. And I'll be hopefully going to Germany pretty soon after that, so it won't be an issue. She started leaning in, back toward him.

OK. He sighed. So it was you, after all, with the feather?

What? That thing Patrick was talking about? Oh no, I have no idea . . .

In my pocket? You didn't put the petrel feather in my coat pocket?

No . . . She patted her front, his coat. Which pocket?

Bottom right.

She felt around, came up with the feather. It's nice, she said.

Thanks.

And so are you, she said. Just tonight. Just nice for tonight. She tucked the feather behind his ear, leaned in, all the way this time, and kissed him. Harder than before. He let her. And he let his arms do what they wanted and pull her down heavy and warm over him. As he did the wind pushed through the rain, took the feather from his ear and blew it off, away, down the coast, into the night.

Aidan was out on-boat the next night. It was calm when they set off. Calmer than usual for that time of year. Calmer than is right, said Dwyer, untying the mooring knots.

Yeah? said Aidan.

Yeah, said Dwyer.

It's a really beautiful sunset, though, said Aidan.

It is, said Dwyer.

Aidan was singing when the wind picked up and changed, started blowing the wrong way,

Windy weather, boys

starting low, just barely brushing his hair,

Stormy weather, boys

growing stronger, pushing the clouds in, rocking his starboard side up and back and up and back, and through the backward wind he could hear, for the first time, someone else singing, a woman, a girl through the wind growing stronger,

When the wind blows

a mermaid, he thought, oh wow, oh God, and the wind pushed and pushed up and back and up so that Aidan needed to anchor himself and all the movable things to the side to weight against it, and still it came harder and harder and pushed

We're all together, boys

and he tried to position the bow to the storm but it pushed back and he tried and it pushed back and the rain came now not gradual like the wind but all at once and was like ice, was like a blanket, so everything was blurred and even though they couldn't hear him and he couldn't hear them only wind and rain and the singing and the singing he could still see the others upwind of him shouting and waving to each other and maybe to him and he could see their lights moving violent and jagged

Blow ye winds westerly

and he counted them one two three four and then three and then four and then three and then they were gone and he couldn't find

Blow ye winds, blow

the anchor he needed to anchor he needed to stand to get it but the wind the blanket rain he knew where it was it was just

● ● ●

Steady she

and then lightning and he saw and then he didn't and he stood and
it pushed he slipped or the anchor or the wind pushed and knocked
him knocked his weight the wrong way the wrong side and the wind
pushed and

Steady she

the rain was a blanket no not rain the water all the cold all the
water around him kicking and he's kicking and it's kicking and find
something to hold, remember, always, find something to hold, and the
lights no more lights not a light not one not one.

It was still clear and calm when Martha tiptoed out, a beautiful night, so she didn't bother putting on her father's heavy jacket, just the rubber boots with her dressing gown. She untwisted her net from between the rocks and sang along with the mermaid as the wind picked up and grew strange.

It was a backward wind, so the more it picked up, the harder it was to hear the mermaid's singing; Martha sang louder to try to encourage it, to try to give it something to latch on to. Maybe it would recognize her voice. Know where to find her.

When the wind blows we're all together

The wind grew and grew and whistled and howled as it passed through the cracks in the rocks around her. It was getting colder, but she didn't want to walk back up to her house to get a coat; if she let go of the tiny bit of song she could still hear she might not find it again. Instead, she wrapped herself into her net to keep warm, with just the end free to work on. And she kept singing.

Windy weather boys, stormy weather, boys

By the time the rain came, all at once like from a bucket, her fingers were too cold to work the needle properly and she had to stop. The wind whipped her wet hair into her mouth and she had to keep spitting it out to sing.

Back in the village, Young William, who wasn't too young, thirty-five or so now, but who was younger than Old William, his father, woke with the first clap of thunder. He sat up and checked the window.

Is it bad? asked his wife, her eyes still closed.

It seems bad, he said, pulling on his seal-skin socks. The wind's back to front and strong. And there's lightning. The water's up. Up and moving.

OK, said his wife, opening her eyes and pushing back the quilt. OK, let's go.

Every able-bodied person aged 18–50 in Big Running took turns being Volunteer Sea Rescue Scouts when they weren't out working themselves. If the sea turned to storm, it was their job to be sure all boats were safe and all bodies accounted for. As much as they could. As much as could be expected. Tonight was Young William and his wife Charlotte's turn. They put the bright yellow VSRS vests on over their coats, checked that their official VSRS flashlights had working batteries and headed down to the water, careful not to wake Old William as they passed him sleeping downstairs in his chair. If we wake him he'll want to come, said Young William.

He is not coming, said Charlotte.

No, no, he's not, that's what I'm saying.

OK.

OK?

OK.

The official flashlights were huge and heavy, with a face the size of a family pie. If it was OK to take the rescue boat out, they were to use them to scan the water for debris and bodies. If it was too rough, they were to stand on the coast and flash them long-short-long-short, long-long-short-long, over and over until either they got a response and it calmed down enough to take the boat out, or it got so bad that they needed to go take shelter at home. They had both been volunteer scouts for years, since before they were married, but this was the first time either of them had actually gone out on a call. It was exciting.

Be careful of the lichen, said Charlotte. In the dark and the rain, with the heavy lights, their footing was clumsy and rough. As well as a VSRS, when Charlotte wasn't working packing fish, she was the town's self-appointed rare lichen preservation officer. It's having a tough year, she said, be gentle.

OK, said Young William. I am, I am. They had to shout to hear each other through the storm. He reached across and took her hand. They were almost at the water, the sound of it striking the rocks as loud as the thunder, just coming down to the point where they'd have to decide whether to go out on-boat or stay onshore, when Charlotte said, Listen.

WHAT? shouted William.

LISTEN, shouted Charlotte.

They stopped moving and listened. Wind. Thunder. Rain. Water. And then,

Steady she

singing.

Steady she

What? said William, and he swung his flashlight around to point toward it.

At first she didn't even look human, all draped and roped in a landed dory, a net-trapped sea-ghost. Young William pulled back, away, and Charlotte stepped closer. Hello? she called, and then louder, HELLO?

The singing stopped and the figure turned abruptly around, tangling.

William exhaled. Oh, oh, he said. It's—

A person, said Charlotte.

Martha, said William. It's Martha Murphy.

They shouted, MARTHA! STAY THERE! WE WILL COME GET YOU! MARTHA! CAN YOU HEAR US? and waved and picked their way slowly down until they got to her.

My God, girl, said Charlotte, what are you doing out on a night like this?

Martha tried to answer, but as soon as she had stopped singing her mouth had let the cold in and everything started shivering and she couldn't control her lips to form words.

William set his flashlight down on a low, flat stone, careful of the lichen, and set about trying to get her untangled from her own net. The bright, round light illuminated them like a spotlight, like they were onstage. Martha's whole body shook as he peeled the rope around and off, around and off; anytime she tried to help it made things worse.

Well hell, that's a mighty tangle, said Young William. This yours?

Martha nodded.

This? he said, pulling up a handful of net. Bunched, tangled. Martha shrank. This, he said. Yours?

She nodded again.

You knot it yourself? He pulled up more, up close to his face, his orange-like-sunset beard.

She nodded.

Wow, he said. Oh wow. All on your own?

She nodded.

I'll tell you what, Martha Murphy, he said, this is some of the finest net I've seen. Just fine, really fine. His eyes were the washed-out blue of morning. With the orange hair they gave him a young look, true to his name, truer than the truth.

Really? said Martha, finding her words again.

Yeah, said Young William. I'll tell you what, I'll buy this off you, if you don't mind, fair price.

It's not done yet.

When it is. Won't be long now. I'm on-boat next week, how 'bout if I come get it the week after that? What do you say, Martha Murphy?

Well, said Martha. She had never thought about selling her knots. About profit from sadness.

Well? said Young William.

OK, said Martha.

Yes?

Martha nodded.

Good, said Young William. Perfect. He went back to unwrapping and untangling the net from around her. Good, he said again. His hands pulling the twine away and off were strong and sure and hard-skinned like her father's. Every now and then his beard would brush her neck. Martha didn't feel the cold anymore. She closed her eyes and fell into something like sleep.

They decided, because Charlotte would have a harder time carrying Martha, that she would take the rescue boat out and William would take the girl back to theirs to dry off and warm up and sleep. Are you sure? asked William. You could just stay onshore and do the light signal . . .

The storm's pulling off. I'll be OK.

You're sure?

I'm sure.

Because if anything happens, Charlotte, I'll—

I'm sure, Young William.

OK, OK. Be careful. OK. He kissed her quickly. Rainwater dripped down everything.

Once she was gone, William folded the net and tucked it away between the stones, picked up shivering, sleeping Martha Murphy, and carried her back to their cottage, careful of any lichen he could see, especially the most delicate golden-orange patches.

Because the rescue boat had a motor and no fishing kit, it was much faster than the cod boats out on the water. Charlotte stood a chance of catching up with them, so long as she kept true north. She positioned herself so she could see both the Big and Little Running lighthouses and used those to navigate. Out and out and out, north and north, as the storm pushed in front of her, away.

And out and north for miles and miles until, finally, Charlotte noticed an upside-down bucket flicker past her, momentarily bright against the dark water. She cut the motor and shone her light all around, to the north, the south, the west, and there, to the east, onto something else, something other than water. She drove to it, a piece of broken board. She did the same again, motor cut, look north, south, east, and found more, a floating nest of them, and from there a crooked, bobbing trail that led her, one broken bit of wood at a time, finally, to a capsized vessel, and, behind it, a boy clutching its side. The slow circles of his treading legs made whirlpools in the water up and out around him. Alive, whispered Charlotte. He's alive.

His coat was ripped and caught around his neck. There was blood on his face and in his hair. He didn't turn when she drew up to him. His eyes were wide, open, but glass. He was in sea-sleep. When your body knows it must stay above water, stay conscious enough to tread, but shuts everything else down from cold or hunger or thirst or loneliness or shock. He had tied himself to the boat with net twine and small fish were trying to eat the loose fibers off it. They scattered when Charlotte reached down with her boning knife to cut him free.

She cut the twine from around his waist, then closed the boy's eyes and hefted him into the boat, careful to counterweight. She took off his wet, cold clothes and spread a thick wool VSRS blanket over him. She took off her volunteer vest and wrapped it around his head and neck. You lost your hat, she whispered. Without his clothes, he was thin and pale like a child. This is no job for children, she said to no one. This is no job.

She shone her light all around and all around again and again but couldn't see any other boats or boys. She didn't have time to look further, now that she had this one. She turned the boat around and pointed herself back toward the Big Running lighthouse.

Young William put Martha in the small bed in the small upstairs bedroom, where they had originally hoped, one day, to put a baby. She was soundly asleep when Charlotte arrived with the boy. William and Old William, now awake, helped her bring him in and put him in the bedroom Old William never used, that shared a wall with the never-baby's. They coaxed warm honey-water into him, gave him new, dry blankets, and then went back downstairs to dry clothes and wait for news by the fire, falling onto each other's shoulders and into sleep almost immediately.

And everyone slept while the sun rose.

Martha woke first. She needed to get home, to get to her sisters before they noticed she was gone. She had on a too-big flannel nightshirt. Probably Charlotte's. She looked under the bed and in all the drawers in the room, but the only things there were tiny, infant-sized; her own things were nowhere to be found. She stepped out into the hall. There was another door beside hers; it wasn't quite caught closed. She pushed it in a bit and peeked through. There was a boy inside. Sleeping. He looked terrible. She pulled the door back almost closed and went downstairs.

Everyone was asleep there too. She found an old envelope and a pencil in the kitchen and wrote:

I had to go. Thank you for finding me.
You are both very kind and your net will be ready soon.

Martha M.

PS I have your nightshirt, and I think you have mine.

She made it home and was just crawling into bed as Molly woke up.
Just went to get water, said Martha.
OK, said Molly. Is that a new nightshirt?

Meanwhile, across at Little Running, a quiet and slow parade of boats-tied-to-boats pulled up to shore, all there, all tied to one another in a safety line like bath toys, all except for two, Joe Dwyer's and Aidan

Connor's. Those two had just disappeared. Just disappeared, Rupert Quinn told the first people they met, the old Spence couple out picking through what the storm had washed up. The storm came up and they just disappeared, he said. Gone, both of them, gone.

Just disappeared, Mrs. Spence said, her voice more air than sound. She'd run as fast as she could to the Connor house, had woken Aidan's mother up knocking. She'd be eighty-eight that spring and didn't often run like that anymore. She steadied herself on the porch fence. Her husband, Mr. Spence, was off running to the Dwyers'.

Come in, come in, sit down, said Mrs. Connor. Say it again, more slowly, I can barely hear you.

But Mrs. Spence didn't come in, didn't move. Just disappeared, she said again. They don't know, they don't— her breath rattling and whistling.

Oh my God.

They don't—

Oh my God.

Not yet—

My God my God my God.

She pushed past Mrs. Spence, down the steps, down the road and down the rocks, down to the water. The Dwyers were already there, pushing boats out. Come with me, said Mrs. Dwyer, his wife. Come out with me.

The rain turned light in the air, half mist.

They'd pushed out past the dip of the cove, were almost to open water, when the Big Running scout boat caught them. It was driven by a man with a beard, someone's son. He waved them down to stop, then pulled up alongside. I'm so glad I caught you, he said, cutting the motor. It's OK. We have him; it's OK.

And both women closed their eyes and let the tightness, the weight, slip away from their shoulders, their arms, their lungs, their hearts.

Your son, the man continued, he's with us, we found him.

Mrs. Connor exhaled.

Mrs. Dwyer inhaled. Son? she said.

Young William took Aidan's mother in the fast boat with him back to Big Running.

And then I'll come back to help you, he said to Mrs. Dwyer. I'll come right back.

At shore they tied up quickly, temporarily, and he pointed Mrs. Connor to his house. Right there, he said. With the white paint. With the green door circle. There was a cat on the doorstep.

Oh, she said to the cat. Thank God thank God.

Charlotte led Mrs. Connor to her son. He's not woken yet, she said, but the doctor says he should, says he will. Old William watched from the door. He had taken off his hat and was holding it in front of him, worrying the tattered brim.

They didn't wake me, he said. If they had, I would have stopped it.

You couldn't stop this, Dad, said Charlotte. This was a boating accident, nothing to do with you.

They should have waked me, said Old William. I could have stopped it.

In the bed, Aidan's face was beginning to bruise around one eye, spreading down across the cheek and jaw. There was a white sock with a blossom of red tied around his head.

We've been changing it every hour, said Charlotte. It's clean.

I'm so sorry for your loss, said Old William.

He's not dead, Dad, said Charlotte.

If they had waked me—

Dad.

It's OK, said Mrs. Connor. It's fine. She sat down on the edge of the bed, leaned over and brushed her son's hair away from his eyes, the bruise.

They stayed like that for a few minutes, Mrs. Connor on the side of the bed, Charlotte and Old William stood by the door. Then, without looking up, Mrs. Connor said, Do you have his coat?

Yes, I think so. I think it's drying by the fire with the rest of his things, said Charlotte.

Would you bring it to me?

I will, said Old William. I'll go get it.

No, it's OK, Dad. I'll go.

After Charlotte left, Old William stepped over and put his hand on Mrs. Connor's shoulder. How old was your husband? he asked.

My husband was thirty-one, she said. And my son is fourteen.

Old William said nothing, just left his hand there on her shoulder until Charlotte came back in with the coat.

It's still not dry, she said. Sorry.

Mrs. Connor stood and took it. She reached down and pulled out the pockets, first one, then the other. Inside there was a penny, a wet wrapper, a spare button, and nothing else. Is that all? she said. I mean, was there anything else that fell out or that you saw?

No, said Charlotte, nothing else.

The boats searched for Dwyer all morning. They searched as the seabirds rose and then settled again, as the mist thinned and lifted, as the fish beneath them swarmed and shoaled through the refracted pillars of daylight, as the light tilted away again with the falling sun and the seabirds rose up again for their evening flight, until the mist pulled back in with the dark. Nothing, said Matthew Quinn to Donna Brown. Just disappeared, said Teresa Doyle to Frederick Begg. Nothing.

The doctor from South Island came by again the next morning and said that, although he still hadn't woken, Aidan was OK to move back to his own house, back to Little Running. It was a much shorter route to take him by boat, across the bay, than to walk around it, but Mrs. Connor wanted to go by land, so they did. They lined a small dory with woolen quilts and lay him in it, with his clothes and coat folded under his head for a pillow. They took turns carrying it in pairs, front and back, across the rocks, the berries, the bogs, for hours and hours and hours. First Mrs. Connor and Young William, then Charlotte and Old William, who had dressed himself in his best all-black suit for the trip.

Over the next days, Mrs. Connor changed and cleaned Aidan's head dressing and cloth diapers, sat him up to spoon-feed him honey mixed with water and salt, and lay him back down again when she was done. She kept his hair combed and neat for when people came over to see how they were doing or to drop off food. She sang while she did it. Although she wasn't proud of her voice, quiet and breathy, it was fine for just them alone. She quietly sang,

The water is wide
I can't cross o'er

nor have I wings
with which to fly

watching his breath up and down, alive, alive; singing to fill the fear in the spaces between it.

They waited to hold Dwyer's wake and funeral until Aidan was awake, two and a half weeks after the storm. He woke on a Thursday morning when the light was brightest, between seven and eight in the morning. He opened his eyes and saw his room, his window, his coat hung on the door hook, and his mother crouched beside it, wringing a white cloth in a pot of soapy water.

Why don't you do that in the kitchen? he said. And then he felt how much it hurt to speak, to move anything at all, and had to close his eyes again from the shock of it.

When he opened them again his mother was beside him, leaning over him, right over him so their eyes lined up perfectly. Don't you, she said.

Don't you ever, ever,

ever

don't you ever lose a feather again.

She took something from her skirt pocket. Black. Soft. Storm petrel. She walked over, sure he could see her, was watching, and put it in his coat pocket. Then she walked back to him and lifted him up to her and put her mouth to his head and held him close and fast. Don't you ever, she said. Ever, ever, ever.

That night, even though it wasn't particularly cold yet, Martha wore her father's old jacket and a toque and a pair of tall, yellow, knitted socks that belonged to nobody and everybody in the family at once. They came right up over her boots. She was halfway down, picking her way from rock to rock, when she heard a little cascade of pebbles behind her. She turned and there, white against the night, was Molly, not far behind her at all, in her nightgown and boots.

Don't be mad, Molly said. I just wanted to know where you go.

I'm not mad.

Is it to him?

Him?

Young William?

What? No, no, no. No.

Is it another boy?

No, said Martha.

Molly pulled at her sleeves, tucking her fingers away inside. But, she said, I just don't—

Martha sighed. OK, she said. OK, come on, I'll show you. OK. She took off her toque. And put this on, she said. You'll freeze.

She led her sister the rest of the way down to the shore, to the old boat. In here, she said, I sit in here. She helped Molly up and in. They sat side by side on the old warped bench. The sky was huge over them.

I guess this is nice, said Molly. You come here just to sit, at night?

Kind of, said Martha. To sit and to listen.

She told her about the singing, the mermaids. The songs, the wind, the net.

Why didn't you tell me before? I wouldn't mind. It's nice out here. Cold and nice.

You remember, said Martha. Do you remember how before, Mom

and Dad would take each one of us out to the bakeshop for our birthdays? Just the one of us, alone with them? Remember what that was like?

Yeah.

It's like that. That's why I didn't want to tell any of you.

Molly put her head on her sister's shoulder. OK, she said. That's OK. The waves pushed in and out like the water's breath. Everything else was quiet. Maybe, said Molly, they only sing if you're alone.

Maybe, said Martha.

They waited like that until Molly fell asleep, slumping heavy against her sister. Martha nudged her awake and said, They're not singing tonight. Come on, let's go back home.

Will you go again tomorrow?

No, no, I think I'm done now.

The next morning, Martha went down and got her net from between the rocks. She brought it back home and worked on it in front of the fire in the sitting room while, across from her, Minnie worked a quilt, and, in the kitchen, Meredith seasoned and jarred cod liver, and, upstairs, Molly practiced fiddle.

After a few days, Martha finished the net and traded it with Young William for six dollars and a fish for dinner. Then she made another, and sold it to another man on his crew, from further inland, who gave her seven dollars and a pound of partridgeberries. And then another, to his sister, for five dollars and six jars of seal meat, and so on and so on and so on. For Christmas that year, Martha bought her sisters all brand-new socks, knit-fresh, never worn by anyone else.

She could still hear the singing at night, if it was summer and her window was opened and she listened very very closely, but she didn't go out again. Not that year, or the next, or the next or the next.

And when it was fine in Big Running, Martha would take her nets down to sell at the harbor and Meredith would arrange fish on the flake she had built and Molly would teach violin students in the up-stairs room with the windows open. And when it was cold, all four sisters would sit in the fire-room with one of Minnie's quilts spread across them, stretched over all their knees like a circus trampoline, and all work on it together as they grew and lived and worked, just normal, for five years.

According to the doctor, Aidan wasn't well enough to move around yet the Saturday after he woke up, but there was a tacit understanding that he would anyway, just for the one night, for Dwyer's wake. It was the least he could do.

Because there was no body, there was no need for a casket, just a nice framed photo with a golden nameplate that read: Joseph Finnegan Dwyer. It was placed prominently on top of the fireplace so people could pay their respects. All of Little Running was there, and some of Big Running too, and some from further inland, even. There was family from Gander and St. John's, and two all the way from Saskatchewan. Everyone brought whiskey. The music and dancing started before Aidan and his mother even arrived, even before sundown.

It didn't take much for Aidan, in his condition, to get drunk. He was at a wobbly, rowdy table of musicians; there were two fiddles, three guitars, one banjo, one bodhran, three whistles, two accordions, and almost everyone singing, though no one as loud as him. It still hurt to sing, but that was OK. That was how it should be, he told himself. When it got to be too much, he leaned back against the wall and let the pain wash over him in the same way the music did.

At some point, Sophie McKinley appeared and tried to pull Aidan up for a dance. It was around three in the morning. One last time, she said, before I go away forever.

Aidan resisted, stayed sitting. To Germany?

No. Not yet. To the sport-specialist high school in St. John's.

Really?

Yeah.

When?

Soon. Next term hopefully.

That's too bad. I'll miss you.

Not too much . . .

No, no, not too much.

She left him alone and got Patrick Darcy to dance instead. Aidan watched them for a while, then got up to get some fresh air to clear his head of whiskey fog, and, maybe, if he could find one, sneak a cigarette to calm his aching lungs. There were still at least three hours until sunup, and he planned to stay them through. A bunch of people had gathered on the front stoop retelling each other Dwyer's favorite jokes, so Aidan slipped out the back instead, walking a few shaky steps toward the bogs until he came to the low, red rock where he and Dwyer sometimes used to smoke. He sat down and checked his pockets for any stray cigarettes. He found a penny, a wet wrapper, a spare button and the new petrel feather from his mother. He put everything else back and held the feather up so it was silhouetted against the moon, stringy and imperfect. The whiskey pulsed hot through him. His stomach, his heart, his head beat and burned.

Oh God, he said, what did I do?

The darkness of the night was like deep water. He closed his eyes and opened them and it was practically the same. Oh God, he said. Oh God oh God. He closed his eyes and opened them and there was Dwyer, out from the night, walking toward the rock.

Calm down, said the ghost, sitting down beside him.

I . . . said Aidan.

It was my own stupid fault, said Dwyer. I could have held the boats back. I didn't. My fault, not yours.

No, said Aidan, you don't know; I lost the feather. I almost lost myself and I lost the feather.

OK, maybe, said Dwyer. Maybe you did. But that just means your own broken body was your own fault. Not mine. Not this.

Aidan let his hand with the feather drop. You're really sure?

Well, I guess we can't ever be sure, with the sea. But, yep, that's what I'd say.

I guess we can't ever be sure, repeated Aidan.

Dwyer didn't respond. Just smiled and nodded a little, half to Aidan and half to the house, the light and the noise and the music.

I used to sing this, remember? I used to sing this one.

Of course I remember, you sang it terrible.

Terrible and loud, that's the trick.

Will you sing now?

No, not now. Not anymore. I can't. Can't make the right sounds.

They were never the right sounds with you . . .

Still.

Still, you can't?

No, the dead can't sing, Aidan, that's why the living have to.

Oh, oh. OK. I can, I will.

They watched the house awhile more. Dancers had started leaking out onto the porch; the wooden beams dipped and creaked.

Can you smoke?

Nope.

Me neither.

Still, it's not so bad, is it? said Dwyer.

No, no, I guess it's not, said Aidan.

Dwyer left and Aidan sat there, on their rock, for another minute or so, letting the cold night air wake and sober him. Then he got up and went back to the warmth and the people and the music, went back to sing, even though his throat and heart were sick and sore, to sing the night through until sunrise.

After three months Aidan was well enough to go back on-boat, back to work, and he did, and he and his mother and Little Running carried on just as they always had, just normal, for five years.

(1992)

Finn, in his small dory, went out in between and around all the other fishers in all the other boats every day except Sunday school day.

And Cora, finished with the Ryans', moved along and spent every day except Sunday at their neighbors' on the other side, another empty house.

On Sunday they sat at the kitchen table and worked on why-did-Canada-confederate-and-how-many-of-this-triangle-fit-into-that-triangle and Cora would look out the window toward the houses and Finn would look out the window toward the boats.

And, at night, he'd breathe quiet, hold the phone close, listen:
Hello?

Hi, Aidan, it's me.

Hi, Martha, you OK?

I'm just tired, said Martha. The food here is awful.

I know, said Aidan.

• • •

Aidan, no one's caught another fish yet, have they?

No, not yet.

Two Sundays went by, and it got rainier and windier and colder and closer to real winter. And some of the fishers, the oldest and tiredest ones, stopped coming out.

And then three Sundays, and colder and windier and rainier and some of the fishers, those with families to think of or those who struggled most out there to keep their minds off what they suspected to be true, whose thoughts were too fast and heavy for books or song to block out, stopped coming out.

And then four Sundays, and many of the remaining fishers, struggling to keep their minds off what they suspected to be true, whose thoughts grew too fast and heavy for hope to block out, stopped coming out.

And Finn would count the boat lights at night. He counted down night by night, twelve, ten, seven, three. And sometimes Cora would come by and count with him and sometimes she wouldn't.

The first day Finn was completely alone again out on the water was the first day the rain turned to snow. He had worn fingerless gloves, but his hands were still stiff with cold as he held his father's old fishing rod in one hand and played the bass line of "The Ballad of the New-foundland Black Bear" over and over and over again with the other.

Normally he would do a mix of tunes so the other fishers wouldn't get bored or annoyed, but now that he was the only one it didn't matter. After two hours he pulled up his line and, because it was a Friday, an accordion lesson day, he rowed east, across to Mrs. Callaghan's, with no fish in his bucket and no other boats blocking his way.

Mrs. Callaghan lived all alone. She lived in Little Running, across the sound from them, and was the only person in the only house left there. The only way to her was by boat. Until he was ten, his mother or father or, sometimes, Cora, would row him over once a week unless it was too stormy. It took between forty and fifty-five minutes. Then his mother or father or Cora would help him ashore with his accordion case, as heavy as the neighbors' dog, and then they'd sit and wait in the boat while Finn had his half-hour-to-forty-five-minute lesson. Then they'd row him back.

To fill the in-between time, his mother would bring a needle and work nets. His father would bring a small bottle and sing. Cora would bring handfuls of pebbles from the beach to drop one by one and watch sink through the light-streaked top water into the colder disappearing dark.

Then Finn turned ten and was old enough to go alone, so long as the wind didn't have the flags straight or the fog wasn't too thick to see his own shoes or the ice wasn't in. For balance, he would put his accordion in one end of the boat and seat himself in the other end. If it was raining, he'd put a black garbage bag over it. If it was hailing, he'd put two.

All utility services to Little Running had been turned off, so Mrs. Callaghan drank seawater boiled and distilled back into fresh. The purple Kool-Aid she gave Finn always tasted a bit like salt and a bit like fish through the grape flavor. She had a giant gas-powered generator in her backyard that hummed gently under everything. Under everything they said and everything they played. It was a low C, so they mostly played in that key.

Did you know Aunt Molly's gone? asked Finn.

Gone west, I know, I saw her go, said Mrs. Callaghan.

She didn't even tell Mom. Cora just turned up for her lesson and the house was empty. There was a note on the fridge that said, Take what you want, but Cora said there was nothing in there but mustard and gone-off milk.

She left on Tuesday, with Nessa and Robert Doyle, said Mrs. Callaghan. I'm sorry.

It's OK. I didn't see her much. Mostly just Cora did.

I'm still sorry.

Mrs. Callaghan?

Yes?

How do you know that? About who's gone and when?

Maybe I'm a witch.

Are you?

Maybe. Come with me, look, she said.

She led him upstairs, where Finn had never been. They were both still wearing their accordions on their fronts, like heavy, backward backpacks. Look, she said.

The room was empty except for an old wooden rocking chair, a small table and a telescope, pointed out the window. Look there, she said. But be careful not to knock it.

Finn pressed his eye to the round black eyepiece and saw, in surprising detail, the ferry port. There was no one there. No boats until tomorrow. You watch every day? he asked.

Somebody has to, said Mrs. Callaghan. Beside the rocking chair, on the table, were a plain coil notebook and a pencil. The notebook was open and showed a list of names. Molly Murphy was the third-last name. Up, in an earlier column, Finn saw, in Mrs. Callaghan's shaky, penciled letters: Martha Murphy/Aidan Connor. I saw all the fishing boats too, said Mrs. Callaghan. All the fishing boats that came out because of you.

Not because of me, because of the fish.

The fish you caught.

But they're gone now, said Finn.

Boats or fish? said Mrs. Callaghan.

Both, said Finn. Sat like he was, in the rocking chair, Finn's accordion pressed back into his chest and made each heartbeat hurt.

They went back downstairs, took their accordions off and put them away. Snaps and straps and bellows and buckles.

Lesson at the same time next week? asked Finn. He took his sweater down off the guest hook. The arms were inside out. They always were. He reached down each sleeve and pulled them normal.

Come half an hour earlier, said Mrs. Callaghan. The sun is setting earlier.

OK, said Finn. He reached up for his coat next. Sleeves backward, the same.

But wait, said Mrs. Callaghan. You can't go yet.

I can't?

No, said Mrs. Callaghan. You can't. Before you go, I think I need to tell you about St. Patrick and the snakes.

You do? asked Finn. Now?

Yes, said Mrs. Callaghan. It would seem that now, right now, I do.

Finn had one sleeve of his coat on already. He pulled it back off, inside out.

Sit down, said Mrs. Callaghan.

OK, said Finn.

He walked over and sat on the sofa with his coat in a big ball on his lap. Mrs. Callaghan sat down next to him. They faced forward, toward the fire.

OK, said Mrs. Callaghan. She took a deep breath. Once upon a time in Ireland there were a lot of snakes. Loads and loads of them. So many snakes.

Poisonous?

Oh yes. And also nonpoisonous. Some squeezers, too. All kinds. All the snakes. People would want to make a cake and open up the flour jar and there'd be a powder-white snake inside, hissing clouds of flour, or they'd want to go to a dance and would get out their dancing shoes and find small green coils of snake inside each one, with smaller, greener coils at the tips, one where each toe should go. They'd reach out for their husbands or wives in the night, in their beds, and would find a thick black sleeping snake between them. It got so that you couldn't walk in the streets, couldn't open your door for all the snakes. And, the whole time, there was a steady hissing sound that grew, in the background at first, and then louder and louder every day, though nobody could tell on which day, exactly, it went from quiet to medium or from medium to loud.

And then, one night, Patrick, who was older than you, but not by much, maybe eight years, this Patrick, who up until then wasn't doing much of anything but trying and finding it impossible to sleep, every night more and more, from the hissing and from the dream he had night after night of a pale gray snake wrapping itself around and around his arms and legs and neck, a dream he was half-sure wasn't a dream at all, one night, when he was just too too tired, heavy with it, near-dead with it, one night he made his way to the center of the central Irish town, right in the very middle of the country, stepping over and between and through snakes, to the central square, where, pulling himself up onto the announcement platform, he cupped his hands around his mouth, as was custom there, to amplify your announcing, and announced: SINCE NO ONE ELSE IS DOING ANYTHING ABOUT IT, I'M GONNA GET RID OF THESE SNAKES MYSELF, DAMMIT!

And then he did?

He did.

How?

LISTEN! he announced. ALL YOU SNAKES, LISTEN NOW! But, because snakes don't have ears, they didn't understand him and just kept slithering and coiling and hissing and squeezing. And this made Patrick pretty angry, because it's rude not to listen when someone's addressing you directly, even more so if they're announcing, and, anyway, he was probably drunk, so, in his anger, he stomped his feet on the platform as hard as he could, making a quite-loud low banging sound.

Now. Snakes don't have ears, and can't hear words and things like we can and like Patrick had hoped, but they can feel vibrations, and they hear like that, instead, like the way your ribs feel it when you play your low C chord on the accordion. So, when Patrick stomped on the platform, it vibrated out through the wood like through the body of a cello and made a long and low vibration that the snakes could hear, clear as can be. Clear and terrifying. Like something horribly huge must be coming. So all the snakes around the courtyard startled out of their holes and cracks and boots and doorways and cupboards and bread boxes and trouser legs and began slithering away from the platform and the noise as fast as they could. Patrick saw this and stomped again, and more snakes even further off heard and slithered away. By this point people who lived nearby had come out to hear what the announcement and big noise were for and saw what was going on and got up on the platform with Patrick and all jumped together, scaring more of the snakes, who kept moving away from the noise in the center of the central town in giant waves, then more people came and jumped, and more and more, scaring the snakes out and away like the ripples from a rock tossed in water, out and away, out and away until, finally, in great groups slithering over and around and across each other in fear, the snakes hit the shore and, terrified, plunged into the water, some of them sliding in across rock beaches, some of them careening off high white cliffs. This went on until, just as day was breaking on the morning after Patrick had first arrived at the platform, the very last snake, a small yellow boot-snake who was blind in one eye, slid across the hot flat surface of a gray beach stone into the cool water, at which point they were all gone. All the snakes in Ireland, gone. At which point everyone sat down on the platform, exhausted, their legs shaking from a whole night of stomping. Because they were so tired, no one talked, they all just listened and heard, for the first time in years, in whole lifetimes for some of them, silence. No hissing at all. Nothing.

How do you know this?

I was there.

You were?

Oh yes. That's why I left.

Because of the snakes?

Because the snakes were gone. And I wasn't the only one. Lots of us did. Many people, most people, were glad the snakes were gone, and stayed and went about their business as before, but some people, a good number of people, really, we couldn't stand the quiet. The new quiet without the snakes. So we all set off in boats. So we followed them.

And?

And?

And what happened to them?

The snakes?

Yes, the snakes. Did they all die? Drown?

Oh no, no, snakes can swim just fine. They swam and swam and swam away from the island, away from Ireland, they swam for miles and miles and weeks and weeks, making their way west, across the ocean. And, because they were swimming for so long and so far, little by little they became less like snakes and more like fish, growing fins so they could go faster and gills so they wouldn't have to keep coming up for air. The salt water drew the colors out of their skin until they were almost the same shining silver as the water itself. They swam and swam in silver swarms until they reached the coasts of Newfoundland. But by that point, they had turned completely to fish, and couldn't climb back up onto the land again. So they stayed there, in the water, in our water. Hundreds of thousands of hundreds of them.

And you all landed here with them?

We did.

It must have been so beautiful.

It was.

But they're gone now.

The people or the fish?

Both, said Finn.

Mostly gone, said Mrs. Callaghan.

Mostly gone, said Finn. He waited, but Mrs. Callaghan didn't say anything more.

It is very important, said Aidan. It is very, very important that you keep up your music, and that's all we're saying about that.

Yes, said Martha, over the phone, from far away. It is important.

Cora took fiddle lessons with Aunt Molly. She had started when she was three, on a small oatmeal box with strings drawn on in pencil. Finn had started accordion when he was four, on an old repurposed fire-bellows painted red and green like Christmas.

But Dad, is it more important than new shoes? asked Cora. Is it? Really?

It is, said their father.

It is, said their mother, over the phone.

Don't you like your fiddle? asked Finn.

A fiddle sells for a hundred dollars, said Cora.

Who do you know who has a hundred dollars? asked Finn.

To your room, said their father.

Me?

No, just Cora. You can go back to your boat, your fishing.

It makes no sense, you know it doesn't . . . Cora's voice got smaller as she walked upstairs, away.

Hello? said their mother, from the other end of the phone, forgotten over the edge of a kitchen chair's arm. Hello-hello? Just footsteps and kitchen noise. She stayed on the line anyway, stayed long enough to hear the long, slow violin notes slipping from Cora's room down the stairs, across the water, and across the country to her. A lament or an air. Made up. Cora never played the tunes Molly gave her. Martha stayed on the line right up until her lunch break was over and it was time to tie her hair back up under her hard yellow hat and go back to work.

Martha didn't go right away; she didn't put the phone down right away. She stood, with the hat proven safe to eight hundred and fifty pounds of impact, to minus thirty degrees of cold, on her head and the phone still in one hand. She watched the flashing amber light of a reversing excavator, on-off-on, its rhythm almost biological, on-off-on, almost comforting.

Your hand is clenched, said the boy. He was twenty-five, maybe. Blond. Fairer than her son. He'd come to use the lunchroom phone, once she was done. This was the first time Martha had seen him there, waiting. It always is, he said. Whenever you're not using it for work. I, I've noticed.

Oh? said Martha.

Yes, said the boy. And that can't be good. The tension. Up from there to your wrist. From wrist to shoulder, from shoulder to neck, to head . . .

Really? said Martha. She looked down. Her left hand, the one with the ring, without the phone, in a tight fist. A hard, safe ball. Oh, she said.

Yep, said the boy. Something to look out for. Worth mentioning. Anyway, I'm John.

The lunchroom was really just a trailer. Walls and floor cheaper than the plastic in kids' toys. Something heavy drove by and for a minute it was too loud to talk. Then,

I'm Martha.

From out east?

Yes. You?

From here.

Here? I didn't think anyone was from here.

I am.

Huh . . . it's nice.

No it's not. But it was. It has been nice. What time you on dinner break, Martha?

Eight p.m.

I'm eight fifteen. Maybe I'll see you then.

Maybe. His hair like honey in the sun that strained through greasy Perspex windows.

(1972)

Something shifted.

Something changed.

Something with the nets or the water or the wind. Before, often, the nets would come up bursting silver-green, more fish than the boats could hold, so many fish that they'd carelessly throw small or strange ones to the shore cats when they pulled in. But this year something shifted, something changed. Some nets started coming up only three-quarters, only half-full. Once Jim Darcy pulled up a net with nothing in it at all but itself. There are good years and bad years, Aidan told his mother. This year is not the worst, it's just not the best, either.

Of course, she said. She was tying up a pudding bag, lowering it into their deepest pot.

But I really don't think it's anything we should worry about, he said.

No, no, she said, as the bag broke the stew's surface and released a cloud of steam around them.

His voice was lower now, more like his father's than he was comfortable with, but he still sang. Still chose the *Solitary Confinement* boat whenever he could.

•   •   •

She's like the swallow

He sang to keep himself company,

That flies on high

and to distract himself from thoughts of Sophie McKinley

She's like the sunshine

and others like her

on the lee shore

and of what might happen

I love my love but

if his net came up empty.

My love is no more

(1992)

Hey, Finn, said Cora, before bed, after looking for lights.

Yeah?

Are you going out fishing tomorrow?

Yeah.

Come with me first. I want to show you something.

Tomorrow morning?

Yeah, tomorrow morning. Come with me first.

Like at the Ryans', they climbed through the front window of the other neighbors' instead of using the door. This time they had no choice, as the front door was locked and they had no key. They won't mind, said Cora. They were nice. And anyway, they're gone now.

This time everything was blue and red and white and gray. Union Jacks on the walls, a beautiful big clock tower taller than Finn all the way up the side of the fireplace.

That's Big Ben, said Cora.

A gray-stone castle wrapped around the hall to the stairs.

And that's Edinburgh Castle. Technically, it's in Scotland, not England, but they're close. That's why it's in the hall, and a red phone-box facade on the door leading to the kitchen, so that it looked like you'd be going into that instead of into the kitchen. The couch was done up to look like a double-decker bus, also red.

Is this all library pages? asked Finn. Cut from the books?

No, said Cora, not enough there, else there'd be no books left. Perry McNeil, who used to do the day care, left stacks of construction paper, still new, still in plastic. And there was some old wallpaper here, so I used that. And ferry timetable leaflets, loads of those. I figure paper's one of the fastest things to break down, ecologically, so it's OK to use it. It won't last anyway.

I guess, said Finn. OK.

She led Finn into the phone-box kitchen. All the teacups were out of the storage unit and were laid out, along with the teapot and sugar bowl and cream pitcher, all out on the table. Beside each cup was a small, triangular sandwich.

You want some tea? said Cora.

Sure, said Finn. Thanks. And then, It's not as hot this time.

Nope, England has a very similar climate to here.

Neat.

So that part was easy, this time.

It's still really good.

Thanks.

And then it was November and Finn's mother came home and his father left. More people left with him, saying, We'll be back, we'll be back. Leaving trucks and cars and curtains and boxes of cereal. We'll be back, they said, walking onto the ferry with just suitcases and plane tickets, with just backpacks and heavy boots. The wind pushing their voices west, away.

There were twenty-two empty houses in Big Running now and six full ones, including Finn's. Three-quarters full, said Cora. Ours is just three-quarters. As the winter pulled up and over them she moved through each, one at a time, some for weeks and some just for a couple days. China! Texas! The Philippines! South Africa! Italy! Finland! Egypt! and so on.

Using her telescope and lists, Mrs. Callaghan helped Finn draw a map of them, of all of the Big Running houses, with color coding for which were empty and which weren't. Finn drew little flags beside each of the ones Cora had been in. You should really come see, he said to Mrs. Callaghan. Some of them are really good; she's really good. Finland has a sauna in the bathroom, even.

Sounds super, said Mrs. Callaghan.

They both knew she'd never actually go. What happens when you leave the place you love, she said, is you immediately grow old and die.

So Finn just told her about them all and they used the telescope and worked on the map and on "The Ballad of the Newfoundland Black Bear" and some of the other songs too.

And then it was December and his father came home and his mother left.

And Finn still went out fishing whenever it wasn't too cold or too windy to hold the rod, carefully pushing his boat out around the ice chunks, breaking them up with the paddle if they encroached while he sat there, hoping the banging wouldn't scare away swimming things underneath, whispering, Please, please, please.

(1974)

Martha's oldest sister, Minnie, got married. To Robert Keane, whose family had the best-producing potato trenches in Big Running. He was a little bit soft in the face and round in the body, but Minnie liked that. He's warm, she explained, when she told her sisters she'd be marrying and then going to live with him. I never feel cold with him.

The morning she left, the morning after a sleepless night of ceilidh and brandy cake and shoes thrown off and some lost altogether, Minnie gave each sister a heavy, rectangular package. They're all the same pattern, but different colors, she said. I've got one too. The quilts inside had a mosaic of diamond shapes slotting into more diamond shapes. They were made from all the clothes they had grown out of.

As Meredith unfolded hers to show them all, Martha noticed, for the first time, a large purple bruise on the inside of her arm, just above the elbow. Meredith saw her looking and closed her arm up again.

Because Minnie had been the oldest and because she had almost always been working inside, in the main room, even when the others were out in the garden or onshore or on-boat, the house developed a kind of hollowness once she left. Not as acute as when their parents had drowned, but a subtle, low, long ache instead. It was nothing too dramatic, nothing that got in the way of their lives carrying on.

And then Meredith came down with a cold that turned to flu. She slept in their parents' old room now, and Martha and Molly brought her shallow bowls of golden broth and braced themselves for when the virus would hit them too. But this time, neither Martha nor Molly fell ill and Meredith didn't get any better. The bruise Martha had seen before, on her arm, spread up and across Meredith's shoulder and chest and neck. The tissues in her dustbin crumpled red like carnations. She was leaving more and more of her broth uneaten in the bowl, where it would skin over and grow cold.

Martha didn't call for the doctor until the day Meredith didn't take any soup at all, couldn't even hold it in her mouth. The bruise had spread up her chin and cheeks and it hurt too much to take the broth in. Meredith had been sick for almost three weeks.

This is not good, said the doctor, her hand just under Meredith's ear, patting down and around in a slow circle. Oh, she said. Oh, oh. You should have called me sooner.

I'm sorry, said Martha, it was just the flu, we didn't—

The doctor pulled the blanket back, away from Meredith in one quick swoop. Her torso and legs down to the ankle on one side and to just below the knee on the other were purple-gray. One side of her stomach puffed big and strange. Molly took a step backward, away from the bed. Much, much sooner, said the doctor.

I didn't— said Martha.

She's going to have to come with me now, to South Island. We need to test blood.

I'm sorry, said Martha, I—

How were you to know? said the doctor, you're only just children. Children all alone.

I'm sixteen, said Molly, from the other side of the bed.

Can we come with you? asked Martha.

Not right now. Today you'll only get in the way. She was packing things back into her bag without looking at them, hurried, frazzled. I, she said, I'm sorry. Martha couldn't tell if it was to them or to Meredith. Come the day after tomorrow, said the doctor. You can come then. I can have someone sent by, before then, if you need help.

No, said Martha. We don't need them.

No, said Molly. Thank you.

You're eighteen, said Molly, after the doctor had bundled Meredith in her quilt and walked her shakily down to her boat and rowed off toward South Island. You're already eighteen, she said to Martha. She said quiet as sinking stone, You should have said.

Martha and Molly slept in different beds now, but still in the same room. After they'd turned off the light but before falling asleep, Molly said, I miss Mom and Dad.

Martha didn't answer, pretended to be asleep, because she knew if she tried to reply her voice would crack and break and Molly would have no one, no one at all.

She waited until she was absolutely, totally sure that Molly was really sleeping, until she could see her eyelids fluttering with dreams, before she got up, put on her dressing gown, walked downstairs, put on her boots and her father's raincoat, and walked out to the water.

It was raining, but only lightly, halfway between real rain and mist. Martha welcomed it onto the heat of her face and hands. The mermaid's song was strong tonight, steady and full. Martha tried to sing along, tried to follow.

There is a ship

That sails the sea

She didn't have her net or needle or card with her. Instead, she picked up an old oar wedged between some rocks on the beach,

It's loaded deep

put it in her small sitting-boat and pushed it out to the water.

As deep can be

She rowed and rowed and rowed until the waves stopped pushing her back and started pulling her out

But not so deep

and the water turned from shallows and sandbars to the deep dark of hidden and forgotten things,

As the love I'm in

and the mermaid's voice grew fuller and realer, and closer and closer,

I know not if

until, just as the dawn sky became dusty with the idea of light,

· · ·

she saw him. Not a mermaid. A boat and a boy. She rowed all the way to him.

Just a boat.

Just a boy.

Just a boy, she said.

He stopped singing, turned around. Oh! he said.

You're not a mermaid, she said.

Are you a mermaid? he said.

No, she said, I'm Martha, just Martha Murphy.

Oh, he said. I'm Aidan. Just Aidan Connor.

You're the one singing.

Yes.

All along, it was you singing?

I suppose.

How many years?

Singing? How many years have I been singing?

Yes.

Um . . . five. I suppose it's been a bit over five years.

Oh, said Martha. And then, It has. It has been five years. Just a bit over five years. She let her hands fall away from the oar, her fingers still showing the grain of it, raised and red.

Do you want to come in? said Aidan. To my boat, I mean. Come in for a while?

OK, said Martha.

They tied their boats together and Martha climbed over, into Aidan's. They sat side by side on his bench and watched the rising sun.

Are you OK? said Aidan.

Yes, said Martha. Her right hand was clutched into itself.

OK, said Aidan.

But you should keep singing, said Martha.

You want me to?

Yes.

So Aidan sang. He sang

"The Water Is Wide"

and

"The Bog Flower Waltz"

and

"She's Like the Swallow"

and when he got to the end of this one, before he even had a chance to take in breath, Martha, without turning her head to look at him, still facing straight on to the sun, unclutched her hand, reached over and put it on his, and his insides twitched and flipped and then melted down, right down, and he knew, for one terrifying second, that this would be it, that this would be the gentle, terrible, perfect undoing of everything.

I hope you catch all the fish, she said. I hope your nets are full to bursting. Then she stood up and climbed back over to her own boat.

Martha Murphy?

Yes, Aidan Connor?

I'd like to see you again, on land.

Yes.

Yes?

Yes, I suppose I'd like that too.

After Martha was five or ten minutes away, back toward the mainland, the water churned, rocked beneath her in the way that meant whales.

But the season wasn't right for whales. Not for months. She looked around, back over toward the fishing boy's boat. Beyond it, maybe fifty meters further out, was the biggest ship she'd ever seen, a dragger. Bigger than a whale. Rocking in its wake, Aidan Connor's boat looked tiny, looked like almost nothing at all.

Molly was waiting for Martha on a high rock. Was awake now, already, and was down, waiting for her, watching for her. The sun lit her from behind so she was just a silhouette. From Martha's place in the boat, Molly looked like a sculpture, like someone had thoughtfully and carefully placed her there. If I can see her, she can see me, Martha knew. But they were still too far, much too far apart, to be able to call out, to hear or say anything. It would be half an hour at least until they could, or would have to, say anything at all.

As Martha pulled the boat up, Molly came down to take her hand and steady her step. She stayed silent. Just kept her hand in her sister's like that, all the way back across the rocks and up and across the road and down the lane and up the steps to their house. She didn't say anything at all, so, finally, just before they opened the door and stepped back in, Martha said, I miss them too.

And they stepped in, home. Molly had the coals going and cooked oats and berries, now cold, on the table.

Hey, Molly?

Yes?

Do you think it's true that all Connors are cheats?

When young Aidan got home from his shift out on-boat, he took off his boots, hung up his coat, kissed his mother's cheek, dusty with flour, and asked, Can a body change his name? Take his mother's instead of his father's?

Do you mean is it legal? She dusted flour over a bowl of dough. Or to what extent it would work? She picked up a wooden spoon and pressed its back into the mixture, again and again.

Both, I suppose.

It's perfectly legal. She put down the spoon, added more flour, picked it back up again and pressed it back into the mixture, heavier, more resistant. But you know as well as I do that it wouldn't make any difference what people know you by, or what they know you as, unless you leave this place. She divided the dough and gave him half.

That would defeat the purpose, I suppose, said Aidan. He kneaded his half down and she hers.

Not to mention I'm not ready for you to leave, not yet, said his mother. I'll die eventually. You can go then. Her hands in and out of the dough in an easy rhythm, like music without music.

OK. His hands more slow, more careful; he was always sure he would do something to ruin everything at this point.

So, who did you meet out there? A mermaid?

The next morning, Martha got up early. She made two cups of tea and went and sat with them, with a book over each to keep them from cooling down too quickly, on the front step. She was waiting for the paperboy to pass by. The paperboy was actually Nuala Doyle, a girl, but everyone called her the paperboy anyway, out of habit. There was only one paper a week, and the Murphys didn't get it, so Martha had to watch carefully to catch her between other houses. She caught sight of her just after six a.m., jogging away from the big merchant house at the end of the lane; she waved until Nuala noticed, confused, and jogged over. Martha handed her a dollar, the second cup of tea and an envelope that said

Aidan Connor

on the front. She was sure Nuala must be able to see her chest pounding under her sweater, but if she did she didn't mention it. Jesus, Nuala said instead. I'm not a flippin' postman. What people don't seem to realize is I'm on a tight schedule. But just this once, OK? And thanks for the tea.

She sat down on the step next to Martha to drink it, sticking the letter in with the small pile of rolled-up newspapers in her bag. It is real good tea, she said.

Her paper route covered Big Running first, then Little Running after that. Halfway up the track between them, on a part-rotted stump she often used for sitting and smoking, Nuala stopped, sat and breathed warm onto the seal of Martha's letter until it came up. She pulled out the folded paper inside, unfolded it and read:

My Sister Meredith (the serious one) is sick and at South Island. I've gone to her.

I'll be back after that.

I think I would still like to see you again, then.

Martha M.

before carefully refolding the paper, resealing the envelope as best she could, standing and continuing on her way, quick to make it before the tide came in.

Martha and Molly arrived at the South Island clinic that afternoon. There was a row of beds out front, each with a patient on it with a sleeping bag pulled up to their chins and a toque pulled down to their eyes. They looked like fish-bait worms. Some were asleep and some silently watched them go past, up the walkway.

The sea air, said the doctor, a new doctor, walking over to meet them. It's good for them. For everyone. Of course, I bring them in if it's raining hard. She put a firm hand on Martha's shoulder, steered her around and to the left. Or hailing, she said. Anyway, here she is. You can take a few minutes and then come and see me at my office. It's just over there. She motioned toward the side of the clinic where there was a little boardwalk with a desk on it. On the desk were a number of fist-sized stones holding down piles of paper; the stacked corners were pulling and flapping in the wind. The doctor strode off toward it.

Meredith was asleep. Her toque and sleeping bag were pink. Matching. Looking up and down the row, Martha realized they all were, each patient had their own matching toque and sleeping bag set. Meredith's neighbors were orange and blue respectively.

Meredith hates pink, whispered Molly.

It's OK, whispered Martha. Since the pink's on her, she won't have to look at it on anyone else. Her sick sister's face was all yellow-gray now. All bruise.

Should we wake her?

No, I don't think we should.

Just stand here for a while?

Yes, I guess so.

So they stood. Molly smoothed out all the rumples on Meredith's sleeping bag, bottom to top. Once she finished, at Meredith's chin, the bag would bump back up again at her feet and Molly would start over. Martha watched Meredith's face for anything, a tremor of her eyes under their lids, a movement of the lips in breath, anything at all. In her peripheral vision she could see Molly's hands moving up the pink fabric and back down again, up and down.

She's going to Gander, said the doctor. They were sitting on some moss-covered stones the doctor had positioned beside her desk. They're sending a boat. It'll be faster than the ferry, easier. A boat, then a car.

What will they do there? asked Martha.

The doctor lifted a rock off some papers, fingered through until she found the right one, glanced at it quickly and said, Tests.

I thought you did tests already, I thought that's why she came here, said Molly.

She needs more, said the doctor. We can do blood, but we can't do bone. She needs bone. She picked up the rock and put it back onto the papers. I'm sorry, she said.

Bone? said Molly.

Yes, said the doctor. Marrow. It's, it's standard, she said. In cases like this. It's not as bad as . . . I mean, it doesn't hurt as much as—she paused a moment, then started again, I am sorry, she said. They don't have as much sea air there, in Gander, but there is a lake. She'll be taken care of there. She will be OK. She lifted another rock, took a pamphlet out from underneath and handed it across the desk, toward them.

YOUTH
AND
CANCER

Martha reached out, put her hand over it.

She'll be OK? said Molly.

Leukemia, said Martha.

They'll call you once the results are in, said the doctor. I can ask them to. I will ask them to.

Leukemia, said Martha.

Leukemia? said Molly.

They'll call you. I'll ask them to call you. The doctor stood up again. I need to make my rounds, she said. But you can go say good-bye if you want. To your sister. For now. Good-bye for now. You can take as long as you want.

Meredith was still sleeping. They stood on either side of her.

Good-bye, said Molly.

Good-bye, said Martha.

As they turned to go, Martha felt warmth, a hand, taking her own. She looked down and saw that it belonged to Meredith's neighbor, all in orange. A very old man. Good-bye, he mouthed.

They stayed overnight on South Island, with a crabber who had known their mother once, and didn't get back home until almost nightfall the next day. There was a folded note stuck to their door with a bit of chewing gum. It said

Martha M.

on the front and, under that, in smaller letters, in a different hand,

(He gave me $3 and a Coke. NOTE: This is not a
regular thing. I am NOT a postman.—N)

Oh? said Molly.

I'll show you later, said Martha. If it's important. She took the note down off the door and folded it into her skirt pocket.

Later, when Molly was in the bathroom getting ready for bed, Martha went into Meredith's room, their parents' old room, closed the door behind her and took the note out of her pocket. Some of the gum had stuck to her skirt's lining, so she had to unstick it carefully to get it out without ripping.

You should have told me. I would have taken you in my boat. Not that
there's anything wrong with your boat. Still, I would have. If you need
to go again, South Island or anywhere, you can always ask me.

Aidan C.

There was a knock on the door.

Martha?

Yes, Molly. Through the old, cracked wood.

Do you think you'll move away? Leave to be with him?

We only just met, Molly. Just one time.

Still, will you?

If I leave, it won't be for ages, Molly, not for years.

OK.

Martha heard her get up and walk away, into their bedroom, into bed, then nothing but the wind on the water outside. She opened the door and went to bed herself, taking the note with her.

The call from Gander came three days later. Molly was inside, preparing wax for jars, so she was the one to answer it. Martha, who had been out on the porch untangling old twine and rolling it back into neat, ordered balls, heard the ring and came in and stood beside her sister. The twine that had been on her lap fell off and rolled down the front stairs, undoing itself in a straight, gray line. Normally, their phone never rang. If people had things to say, they would come to the door.

OK, said Molly, pulling a chunk of her hair free from between her ear and the receiver.

. . .

OK.

. . .

OK.

. . .

No, I— OK.

. . .

OK, thank you.

. . .

No, it's OK, thank you.

...

We will.

...

We will.

...

We will.

After she hung up, Molly looked over to her wax, in a pot on top of another pot. It had cooled over, all gone hard. Goddammit, she said.

What did they say? said Martha.

Now I'll have to start again.

Molly, what did they—

And I'm no good at getting it right, I'm too scared of burning it; I'm no good—

Molly. Martha reached over and stopped her sister chipping at the hardened wax with a spoon. Molly, what did they say?

Molly let the spoon go. It stuck into the wax, almost upright. She's moved, she said. They got her to Gander, did some tests, and the tests were positive, which means negative, which means bad, they were bad, and they moved her again. Further away again. To St John's. I don't know why she had to move again. They didn't say why. I don't know why.

Oh, said Martha. Did they—

Molly sat down on the floor, pushed her hand against her eyes.

Martha sat down next to her. She reached over and took Molly's other hand. It was wet and warm from the wax and the steam. For a while she didn't do anything, didn't say anything, just sat like that. The floor was dusty; there were two dead flies in the corner, against the wall. She wanted to look at Molly, at her sister, but couldn't, couldn't stop looking at the flies. We'll go see her, she said. We will. I know a way. We'll go. She'll wait for us.

Martha rocked her weight from one foot to the next. There was something in her boot, something poking up under the ball of her foot, but she didn't want to bend down and be in an awkward position when Mrs. Connor came to the door, so, instead of trying to get it out, she was looking for a way of balancing so no weight was on that part of that foot. It was sharp, whatever it was. Urchin shell, maybe. She'd never been to Little Running before. Had to ask Nuala the paperboy which house to go to and how to get there.

Yes! Yes, sorry, hello! Hello? Martha could hear Mrs. Connor, calling from the kitchen before stamping out, toward the already propped-open screen door. She pushed it open further with her foot and wiped her hands on her apron. I'm sorry, she said, noticing Martha notice them. I'm jarring meat. Her hands and arms all the way up to the elbow were stained bright red.

Martha rowed back home ten minutes later with a jar of new seal meat and the promise that Aidan would come see her in five days, when he was back on land.

Just be careful, Mrs. Connor had said, handing her the jar. Just be careful with him, OK?

Martha sat on her front step and worked on a net. She didn't know why, but she didn't want to meet Aidan in the house, didn't want to bring him in there yet. The wind was indecisive and bad-tempered and kept blowing the end of her twine the wrong way. It made new knots where she didn't want them. From the steps she could almost see down to the water, and, normally, would be able to hear anything like a boat being pulled up or boots on rocks, but today the wind was too erratic, too disordered to hear anything but it. She squinted toward the water like Meredith had taught them as children, but, as always, that just made her vision fuzzier, not better, so that the first thing she saw of Aidan was just a blot of green. She widened her eyes properly to see his green coat and navy toque. She stood up, waited. He walked a little closer, saw her and smiled. She did too, exhaling. She didn't realize until then that she had been holding her breath, didn't realize that she mostly didn't expect him to come at all.

Hello, Martha,
   Pardon?
   Hello . . . Martha?
   Hello?
   Pardon?
   PARDON?
   The wind was louder than they were.
   HELLO, MARTHA MURPHY.
   OH, HELLO, AIDAN. HELLO, AIDAN CONNOR.
   Her hair was in its usual braid and the unfastened ends of it blew toward her mouth when she spoke and she had to spit them away. Aidan's hair was mostly under his toque, but a few of the front bits blew out in wisps, the wind straightening the curls. Martha reached up to him and brushed them away, aside. She could feel the gentle stubble of salt on his brow.
   I'M GLAD YOU CAME, she said, turning and leading him up the stairs. PLEASE, COME IN.

•   •   •

Martha shut the kitchen door behind them. She knew Molly was up-stairs, was listening.

It's further than Gander. A lot further.

Yes, I know.

It must be a hundred miles, at least.

A hundred and fifty nautical miles.

Our boat could never make that.

The Grass Widow can. Mine can.

And Molly, what about her? Molly will have to come too.

That's fine, there's space.

You'll miss a lot of work.

You will too. Anyway, we can fish on the way back.

And I guess I can make nets on-boat. I can do that almost any-where.

Of course. Tomorrow, then. Let's head off tomorrow, first thing, so long as the wind dies.

Do you think it will?

I think it will. He still had his coat and toque on. It was warm in the kitchen, verging on uncomfortable, but he kept them on.

OK, said Martha. Me too. I think it will too.

I'll come a half hour before sunrise.

We'll be here.

OK.

OK.

He stood to go, stepped toward her. She stepped back.

Thank you, she said.

Always, he said.

Pardon?

Anytime, he said. He stepped away, toward the door. Anytime.

Before going to bed that night, Molly and Martha gathered their things. Raincoats and clean socks and underwear and an extra bra and warm sweater each for the two of them and for Meredith. Three dark berry tarts and three hard tack breads and three dried fish and three large jars of water for them and for Aidan. And he will bring things too, said Martha. He said he would, so this is just in case.

Molly nodded, pushing the toes down and in on a pair of balled socks. They were Meredith's; Molly had them in an almost perfect sphere. It's nice of him to take us, she said.

It is, said Martha.

And for you two to bring me along.

Of course, said Martha. She stopped tightening the jar lids, looked up. Of course we're bringing you along, Molly. That's the whole point. For us to go. Both of us. Of course.

OK. I just thought that maybe you might want—

No.

OK. She stuck her fingers down and into the socks.

Molly, said Martha. No.

OK.

On the tops of the piles they put Martha's needle and card and twine, Molly's score book and pencil, and, unwrapped from tea towels behind the broken cupboard door where their sister thought nobody knew she hid it, Meredith's splitting knife.

Aidan arrived half an hour before sunrise. Martha and Molly were waiting on their front step.

READY? he called up to them.

READY, Martha called back.

Ready, said Molly, more to herself than anyone else, reaching over to pick up her pack.

The morning was calm and still enough for the predawn birds to be easy high up and across the dust-blue sky.

Martha and Molly and Aidan took turns rowing and sleeping and talking and netting and fishing and eating and writing and drinking, careful, aware that they might need to make what supplies they had stretch out over days if it didn't rain. But it did rain, and they pulled up their hoods and put out their jars, lids hanging open, to catch all they could.

You've taken this boat out this long before? asked Martha.

She was rowing and Molly was sleeping and Aidan was checking the compass.

Sure, all the time. Whenever it's my shift. Which is most of the time, in the seasons, said Aidan. He squinted at the place in the clouds where he imagined the sun should be.

For days? said Martha. And nights? In a row?

Of course. That's how you get the fish in.

They don't spoil?

Only sometimes. Rarely. We keep them in seawater and dry on board. See? He pointed behind where Molly was curled against a pile of net, to a ladderlike structure. Wood on wood.

It's different in Big Running. We dry on the flakes. We all come back to the stages at the end of each day. Everyone does.

Every day? said Aidan.

Every day, said Martha.

You all must get pretty sick of each other, hey?

Martha stopped rowing.

No, I mean, I just mean, it's nice to be away. To miss people.

It's also nice to be together.

Yes, yes, of course it is, I just meant—

I just wanted to be sure it was safe, said Martha. I've never been on this kind of boat before.

The Grass Widow is safe, said Aidan. I've worked hard on this one. It's safe. It has to be.

And each sunset, the jellyfish would congregate and float all around their boat like loose, orange clouds and Martha would lean over toward them and tell everyone's fortune from the patterns.

Aidan was rowing and Martha was sleeping and, even though it was dark now, Molly was writing in her notebook.

What are you writing?

Music. Violin music.

Aidan stretched out his neck to see over onto the page while still rowing. It was covered in shapes. Each with a number inside. Circles, triangles, squares and diamonds of all different sizes.

I've never seen proper music-writing before, he said.

Oh, neither have I. This is just a way I made up to do it. Each shape is one of my strings and the numbers are a finger and the size is duration.

What about there? There it says small circle seven. But you don't have seven fingers.

That's for if I want to go higher. That's where my seventh finger would be if I had seven fingers. Or more. It's all pretty easy, when you think about it.

I guess so, said Aidan. He rowed and they were silent for a while. Then he said, Hey, Molly?

Yeah?

Could you write out something that already exists? Like, if I sang something?

Sure.

Like,

The water is wide,

he sang,

I can't cross over

quiet and low so as not to wake Martha.

OK, said Molly. Yes, I can do that. But you have to go slowly.

The
water

sang Aidan.

Good, said Molly. Got it.

is
wide.

Good, said Molly. Good, good. Got it.

He sang a bit more, and she wrote out a bit more, and the same again, and again, and again, the song a duet with the rhythm of his rowing.

Aidan sang and Molly transcribed and Martha slipped in and out of dreams of mermaids until the fog pulled in tight and dense, wetting Molly's paper and making it hard for her to see her pencil. Well, said Molly, closing the notebook and tucking it up against her chest, under her waterproof jacket, I've got most of it I think. I think I can figure out the rest from there.

For a while the oars against the water were the only sound. Molly was sitting so still Aidan thought she had fallen asleep like her sister. Until,

Is it true? she said.

Molly, I thought you were asleep.

Is it true, Aidan?

Is what true?

That all Connors are cheats. Is it true?

They said that in Big Running?

Yes, said Molly.

They say it in Little Running, too. I just thought. I hoped . . .

It doesn't matter if it's not true. Right?

To some people it does.

That doesn't count. Overall it doesn't matter unless it's true, right? So . . . is it?

I . . . No, Molly. I don't think it is. I don't think it has to be.

Me neither. She smiled and closed her eyes and went to sleep for real.

And sometimes the water was blue, more blue than sky, and sometimes it was dark and green and thick, and sometimes it was hardly any color, changing and moving and pushing and pulling like breath.

• • •

Aidan was sleeping and Molly was rowing and Martha was washing her hair with bucketfuls of salt water from over the side. It was cold but good, like waking up over and over and over again.

You know, said Molly, sometimes I forget about Meredith. I forget where we're going or that we're going anywhere, that this isn't just normal life. Sometimes I forget her.

A lot?

No, just sometimes.

We're almost there.

Are we?

I think so.

First came the lightning, when they were all asleep.

Martha woke first. Something is broken, was her first thought.

Then the thunder, rolling out like slow motion, and she remembered where she was, who she was with, and that she wasn't meant to be sleeping at all.

First the lightning, then the thunder, then the wind and the waves, the waves and the wind and the night-white water, all of which were the same, all one, pushing and reaching and pulling and pressing in on them, on every side, wind, waves, water, everything wet and loud and black and white, deep night, then light, then night, then light, and everyone was awake now, Aidan's mouth moving like talking but just the sound of the wind and the waves and the water, just a moving mouth, only visible when the light hit, then gone again, his arms up and grabbing things, something, a snake, a rope, just a rope, Martha stepping out, toward him, black-white, the wind grabbing her hair, punching her back, deep, heavy against her gut, and something, something else, on her arm, pulling her back, a hand in unison with the wind, pulling her, sudden, and she fell back, away from Aidan and back inside and the hatch banged shut. No, said Molly's mouth, in lightning flashes, full of the sound of wind. No.

They watched Aidan through the small rain-streaked window, slow motion in the black and white. Martha counted to a hundred under her breath. If she could get to a hundred and back down again he would be safe. Her hand balled into a tight fist.

Aidan pushed through the hatch, all wet and wind, at ninety-eight.

That's it, he said, and they could hear him. I think that's it now. I think that's the worst of it over.

You could have died, said Martha.

No, said Aidan. I'm safe.

Sometimes the mermaids save people, said Molly.

Sometimes they don't, said Martha.

By the time the sun rose, the water was as calm as if it were frozen. It shone orange-pink all around them for miles and miles and miles.

Martha and Aidan made a list of what they'd lost. Two water-gathering jars, two packets of hard biscuits, one oar, one pair of mittens, one rope, the compass.

Do you know where we are? asked Martha.

She was whispering. Molly was only ten feet or so away, picking up fish that had been tossed into the boat by the storm. If they weren't moving she threw them back into the sea; if they were, she put them in a bucket of cold water, for later.

Yes, whispered Aidan. Kind of.

Kind of?

Well, not exactly. Not like before, but . . . we know the sun is east, and the north star is north.

Aidan, I—

Please don't worry,

Aidan, she said.

We are, we are moving.

And—

It will be OK, I know, just . . .

She put a hand to her face. Row away from the sun in the morning and away from the star at night, she said.

Yes.

Just that.

Just that. He stepped in, carefully took her hand away from her eyes, held it.

Look at this one! Molly came up beside them, her bucket swimming with confused and crowded fish, one of them gleaming bright green all down its back.

Deep water, said Aidan. Deep-water fish.

They aligned against the sun. Aidan found and dusted off the emergency oar, to replace the one they'd lost, and rowed hard and long. Much longer than his turn, almost until sunset.

They could usually feel the morning sun, guess at it through the cloud and fog by the gradient of gray in the sky, by the just-there extra warmth on their faces. But night was harder. If the clouds thinned and the fog lifted they could find the north star and point themselves away, but if not, if the clouds stayed dense and the fog stayed heavy, then the stars were invisible and any way could be the right way and every way could be the wrong way and they would squint and point at real or imagined flecks of light in the white-dark and turn themselves around again and again.

It was misting but not raining and after a while their remaining gathering jar stood thirsty-empty. The mist and fog condensed around its sides and in the ridges of its top and they would take turns licking it off. They breathed with their mouths open, drinking what they could through mist, through fog.

• • •

It was night, half-clear, and Martha was rowing. Molly and Aidan were asleep. Molly with her collar pulled up high and her hat pulled down low, and Aidan sat up like he could have been awake, like he could have been in church. Everyone was sleeping more now. But Martha was awake and was rowing through white ribbons of night mist, everything quieter than seemed possible. She was listening to the quiet when her oar, her left oar, slowed in the water, like it had suddenly become thicker, heavier. And then her right oar too, so she had to push her full body weight up and back to pull through each stroke, like fingers through wind-tangled hair. She stopped, balancing the oars down into their resting places, and leaned out to look over the edge of the boat, into the now-heavy water. Oh, she said. Oh, oh, oh.

She blinked, squeezed her eyes shut, and then opened them again and saw the same thing. Things. Hundreds and hundreds, thousands, more than her eyes could count, all around the boat and leading on, out, jellyfish. Glowing and bright like the stars had fallen down into the sea, like she was in the middle of a new and important constellation. Orange, green, blue, each one pulsed in time with the others. One big heart, thought Martha. Like one big heart.

And they were in a line. The clouds of jellyfish weren't random, they formed a line, a trail, two boats wide and endless boats long, leading away, a different direction to where *The Grass Widow* was going, to where Martha was rowing. Orange, green, blue. Orange, green, blue. Martha breathed up and down with them. OK, she said. OK. She took up the oars and pushed carefully through the glowing water, turning the boat around, pointing it down the glowing, beating trail.

She didn't have to row after that, the pulse of the jellyfish pushed them swell by swell down their path. Martha fell asleep to the silent song of it.

When Martha woke, the jellyfish were gone and the water was pitch-dark again. Instead, there were little points of orange-white light higher up, between the water and the stars. Hundreds of them, stretching through the mist. The boat was headed straight toward them.

Martha stumbled up and over to the hatch, down to wake Aidan. It was warm down there, close. She pulled him up and out to where the cold air opened his eyes wide and, even though he tasted of sleep, and she did too, she pulled him close and kissed him.

And all around was cold and wet and they were warm, were warm and dry.

We made it, she said. Aidan, we made it.

And the lights of St. John's pulled them in, easy now, like nothing.

Meredith was still wearing the pink toque, even though she was inside now, in her own little room. My God, she said. You didn't have to come. So far! You look terrible.

You look better, said Molly.

Mostly better, said Meredith.

The bruising was gone, all gone except for a small patch, the size of a closed hand, on the inside of one arm, just above the elbow. That bit will always be like that, said Meredith. Because that's where it started. There's nothing they can do about that.

Like a scar, said Martha.

Like a tattoo, said Aidan.

Meredith turned, started, noticing the new boy for the first time. Who in hell is that? she said.

I'm Aidan, said Aidan.

Aidan Connor, said Molly.

Aidan . . . Connor? said Meredith.

Meredith, no, said Martha.

Hm, said Meredith.

Really, though, you are glad to see us, right? said Molly.

Meredith smiled. Really, though, I am. I am, Molly. Especially as I don't think I'm ever coming back.

Meredith had been asleep, had been away from the world for weeks at the hospital. She hadn't noticed when they stuck her with round and clumsy sensors, and then needles as thin and plenty as hair, some just now and then, some always in her, reaching out like a marionette's strings. She hadn't noticed when they put her under lead blankets and into a slow, dark tunnel, or when they opened her up and took some bits out. She hadn't noticed when they took off her toque and washed it, rinsing away specks of blood, of sweat, tangles of lost hair, or when they'd put it back on again, clean and slightly less pink than before. Meredith slept and slept and then, finally, she woke up. And then what she noticed was the food.

At first all she could eat was popsicles. Frozen sugar and fruit juice that she could just leave on the warmth of her tongue and let drip down her dry throat. But these weren't just simple rectangular or oblong popsicles like the ones she'd made with her sisters when they were young, out in the back snow over winter, these were little ice statues. These were carved. The first one was a fox leaping up, snout at the top, stick coming back through its tail. Orange. The second was a palm tree, leaves pushing out from the top with carefully crafted fruit where they met. Coconut. The third was a seahorse. Apple.

Then solid food. Salads with tomatoes and cucumbers carved like roses and tulips and lilies. A lasagna with each layer a different color, a rainbow when she cut into it. A Jello castle with grapes and melon suspended inside, king and queen, courtiers and servants. Breathtaking, all of it.

Is this you? she had asked, quiet, her voice barely back yet. Is it you who makes these?

No, ma'am, the nurse, tall and dark and not from there, said. I just carry it. He put the castle down on Meredith's bed tray; the servants and courtiers jiggled.

Do you know who does, who does make it?

I could find out. I could try.

Yes please. Please do.

Ma'am?

Yes?

Is the food all right? I mean, if there is a problem maybe you could tell me first.

There is no problem. It's good. It's really good. That's what I want to tell them, the cook.

You're sure?

Yes.

Because it's just that she's a bit shy and if you were upset, well, I think it would upset her very much, so it'd be better to tell me first, and I could tell her, I could pass it along myself.

No, I'm not, I just— Wait . . . so you do know who it is?

Maybe I do. I mean, yes I do, I think. I mean, I will try to find out for sure that it's her, so long as there is no yelling.

There will be no yelling, I promise.

You promise?

Yes.

Half an hour later a woman, also tall and dark, knocked on Meredith's open door. She held a single tiger lily.

Come in, said Meredith.

My brother, the nurse, said the woman, he said you wanted to see me? She walked to the bed and handed Meredith the flower. It's sugar, she said. You can eat it.

Wow, said Meredith. And then, You're incredible. I just wanted to tell you that you're incredible, that's all. Your food is, I mean. It's not like any food I've seen before, ever. She took the flower.

It's nothing, said the woman. Just cooking.

You do this for everyone, said Meredith, for all the patients?

No, said the cook.

No?

No, said the cook. Not everyone. Her face reddened.

Oh . . . said Meredith. Why? Why for me?

I saw you when you came in, said the cook. I saw you coming in on the boat. To the emergency sea-dock. I was checking my mussel ropes. You were laid out in your sleeping bag. You were like the Lady of Shalott. It was beautiful. You were beautiful. And I was so sure you'd die, like her, like the Lady. Lots of people die here, all the time. I make a manicotti and it gets sent back because the patient has died. I specially froth milk or whip cream and still they die. I try really, really hard, and they still do. They die. So, for you, I decided to try as very very hard as I could. Stay on nights, make perfect the smallest details, every single detail. The very very best I could. I can't save everyone. But I needed to save someone. So I chose you. Just because I had to choose someone, and because you looked like the Lady of Shalott. I didn't want you to die.

But you want other people to?

No, no, of course not. I don't want anyone to.

But especially me, said Meredith, and smiled. The sugar flower stem was dissolving in her hand, sticky-crumbly. But you know it doesn't work like that, she said. You know it can't.

I know I can try.

And if you fail?

I can try.

The flower stem had dissolved away completely now, the whole thing coming apart in two pieces. Meredith put it down on her bedside table, wiped her hand on the bed's outer sheet and said, OK. Then I'll try too. And then, I'm Meredith. Meredith Murphy.

I know, said the cook. I'm Rose-Marie Dajuste.

Rose-Marie, said Meredith. I think it's working, you know.

Yes, said Rose-Marie. I think so too. This time, I really think so.

Do you know what else, Rose-Marie? said Meredith. When it works and I get out of here, I'd like to cook you up a fine piece of fish. A real damn good bit of codfish. What do you think about that?

I think yes, said Rose-Marie.

OK, said Meredith. Perfect. Then she fell asleep.

Rose-Marie came by every day after that; she told her brother to watch the pots and brought Meredith her food herself. She'd sit with her while she ate, and after that until she had to, really had to, get back to the kitchen. If Meredith fell asleep while Rose-Marie was there, she fell asleep holding her hand.

So, said Meredith, when I'm discharged next week, I'm going to go back to hers. I'll rest up there. I'll grow strong, and then, in six months or a year or so, we'll start a restaurant together, Rose-Marie and I.

You will? said Martha.

We will. We've planned it. She'll give notice and I've got savings from back home, from my fish. We'll open it here, in St. John's.

And you'll live together? asked Molly.

Yes, said Meredith.

So you won't be lonely.

No, I don't think I will be. I think I'll be OK. I think I'll be happy.

But we'll miss you, said Molly.

I'll miss you too, of course, said Meredith. Being happy doesn't mean I won't miss you. It just means having to choose between two good things.

And you choose here.

I choose here.

Before they left back again, Martha gave Meredith her splitting knife. Maybe you won't need it anymore, she said. But you should still have it.

Of course I'll need it, said Meredith. I will always need it. I will always have this bruise and I will always need this knife.

Meredith and Rose-Marie prepared them baskets and baskets of food to take on their journey home. Pickled beetroot and carrots all carved into little flowers, dark and heavy breads with M-R-M hand-formed along their tops, long strips of dried fish and pork and beef, twisted and braided like ribbon, apples and pears in whiskey and brandy, and a box of perfect chocolate seahorses, dark and milk and white, in a sea-froth of spun sugar.

And water, said Meredith. Bring jars and jars of it. More, this time.

We'll run out of space, of weight, said Martha.

You won't, said Meredith. You were saving a spot for me. Fill it with water.

Martha and Molly and Aidan didn't get lost on the way back to the Runnings, and there was no real storming, but the passage was still long, against the wind much of the time, and Molly became ill with sea-fever from looking at nothing but water for so long and had to take three days off rowing and only look at her books or hands or the floor or close her eyes until she recovered. They sang to pass the time and made wishes on passing birds and imagined drawing lines between the stars to spell out their names and the names of others they knew and missed and rowed on and on and on, toward home.

It was dusk and Aidan was sleeping and Martha was rowing when Molly saw the icebergs.

But it's the wrong season for bergs, said Martha.

I know, said Molly, but they're there. Look, see?

Martha squinted, stopped rowing for a beat. They're ships, she said, not bergs, ships.

Molly squinted too. Big as bergs, she said. Monster-big.

Yes, said Martha. Yes they are. She picked up the oars, started rowing again. But they're far off.

Molly stayed where she was, stayed squinting. Just think how many fish you could fit on one of those, she said. A whole town's worth. A whole sea.

(1992)

It was almost Christmas. Northern Alberta was covered in snow, thick and heavy over lights, under tire treads. Martha wore all her layers to work, bright yellow over yellow over yellow. Had the tiny space heater turned up full. A fire hazard, said a welder, handing in a visor cracked with cold, picking up a new one.

I know, said Martha. Of course I know that.

All the December employees at Bison Trail work camp got the 23rd, 24th and 25th off as well as a fifty-dollar Christmas bonus, so Martha and Aidan decided she should come home early that month, for the holiday. It was a surprise, for Finn and for Cora. It was going to be a surprise.

Flying's expensive, Aidan. Are we sure?

I'm sure. You've got that bonus.

Fifty dollars is enough for a dinner, not a flight.

Still, it's worth it.

And you haven't told them? asked Martha.

No. A total surprise, said Aidan.

OK.

It will be good. It will be absolutely worth it, Martha. It will be.

OK. You're right, I know.

. . .

Is there snow there?

A bit. Mostly sleet. And fog.

There's so much snow here now. It piles on top of the trees like it's fake. Like someone's painted it there. It piles on top of the machinery and makes things look almost nice.

Almost?

Not quite, but almost . . . Aidan?

Yes?

I am excited, I just worry.

I know. It's good. To balance me.

To balance each other.

Yes.

Yes.

She bought a ticket for the overnight flight on the 23rd so she could get the early-morning ferry on the 24th, the last one before they shut down for the holidays. John with the fair hair squeezed her and three others into his truck for the ride to the airport. It had been snowing all day, the flakes thick and heavy, soaking their hair and eyelashes as they worked, becoming finer and denser as evening fell and it got cold. The wind blew it in swirling ghosts around the truck. They could feel John fighting against it with the wheel, though he didn't say anything. Everyone watched out the windows. In front of and behind them were other trucks full of other workers, all going to the airport.

You can just drop us off, said Martha, no need to park.

I might as well, said John. That way I can help you with bags. And just in case—

You really don't have to, said Martha. She was up in the front of the truck with him.

I might as well, said John.

The airport had a giant tree in the entrance lobby, covered with plastic lights made to look like candles. There was red and silver tinsel all over the barriers that outlined the lineup for check-in and a tinny children's choir rendition of "Do You Hear What I Hear?" played over the PA. The mounted information screen was tinseled too, and sprayed with artificial snow around the edges, the blue-white of it matched the blue DELAYED lettering, while the red tinsel matched the CANCELED lettering in red.

Flight 314 FortMc–Gander DELAYED Please Wait

They stood around it like a fire, waiting for the blue to go red or green, joking and talking at first, then growing quiet and restless, taking off backpacks and putting down bags, backs and necks stiff from looking up at the screen as, one by one, flights turned from DELAYED to CANCELED, from blue to red. John took Martha's left hand, tensed into a fist, uncoiled the fingers for her and held it. They didn't look at each other, just up, at the screen.

They stayed there, waiting, watching, while the absent choir sang through "Silent Night" and "In the Bleak Midwinter" and "O Little Town of Bethlehem" and "Once in Royal David's City" before starting its loop over again, "Do You Hear What I Hear?" "Silent Night," "In the Bleak Midwinter," "O Little Town of Bethlehem," "Once in Royal David's City." And again. And again. And then, during,

Snow had fallen snow on snow

Snow on snow on snow,

their flight, the last flight, turned from blue to red. Just like that. Outside the snow whirled and rushed and piled. Snow on snow on snow.

I'm sorry, said the woman at the service desk. It's just not safe. I'm sorry.

And the camp welder with a new baby in Musgrave Harbor said, It's not your fault. We know.

And she said, But I am. I am so sorry.

And the PA sang,

How still we see thee lie.

And one by one, people gave up waiting for answers or vouchers, and got taxis or rides with each other back to their camps, until it was just the two of them left there, under the screen that was now all black except for PLEASE WAIT in small white letters along the bottom, and John said, I know it's no consolation, but you could come have Christmas with us. With my mother and sister and me. You'd be very welcome.

Thank you, said Martha. She didn't let go of his hand until they reached the truck, until he had to get in to drive.

An Act of God, said Martha, from what used to be John's childhood bedroom, in his mother's trailer. They don't give refunds for those.

It's OK, said Aidan. We'll ignore the Advent calendars and radio station countdowns and wait. Save Christmas until you're back.

But then you'll have to go—

Not for two hours, we'll have two hours.

They celebrated at the cafeteria-style restaurant at the ferry dock. It was new. The only new thing on the whole island. They only had the turnaround time while the ferry was cleaned and reset, so Martha met them on her way off and Aidan brought his bag with him so he could go as soon as they were done. Each of them, Martha, Aidan, Cora and Finn, got to choose whichever main course they wanted out of the beautiful steaming silver bins, and either a fountain drink or any of the desserts from the illuminated cooler display.

Though the do-it-yourself drink dispensers were tempting, in the end Finn chose a three-color Jello bowl with a perfect tuft of cream on top instead. The whole family chose the dessert option, since there was a jug-and-glasses system where you could get water for free.

It was Finn's first time there and it was wonderful. Their individual red plastic trays, the smooth metal track they ran along, the little towers that held and organized the jam and peanut-butter packets in case you chose all-day breakfast like Cora did, the red-and-white-striped candies you got absolutely free at the end, all wonderful.

I bet this was closed on real Christmas anyway, he said.

Under the table he could see his dad's hand on his mom's knee. We should do this again, he said. We should do this every year. Although they had taken down their tree, the restaurant still had some of their other decorations up.

It's actually OK, said Cora. She cut into her egg yolk and it spread all over her toast. It's actually not too bad.

(1974)

Time on land is different from time on-water, and once Aidan got home, after he had left Martha and Molly on their side of the bay and had rowed back over to his side and had gone in and kissed his mother, whom he expected to be sleeping that late at night, but who wasn't sleeping, who was up, was sorting mint leaves for drying by the fire, throwing the bad ones in, watching them sizzle and resist at first and then catch and pop like dynamite, sudden and violent and gone, once he had kissed her cheek and she had said, You made it back,

and he said, Yes, of course,

and she said, Well, one never can be sure,

and they had turned the flue down for the night and gone to bed, once he was there and should have been sleeping, could hear his mother sleeping across the hall, her breathing deep and long, almost as soon as he heard her lie down, like a body starving for it, like she hadn't slept for days and days, then, in his bed, in his old bed, Aidan felt time pull out and away from him. He felt too big. There had been people in outer space now, he'd heard, and while they were there, in space, time moved differently from on earth, so that when they came home they were the wrong age. That was him now. He felt so old now, so much older, too old for the smallness of this childhood bed, for the nearness of this familiar ceiling, for the closeness of his mother's grateful breath.

But he did sleep, eventually. And he dreamed of women and waves and how you should not, should never, drink salt water, even when you're so, so, so thirsty.

And then his mother was knocking on the door to his room because it was time, was past time, for him to get up and eat the breakfast she'd made and go to the boats, to work. He had had more than a reasonable amount of time off already.

Back in Big Running, there was one jar in Martha and Molly's store cupboard, one jar of sweet pickles, that was impossible to open. It had been there since before their parents died, since their mother used to seal the jars and their father used to open them. Whenever she remembered it, when she had a minute walking past the cupboard or was in there anyway getting something else, Martha would try to force it, with new angles or hand towels or boiling water, but it always stayed shut, the metal of the lid and the glass of the jar like one.

But this time, the morning after they got back from visiting Meredith, when Martha went to get a jar of bakeapple jam and, as usual, without even thinking, reached out to try and open the impossible jar, one arm over it, the other hand on top twisting, this time, the lid moved. A creaky resistance at first, then smoothed out like a knife past scales through to soft meat, slipping easily around and off in her hand. At once the whole cupboard smelled of vinegar.

And that wasn't all. Although she hadn't noticed at the time, the days at sea, all that rowing, had left Martha's arms stronger than they'd ever been. Stronger than she knew women's arms could be. The wind blew hard and broke the fence and she pulled it back up, alone and fine. One of the beach cats stranded itself up on top of their roof and she pulled herself up from one windowsill to the next to get it down. The knots she made in her net pulled hard and firm like pebbles, like beads, and she made them faster and better, faster and better than ever before.

Do you miss him?

He's out fishing now, Molly.

Yes I know, but do you miss him?

. . .

. . .

OK, I do. Yes, I do.

You do?

Yes.

You should miss Meredith.

Yes, her too.

And Mom and Dad.

Yes, them too.

And Minnie.

Of course, of course.

And me, miss me when I'm not here. When I'm upstairs practicing or out teaching or when you're out by the water—

Molly, I—

And then you can miss him.

Molly, I can do it all at once. I can miss everyone.

Yes, but us first.

OK, you first.

OK?

OK.

Martha had a new project now. She did her other nets, her commissions and orders too, what people wanted and what she had to do to
pay her share of the household costs, but, in between, instead of swimming before breakfast or going for walks at lunch or reading after dinner, she worked on it. She wasn't even sure what she would do with it,
when it was done, if she would want it at all, but still, she worked on
it. And to everyone else, to Molly, it looked just like netting as usual.
It looked like nothing was happening, like nothing was different from
regular, from before.

(1993)

Winter pushed on and Cora made Luxembourg!, Bhutan! and Tasmania! and Finn filled in his map and Aidan and Martha worked and waited and waited and worked and January, then February, stretched on and on and on.

Almost every night, Finn's parents spoke on the phone. Almost every night, Finn slowed and lightened his breath, silent on the upstairs line. One February night, when the fog made everything otherwise quiet, otherwise dark, Finn heard:

We got a notice today, Martha. His father's voice doubled, one downstairs, one on the line.

A notice? His mother's voice was fuzzy, which meant a further away, off-site, phone. A temp office out somewhere darker, somewhere wilder.

A green notice, said Aidan. Like before.

Oh. A—

Yes.

Oh.

. . .

. . .

It's— said Aidan.

I— said Martha.

It's almost exactly the same, said Aidan. The terms, the wording. More money this time. A little bit more.

To where? said Martha.

Anywhere, said Aidan. Anywhere else.

Anywhere real, said Martha.

We're real.

You know what I mean.

I know, I—

I mean, said Martha. Aidan, I mean this could be OK.

. . .

It could be time—

. . .

Aidan?

Maybe.

How long do we have?

Half a year. Until August, said Aidan. Just six months.

As soon as they hung up, Finn hung up the upstairs phone too, pulled off one sock, put it in the pocket of his corduroys and ran down the stairs. His father was still in the kitchen, by the phone. He was holding one of Finn's for-school pencils. He had a notepad in front of him on the table, blank.

I forgot, said Finn. I forgot that I lost my sock down on the rocks this afternoon.

You did? Shouldn't you be in pajamas? Be in bed?

Yes I did. Yes I should. But I need to go get it first. I'll go to bed right after. I promise.

It's dark, and wet.

I'll be quick.

You know where it is?

I know where it is.

Five minutes, then back to bed.

Five minutes.

It wasn't hard for Finn to find a notice, even in the dark. Most of the houses they were delivered to were abandoned, so Finn just pulled one out of the mail slot of a former neighbor. He held it up toward the sky, the moon, but it was too dark and foggy to see anything but the outline, so he folded it carefully in half and then in half again and put it in his pocket. He took the sock out of the other pocket and ran back home holding it.

Got it! said Finn.

His father was exactly where he'd been when he left. Still standing by the phone, like it might ring again any minute.

OK, good. Good work. Now go to bed.

OK. Goodnight.

Goodnight.

Finn ran up the stairs and into his room. He closed the door as much as it would close when the weather was wet, sat on his bed and took the notice out of his pocket. It was on light green paper, the color of early-morning sea.

The first time the notices arrived, seven years earlier, it was Finn's job to collect the mail in the mornings. He was four years old and could read some words and most numbers, but the black lettering on the notice was too tight and too small for him. He brought it up to the house, into the kitchen, where his mother was making coffee in her work overalls. Dark stains all over the legs like the pattern on an eel. Just one thing, he said.

Thanks, said Martha. She was pouring milk with one hand and took the notice with the other.

The milk was old. Finn saw a lump drop down into his mother's coffee.

Mom? he said.

Oh God, said Martha.

The milk, said Finn.

Where's your father? said Martha.

He's on-boat, like always, said Finn. Mom, the milk.

I'm going to the neighbors'. You wait here. Don't go anywhere.

She left the notice on the counter, her coffee and the open milk beside it. Finn poured out the milk, lumps clogging in the drain, then went to wake his sister.

It says: Everyone out! said Cora.

It does?

Basically.

Out of what?

Here. Out of the village.

Really?

Yep. Everyone out! Time to move to a bigger town!

But why?

Not so many fish anymore, not so many jobs, so what's the point of living here?! it says.

But I like it here.

Too bad! it says. Lots of people left already, so off you go!

There are more fish in the bigger towns?

I guess so.

What else? There are a lot of words.

We'll turn off your heat! Your post! Your water! You won't be able to take baths! You'll freeze in winter!

Really?

Really. It says, We Really Will. Don't think this is a fake, it says. Because this is not a fake.

When?

Um. Cora looked back down at the green sheet, ran her finger along to the bottom. There's going to be a meeting, she said. After that.

Soon?

Yep. Very soon.

Four months after the arrival of the first notice, the one Finn couldn't read, he had stood with his sister and father on a large flat boulder and watched their house float away. His mother was out on the water in a dory, helping pull it away from their east-cove village, Little Running, toward the slightly bigger west-cove village of Big Running. She was in charge of ropes and knots. It took two hours and forty-seven minutes to pull it across.

Theirs was the very last of five once-east-cove homes, now west. Resettled. Just like that, said Finn's father. Just like that. There was only one house left over in Little Running: Mrs. Callaghan's. She wouldn't leave. Not even when the government said they'd pay her twice the amount everyone else was getting because she'd been there so long. Not even when they said they would cut off water and electric within twenty-four hours. Not now, not ever, she said. Not now, not ever.

Finn didn't need Cora's help to read the notice this time, but he still went to her room, still woke her up.

Wake up, said Finn.

No, said Cora.

Wake up, you have to.

I don't.

Look, said Finn. Look. His whisper cracked. Cora lowered her blanket off her face, opened her eyes. Look, Finn said again. He handed her the paper.

They were silent while she read. Finn sat on the floor, close enough to follow Cora's eyes but far enough that no part of him touched any part of her or her bed. She finished and folded the green paper in half and handed it back to Finn, still silent. She closed her eyes but not to sleep, sighed.

I'm going to hold a meeting, said Finn. I'm going to fix this.

Yeah? she said.

Yeah.

He made his own notices. On white paper:

NO
WE DON'T HAVE TO
GO.
A MEETING TO TALK ABOUT WHAT TO DO INSTEAD
WEDNESDAY, FEB 17th, 6 P.M.
CONNOR HOUSE
SNACKS INCLUDED.

His father watched him. He stood behind Finn at the kitchen table while he wrote them out one after another after another. Can I help? he asked.

No, said Finn. Thanks, but no.

So Aidan made him hot chocolate and picked up paper scraps and got out a spare black felt pen in case Finn's ran out of ink. When that was done and there was nothing else to do, he just stood there, behind him.

Are you sure? he said.

Yes, said Finn.

Finn delivered them on his bike to the four still-occupied houses first, then to all the others too, just in case. He pushed them through metal-cold mail slots, then stood outside and waited, ten seconds, thirty, sixty, in case he heard anything inside. Anything moving, anything living. When he finished, the sun was almost gone, Wednesday, February 10, almost gone.

Five days before the meeting Finn borrowed the Today's Specials blackboard from the empty bakery, along with two boxes of pink and white chalk he found in a drawer behind the counter. He carried it all back to his house, the blackboard balanced across his back, the chalk in his pockets.

Three days before the meeting Finn drafted an agenda, including seven minutes for greetings, five minutes each for everyone to speak, two minutes each for two votes, should they need votes, and five minutes for scheduling the next meeting and plans. He wrote it out and taped it to the mantel. No fires until after the meeting, OK?

OK, said Aidan.

•   •   •

Two days to go and Finn made reminder notices, drew stars on them, underlined the date and place, pushed them through the mail slots of all the houses. At the third house a hand caught his as he posted it through. Cold, salt-rough fingers around his.

Finn?

Yes, Mrs. O'Leary?

You have time for a tea, Finn, a chat? Her voice was quiet but close; she must have been kneeling down, whispering into the slot.

Thanks, Mrs. O'Leary, but I've got all the other houses to finish.

OK, maybe next time.

Maybe next time. See you Wednesday?

Yes, yes, Wednesday.

One day before the meeting Finn took a rag and wiped all the dust off the shelves and window frames and Cora's violin case and the blackboard, now propped in front of the fireplace. He melted Jello powder into bowls of warm water and carefully filled the fridge with the green and orange liquid, pushing all their other food to the sides.

Is there anything I can do? asked his father.

Don't bump the bowls, said Finn.

Two hours before the meeting Finn made a small pile of all the pencils and pens and scrap paper he could find, neat on the living-room coffee table. He chopped cheese into cubes and put it on a plate to one side of the pencils. He chopped Jello into as close to cubes as it would go and put it on another two plates to the other side of the pencils.

Where's Cora? he asked.

I don't know, said his father. She'll be back soon though, I'm sure.

Fifteen minutes before the meeting Finn wrote:

BIG RUNNING TOWN MEETING

on the blackboard in white and underlined it in pink, leaving lots of room underneath. He sat in the chair nearest to it, rolling a piece of chalk between his thumb and finger. He could see out the front window from there.

Is there anything I can do? asked Aidan.

Do we have enough chairs? asked Finn. He had moved all of the kitchen ones into the living room, and all of Aunt Molly's too.

I think we do.

I guess you could help take coats and arrange boots, when everyone gets here, if they all get here at once?

OK, said Aidan. OK, I can do that.

He stood by the door and Finn sat in his chair and they both watched the window, both waited.

The sun set just before six o'clock, spreading across the evening's mist pink and orange and red.

That's nice, said Aidan. Isn't that nice?

Yeah, said Finn.

It was almost fully dark when Cora got in. Sorry, she said. Sorry I'm late. Where should I sit?

Well, said Aidan.

Anywhere, said Finn.

Can I eat some Jello?

I— said Finn.

Not yet, said Aidan. Not quite yet.

At six fifteen Cora snuck a piece of green Jello. Finn saw but didn't stop her.

At six eighteen there was a knock on the door. Aidan moved toward it, but Finn was there, turning the handle, before he could get to it. Hello! he said. Hello hello hello.

Three people were on the doorstep, Mrs. and Mr. O'Leary and Bill Kelly, who had a guitar case on his back.

Come in, come in, said Finn.

Let me take your coats, said Aidan.

You might want to keep them on, said Cora. Since we're not allowed to have a fire.

The next group arrived just as Bill was finding a place to lean his guitar. This time it was five people, some recognizable, some not.

My cousin, back visiting from out west, said Sheila McNabe.

My sister, said Charlie Brophy, over from South Island.

The cousin carried a flute with no case, the sister a set of pipes.

By six thirty the room, and all the chairs, were full. Cora had been shifted to the floor to make room. Aidan still stood by the door. All the green Jello was gone and most of the orange. Under chairs and across knees and between bodies there were three fiddles and three guitars and two bodhrans and four whistles and two accordions and one flute and one set of pipes. Everyone was talking to everyone.

OK, said Finn. It's time to start.

Everyone kept talking to everyone.

OK, said Finn, louder, lower. He knocked his fist against the blackboard, once, twice. Heads turned, voices dropped.

IT'S TIME TO START, he said. Please.

Everyone went quiet. Everyone looked at Finn.

OK, said Finn. He exhaled, held up a green notice. The thing is, he said, we don't have to go. Right? Not unless everyone wants to. It has to be unanimous. That's what it says.

Near-unanimous, said Cora.

Ninety percent of us.

Of residents.

What does that mean?

People who live here.

Or own property here.

And if they're gone, already gone?

That counts as a yes.

Yes to staying or yes to leaving?

Yes to leaving.

OK, said Finn, still. Still, we are still here, we are enough of us.

When do we have to decide?

Six months.

Less now.

Six months minus a week.

I've lived here sixty-seven years, said Mrs. O'Leary.

Fifty-two, me, said Joe Blacks.

Thirty-six, Sheila McNabe.

Twelve, said someone.

Thirty-nine, someone else.

Sixty-six,

Seventy,

Fifteen,

Forty-eight,

Forever,

Forever,

Forever.

Finn wrote down all the numbers, all bigger than him.

And I'm tired,

I'm so tired,

So, so,

So, fucking tired.

Both Finn and Cora looked over to their father, but he said nothing, just nodded a little.

Finn, said Mrs. O'Leary, I'd still like to believe you could bring them back.

So would I,

So would I.

You caught the last fish, do you think you can catch more?

There are no more.

There might be more.

There are no more.

If there are, Finn can find them.

Yes, Finn will find them.

We've tried.

We're tired.

We've tried and tried.

It's you or nothing, Finn.

Yes,

Yes,

Yes,

Finn or nothing.

The room went quiet again. Finn waited, pressed his fingers around the chalk, imagined he had the strength to squeeze it flat, to squeeze it until it turned liquid and pushed through, between his fingers. A woman he didn't recognize reached over and took the second-last piece of orange Jello. Cora reached after her and took the last one. Still quiet. Finn opened his hand; the chalk was still solid, still normal. He wrote:

Me. (Finn Connor)

on the blackboard.

Does anyone have any other ideas? said Finn. Anything else?

Quiet. Rupert Coffin scratched his leg. Mrs. O'Leary met eyes with Mr. O'Leary, then looked away.

Finally, somebody's sister-in-law said, How about a song? She picked up a guitar that wasn't hers.

Yes,

Yes.

For the fish, or— said Finn.

For now, said Aidan. It was the first thing he had said since everyone arrived. Let's have a song for now.

After the first song there was another, and then another, and then another. Someone moved the blackboard to the front porch and started a fire. Bottles and flasks appeared from coat pockets and fiddle cases. His father went and got Finn's accordion, helped him lift the straps over each shoulder. Arms and legs and voices, fiddles and flutes and drums, all moving together, all in time. It was warm and there was food and there was drink and all the songs were songs Finn knew. Aidan phoned Martha in Alberta and held the phone up so she could hear. Finn played and sang along as late as he could, fighting sleep, leaning into the cold of the wall against his back, the rough of the boards under his legs. He didn't notice exactly when Cora slipped away, out.

When he woke he was being lifted, pulled up by his father. His accordion was on the floor beside an empty Canada Club bottle. Finn let himself be helped, half carried, upstairs to bed. His father was humming; Finn closed his eyes and sank into it.

It was past two in the morning when Cora came to Finn's room. She had her toque and one of their mom's sweaters on, red wool with two twisted braid patterns, one along each side. It hung down well past the pockets of her jeans, almost to her knees. I'm sorry, she said. I just want to show you one more thing. Just one more. Bring a coat.

They walked out to Carissa Stone's cottage, set back a bit from the other houses, away from the water. They climbed in through the window.

Everything, all the walls, the floor, the sofa, the rocking chair, the door, the fireplace, the ceiling, the chimney, everything, was covered in blue, a mix-up of lots of different blues, cut from lots of different pictures, all stuck together so it almost looked like it was moving. On top of this was a combination of people-things and sea-things. There was a little wood cabin right next to a giant octopus, a school of green and yellow fish flowing around a tall city tower, a seahorse floating out the doorway of a post office, a crab pushing a stroller, cars sunk into seaweed. There were jellyfish hanging over the lightbulbs in the ceiling with bicycles and mittens and school buses caught up in their tentacles. They were made of plastic wrap and tinfoil. They made everything shine.

It's Atlantis, said Cora. There were no more Happy Backpacker Guides, so I came up with this one myself.

Oh, said Finn. Oh wow. This is the best one, Cora. This is the best one of them all.

Yeah? said Cora.

Yeah.

. . .

. . .

Hey, Finn?

Yeah?

I wanted to tell you, you can go into any of the houses whenever you want, OK? I know I said before that you couldn't, but I changed my mind. You can.

Thanks, Cora.

You're welcome.

Finn updated his map before going back to bed. If it was right, this was the last empty house; Cora had filled them all now, twenty-four in total now. He fell asleep remembering what it felt like to run his hands down Atlantis's mismatched blue walls, about how it was like being underwater and being able to breathe at the same time.

The next morning she was gone. There was a note

> *Please don't try to find me.*
> *I'll be fine.*

surrounded by empty cups and plates and bottles. Finn read it and felt like his feet were sinking down into the wooden planks of the floor. Like he and his father were the only two people left on the whole island, in the whole world.

Martha was in the temp tool crib on the overnight shift. It was busy and it was loud. The phone was ringing, but she didn't have time to answer it; a steady lineup of men strung back from her open window as one by one she handed them the flimsy blue coil notebook in which to write their names and the equipment they were getting while she went to find their things in the back. Denis, metal saw; Steven, cracked hat (return); Aaron, tube wrench; Ross, heat packs; Stewart, drill bit five; Patrick, drill bit six; and then John, not writing anything, just standing there. In his safety hat and glasses it took her a moment to recognize him; everyone here looked the same.

Come for a walk later? he said.

I don't get off for another seven hours.

After that?

Where is there to walk? All around them concrete, steel, lights, trucks, noise.

I know places.

OK.

Is your sister doing better? At Christmas dinner, John's sister had stayed in her room the whole time, door closed.

She's a bit better, said John, thanks for asking. It's been a long winter.

They were walking through the site, up toward the northwest corner. The machine noise was loud and his voice was soft, so Martha had to lean in to hear.

This is the quickest way out without a truck, he said. It was all concrete, lights, noise, and then trees, the development drifting off into forest like a beach to sea. We're still technically on-site here, said John, but it doesn't feel like it, hey? They stepped into the forest's shadow, the snow reaching up past the tops of their boots. The insulation of the trees muffled the site noise down, like it was under snow too.

John, said Martha.

Yeah?

What was it like here, before?

There were a lot of trees.

There are still a lot of trees . . .

There were only trees.

I'd like you to tell me about it.

Martha Murphy, I'd love to tell you all about it.

Back in her room, like it had in the tool crib, Martha's phone rang and rang. Once every ten minutes, again and again and again, from the end of her shift, at six in the morning, through to seven and eight and nine, until, at ten minutes past nine, she heard it ringing from down the hall, still ringing as she tried the wrong key in her room door, they all looked the same here, all the small, flat, cheap kind, still ringing as she finally got it unlocked and pushed open and reached out to it before even taking off her boots or shutting her door.

It didn't say where she was going?

No, I read you the note. That was the whole note.

Did anybody see her? Somebody must have seen her.

No one has. I've been around to everyone, no one has.

Did you check the empty houses?

He did, Finn did. She's not there.

She can't have just left, Aidan. She's only fourteen. She can't have just left. Did you check the boats? Are there any missing boats?

No, I didn't—

Damn it, Aidan. You have to check the boats. Always check the—
I haven't—
My God, is it stormy? Did you let her go out on a—
I didn't—
Oh God.
I didn't—
Oh God.

When Finn came back from double-checking the houses for Cora, in case she actually was still there, in case he had missed something the first time, his father was standing in the kitchen, just like he had been an hour before. Only now he was wearing his old green jacket and, instead of holding the phone, he was holding a very small, very worn feather. It was missing most of its vanes. He didn't turn around when Finn came in.

She's not there, said Finn. Not in the houses, still. I checked really carefully, I checked again.

OK, said his father. Thank you.

Finn was afraid that he was going to offer to come along, to go check the houses for himself, but his father didn't say anything else, didn't move.

Do you want me to go check again?

No, no, it's fine. Thank you, Finn.

Silence again. Aidan and the feather and Finn. It wasn't any kind of feather Finn recognized.

Finally, his father looked up again and said, Do we call the Sea Rescue volunteers? The police?

I don't know, said Finn.

I don't either, said Aidan.

There weren't enough people left in Big Running to have their own Volunteer Sea Rescue Scouts anymore, so they had to wait more than an hour for them to arrive from South Island, even with the motor in their boat as they had to fight the wind and cut through the floating ice. Finn and Aidan met them at the water.

I'm Mavis, said one.

And I'm Violet, said the other.

They were older than Finn's mother, but younger than Mrs. Callaghan. They both had the same white-silver hair, cut short, just barely sticking out from under their SIVSRS toques. Their eyebrows and eyelashes were crusted in matching salt-ice. Sea widows, the both of us, said Mavis, cutting the engine.

This water can be a right bastard, said Violet, throwing a rope out so Finn and Aidan could pull the boat to them.

But we'll do whatever we can, said Mavis.

Whatever we can to help, said Violet.

Their SIVSRS vests shone bright yellow against the water.

I'm going with them, said Finn's father. Can you go back around to see if anyone's missing a boat?

And even though Finn wanted to go out in the fast boat with Mavis and Violet, wanted to sit right in between them, wanted them to put their arms around him or squeeze his hand while they all looked, all looked together, he didn't say it. Instead he said, OK. And he turned to walk away, back toward the houses.

AND WE'LL MEET BACK AT HOME AFTER! called Aidan, over the motor's cough.

OK, said Finn, though he knew it was too quiet for his father to hear.

He had already been to the four neighbors who still lived in the Big Running Greater District twice that morning, and, of course, they had already checked their boats, and nothing was missing, nothing was gone.

Mind you, said Bill Kelly, slurring a little, still hungover, there's nothing would have stopped her taking one of the old ones rotting on the rocks. Dozens of those up and down the water that nobody's counting or keeping track of anymore. Doubt any of them would hold up for more than a few miles out, bumping with the ice though, and Cora's a smarter girl than that.

She is smart, said Finn.

We know, said Bill.

She is.

Yes, we know.

After checking with everyone, again, again, Finn went home and got his accordion and took it out of its case and strapped it onto his front. Then, without bending over, he slipped off his shoes and stepped into boots, tall black rubber with red soles, and set out across the marshes the two miles to the tallest plateau with his cairn on it. The weight of his accordion made his feet stick in the half-frozen bogs more than usual and he had to flex his toes with every step to keep his boots on.

His cairn was still there, still standing. There was a new orange spot of lichen blooming across its lower stones. A lonely lichen is a happy lichen, Charlotte from the fish-packing plant had told him once, before she and her husband went west. The fewer of us around there are, the better for it. Finn kicked at it with his boot, first just a little and then hard, so that the whole cairn fell over, some stones tumbling down the side of the plateau into the marsh, others falling into and onto themselves in a messy pile.

He stayed standing up to play. He wiped his eyes and nose with his already-wet sweater sleeve, positioned himself facing west, looking into the foggy sun, and began to play one of the Local Jigs, Reels and Airs Based on the Flora and Fauna of the Region. He knew them all by heart now. It started raining, which wasn't good for the accordion, but he kept playing anyway, right through, right until he had played through them all. At one point, in the middle of "The Cotton Grass Air," three caribou appeared from the northwest, about a hundred meters away. They stopped and stood lichen-still for the rest of the air, then two reels and one more air, then left again the same way they had come.

Martha still had ten hours left before her next shift started. She sat down on her bed and looked at the phone. She had no reason to pick it up. No news, nothing to say. More than sleep, more than crying, she wanted to pick it up, but had nothing.

Mavis and Violet dropped Aidan off as close as they could to dry rocks, but he still had to wade in from shin-deep ice water, the cold of it first shocking, then numbing him. Once home, he took off his boots and wet socks and left them by the front door. He could see that Finn was there already, his smaller boots fallen over in the entranceway, his accordion out of its case, wet sock marks on the rug up the stairs toward his room. Aidan walked past them, into the kitchen, and sat in the chair nearest the phone. He had no news, nothing to say. But he didn't know what else to do, so he sat there, just sat there.

Finn stretched the phone cord the other way, out along the hall, around the door and into Cora's room. There were no lights on in their house or any house, no boat lights on the water. He sat on the floor, back against her bed.

More? asked Mrs. Callaghan.

Please, said Finn. Please.

(1974)

After their journey, once everyone was back and things were normal and Aidan was out fishing again for long nights and days and nights, after that, when he came in to drop off his catch in wet and shining piles like pirate treasure, then, before going home, before seeing his mother, Aidan would row over to Big Running, to Martha. She would meet him on the shore, working nets, or, sometimes, if she saw him coming a long way off, in her own boat, she would row out to meet him. It was almost always morning, almost always early.

In clenched fists, Martha would bring Aidan sea glass, round and smooth and blue and green and clear as sky. Mermaid's tears, they called them, in the Runnings. Cried for people left back onshore, hardened by distance.

So many tears, said his mother. Aidan arranged the glass on the mantel over their fireplace, sorting it so no two of the same color were next to each other. When the fire was lit the light shone through them and onto the walls and ceiling and onto their hands and cheeks and mouths, blue, green, clear as sky.

In buckets of cold seawater, Aidan would bring Martha the strangest, most wonderful things he found in his nets. A tiny, bright red fish like a spark. A sea snake black as tar spiraling around and around itself. An explosion of a sea urchin like a living firework.

Martha built rock cages for her creatures. She'd wade into the water and use small and medium rocks to build circular cages in the shallows. She poured the fish, the snake, the urchin out into these. She made them in a row so she could walk along, like a zoo. She brought Molly down to see. Do you think it's cruel? she asked, the water pushing and pulling into the rock cages, in and out, against their calves, bare, trousers rolled up.

I don't know, said Molly. Do they escape?

They all do, eventually, said Martha. Does that make it better or worse?

Hm, said Molly. I'm not sure. Better, I guess.

(1993)

The next day was a Friday. An accordion lesson day. Should I go?
asked Finn, downstairs for breakfast. They were out of cereal and the
milk was bad so he was eating crumbled up jam-jam cookies with
water.

Of course, said his father. Why wouldn't you go? He wasn't eating
anything. Just drinking black coffee in his bright orange SQUIDJIG-
GINGGROUND! mug.

What will you do?

What I normally do. I have things to do.

Go fishing?

Maybe. Maybe stay in and work around here. Make things right
for when your mother and Cora come home.

I could stay and help?

No. No, you should go. Go.

OK.

Because it was always freezing now on the boat out to Mrs. Callaghan's, and because Cora wasn't there to get mad at him for it, Finn
went into his sister's room and got her bigger, caribou-head sweater
and put it on over the top of his own fish one. He wrapped up his accordion, too, first in its case, then in one of Aunt Minnie's old quilts,
then stuffed it into a black garbage bag that ripped a little from the

expanded bulk. He carried it like a big, ungainly baby down to the ice-docked boat. Once on the water, the double-thick wool over his arms made it hard to bend at the elbow, so Finn's rowing was slow and clunky, pushing frozen-fingered through patches of sugar-thin ice that cracked against the boat like cellophane.

Well, said Mrs. Callaghan, once Finn had unwrapped all the layers off his accordion and himself. That's fucked.

What?

Fucked, said Mrs. Callaghan. Look here, she said, and pointed at one of the dark splotches blossoming along the instrument's bellows. Or here, pointing at another. Or here, another. Got wet, didn't it?

Not today . . . said Finn. I wrapped it. I double-wrapped it.

No, not today, yesterday, said Mrs. Callaghan. After Cora left.

You, said Finn. You know?

Your dad phoned me right away, right away that morning, checking she wasn't here with me. Of course she wasn't here with me, said Mrs. Callaghan. That wouldn't make sense. That would be the opposite of making sense, of Cora.

I don't— said Finn.

Look, said Mrs. Callaghan. She braced herself with one hand on the wall and the other on her chair and shakily stood up. She took his hand and led him up the stairs into the spare room. The telescope pointed out the window. The notebook was open on the table beside it, full of names, of people gone. In fresh letters in the second-lowest slot on the right-hand page it said:

Cora Connor

in careful, black pen. Finn ran his finger over the ink's impression.

I'm sorry, said Mrs. Callaghan.

Finn didn't say anything.

I'm sorry, said Mrs. Callaghan again. I don't have the power here for a hair dryer, with my little generator, but if you have one at home you could probably still save it. Still dry the bellows out OK.

Yeah?

Yes, I think so.

OK.

They went back downstairs and Finn put his accordion in its case and its quilt and its garbage bag. Then he pulled his sweater on over his shirt and took Cora's down off the hook where he'd hung it.

Soon there'll be proper ice, I think, said Mrs. Callaghan. Soon it'll be too froze up for you to come see me for a while.

Not yet, said Finn.

Yes, but soon.

I'm getting stronger at rowing, better at breaking ice, thin ice at least.

Well, just don't get stupider while you're at it.

Stupider? No, I won't, I mean I'm just—

Oh, you probably will. You almost certainly will, eventually. The sea does that to men. To women, too. Come on, come on, it says, you know me, surely you trust me by now, by now. And eventually they do, you do, even though they know they shouldn't, they can't. It comes from swallowing seawater when you're young. When you're a baby, usually. Something we almost all do, inevitable, really. Then it's in you, and you can't resist, you can't think right, when you've got it like that, calling you from inside and out . . . She stopped and looked at Finn, put one arm out over his head, measuring. Though you're probably fine for a few years yet. Probably until you're a bit further grown.

And Cora?

I don't know. I don't know about her.

And what about you? said Finn. How come you know better? Haven't you ever swallowed some water accidentally?

Of course, said Mrs. Callaghan. Of course, of course. We all did. We all do. She let her arm fall back down, away, to her side. We all do.

She left time at the end of her voice, like she was going to say more, like a bridge to somewhere, but instead she was quiet and the bridge ended before going anywhere.

Anyway, she said after a beat, think of the poor Spaniards. Remember them when you think about visiting me in storm-time.

The Spaniards? All Finn knew about Spain he knew from Cora's house. Bulls and sun and tomatoes. Nothing about seawater, about storms.

Mrs. Callaghan sighed. Sit down, she said.

Finn had one sleeve of Cora's sweater on. He pulled it off, inside out. OK, he said. He walked over and sat on the sofa with the sweater in a ball on his lap. Mrs. Callaghan sat down next to him. They both faced forward, toward the fire.

The Spanish have the sea too, she said. Not all of them, but a lot of them, and one year, one winter, it was especially high, much higher than usual, and it rose and rose all around the Spanish coast and trickled inland down roads and paths and into grain stores and under nursery doors until their bread was soaked in it and their babies licked it off their fingers and toes and their wine tasted of salt and got them drunker than ever before. And they danced and laughed and splashed and decided, that year, to send out ships, three hundred and thirty-three ships.

Three hundred and thirty-three?

Yes. Three hundred and thirty-three, out, west and north, to explore and discover, since this was when people were still exploring and discovering. And, see, because they were from a warm and welcoming place, and because they were stupid with the sea, they pushed off, all three hundred and thirty-three of them, each with a captain and a crew and a cat, because cats were lucky and because the cats had lapped up seawater too, from the puddles and ponds, they all pushed off to explore the North Atlantic New-Found-Land that year, smack dab in the middle of March.

She stopped for a moment. Turned and looked at Finn. In March, she said again.

In March?

Yes. In March. But being on the sea in March here is not the same as it is in Spain, is it?

I don't know . . . no?

No. But it called them, lured them, and they were so excited and inflamed and stupid that they didn't stop to think about the difference between there and here, what it could be, what that could mean for them. Instead they just sailed happily north and west and north and west and then, of course, once they were north and west enough to be almost here, the storms hit, of course, the March storms. Still they tried to push on, north and west, as the storms hit harder and harder and as, one by one, the sea reached up and pulled the ships, the sailors, the captains, the cats, down to her. One after another after another after another, on our rocks and our shoals, one by one by one. The sea needed them, so it called, and when they came it took them, all three hundred and thirty-three, just like that.

Just like that.

Just like that. The sea is different from the devil, because it doesn't offer a bargain; it just asks and gets.

Why did it want them?

Hm?

You said the sea needed them. Why? Why did it need them?

Oh, always different reasons, always. But always a reason. That's another way it's different from the devil, it always has a reason. In this case, the fish were coming, the sea could feel them moving this way, pulling through it, and it knew they would need places to live and eat and hide once they'd arrived. They need that, the fish, codfish especially, a dark and sheltered place to feel safe, especially in the daytime when the sun is too bright. And the sea loves its fish. Needs its fish. And, of course, the codfish aren't the only ones who like wrecks. The plankton, the barnacles, the mussels, the littler lives gather and grow there too, where there's something to hold on to, and the fish like that even more because they get to eat them. The little lives don't mind too much because they multiply so quickly, covering over a single wreck in no time, a garden of them across the bones of an old ship, so many new lives in exchange for a few.

So . . . it was good, what happened to those Spanish ships in the end? It was good that they all sank because it meant the fish and the barnacles and the mussels and crabs and things could all stay and live?

It's not good or bad. It just is. But that doesn't stop us feeling bad when a body gives in and the sea takes them away. So, even if it's not bad, or good, I don't want you being stupid. Not yet. OK?

OK. Finn pushed his fingers through the place where the knit was loose in Cora's sweater. Mrs. Callaghan?

Yes.

It's almost March now, isn't it?

It is . . . and the storms and the ice are real, Finn, not stories, real. OK?

OK.

•   •   •

The ice-rain settled into mist as Finn rowed back to Big Running, like a filter of gray-white over everything, like a cold and constant cloth against his mouth, his nose, his eyes.

Instead of going home after Mrs. Callaghan's, Finn went to the Italy! house. He knew they had left a hair dryer; Cora had used it on her Sistine Chapel ceiling painting so it would dry quickly and not drip on the carpet. He hoisted the window open, lifted his accordion through and in, and then climbed in himself.

The hair dryer was in the bathroom. Cora had put it back once she was done with it. Finn took it out again and plugged it in the living room next to the lamp made to look like a leaning tower. He unwrapped his accordion—bag, quilt, case—stretched the bellows out as wide as they'd go, and hummed along to the steady hum of warm air like Mrs. Callaghan had told him to. You can still sing, when you don't have an instrument, she had said. Even when you don't have anything, you can always sing.

Cora went the long way, across the dark marshes. She went the dark way, away from the road, over the moss and mud and slush and rocks, to the combination grocery store/gas station. It was the only one on the island, at the ferry lot. Eleven kilometers or nearly seven miles away. It was rainy and windy, so her footsteps washed and blew out of any snow or ice she crossed. She had a portable reading light that Aunt Minnie had sent her for her birthday that she used as a headlamp, like the cavers in Mexico. She attached it to the top of her coat's hood so she could have one hand free for her violin and one for her suitcase.

The ferry station was right at the midway point of the island, where the rocks met the trees. Cora switched off her headlamp and waited in the darkness between two firs for a car to pull in. It was almost morning. Only an hour until today's boat.

Eventually the O'Learys pulled in, in their battered, wine-red station wagon, Mrs. O'Leary driving and Mr. O'Leary asleep in the passenger seat. When Mrs. O'Leary, tired-eyed, sad-eyed, went into the office to pay and to chat, Cora slipped out, away from the trees. She carefully, quietly, opened the back door on the car's far side and pulled the latch that dropped the seat forward and exposed the trunk. Carefully, quietly, she pushed her violin and suitcase through and in, then climbed in herself, closing first the car door, then the back seat hatch. She sat in the trunk's cramped darkness, between her own things and the O'Learys' suitcases and boxes, with just one finger hooked out so the hatch didn't quite latch shut, so she could escape if she needed to. Just one finger, not quite invisible, but almost. She had practiced everything at home, in their car, was good and fast and silent. Mr. O'Leary slept and slept. Didn't wake when his wife came back and closed the driver's door more loudly than she meant to. Didn't wake when she started the car and drove it around to the waiting area. Or when the gulls started circling and calling and calling and circling in the wake of the ferry pulling in.

Of course the car was going to the boat. Was going west. That's where they all went now.

No news? John leaned into the frame of Martha's room door. No news about Cora? He had just got off work. She could tell by the way his face sparkled under the fluorescent light with bits of dried sweat-salt.

No news, said Martha. But you don't need to keep checking up on me like this. You haven't been to bed yet.

Have you?

No.

You going to stay up much longer?

Probably.

Let me teach you how to knit.

Now?

It will be good for you. For your tense hand.

I already know how to make net, it must be pretty similar.

I've never seen you do that.

Not much use for it here, is there?

I don't know, maybe there is. You should teach me.

To net?

Yes. I'll teach you to knit and you teach me to net.

OK, OK. Come in, John.

He came in, shutting the door after him, and sat next to her on the bed. Martha lifted a hand and ran it down the side of his face, across the salt. You didn't have to come, she said.

I know, he said.

Cora sold her violin in Toronto. She also had a couple credit cards she'd found in houses back home that she could try, if she had to. She kept the violin case and filled it with food, supplies. She hitchhiked. She'd been on two boats and in six cars so far. If anyone asked, she gave a different name each time. She held a small boning knife hidden and ready in her pocket whenever she got into a new vehicle. She was almost there.

The police came from the mainland. They knocked on all the doors Finn had already knocked on. They checked all the boats Aidan had checked. They searched all the water Mavis and Violet had searched. They did it again and again. They asked Finn questions, the same questions, again and again. Finn watched his father, on the other side of the kitchen, leaning into the counters with his eyes shut, saying, I don't know, I don't know, I don't know.

And the ice pushed in and out and in, and the days went by.

The police left, promising phone calls and databases, promising anything when there was anything, anything, anything, anything at all.

Then Finn's father went too, off to Alberta, and his mother came home. The ferry was late because of the ice, and needed a quick turn-around to make up time, so Aidan and Martha only had a minute in the parking lot, just a seconds-long embrace, her head into his shoulder, his hand on her back, until Martha pulled away.

You've got to go, she said.

I know.

They won't hold it for you.

I know. I'll call.

I'll call too.

OK. Tell Finn. Tell him I'll call.

Yes. Go, go.

Finn waited in the car, his hot cheek against the frozen smooth of the window.

In a ditch, down between the marsh grass and weed that stuck brittle out of the snow, Cora didn't move, she breathed as shallow as she could. She could feel cold-wet melting into the gap between her coat and jeans; the side of her face was numb where it lay against the drift. Through the fogging of her breath, out and up, she watched a pair of boots trudge along the road above her, heard them crunch the gravel through snow, now closer, and,

Girl?

Now away,

Girl?

Drunk. Or, worse, not drunk.

Girl!

Up and back, again,

Girl, I only want to . . .

And, as Cora watched through the cloud of her breath and felt the plastic handle of the boning knife in her hand, and as the ice dripped down, through her pants, her underwear and her socks, as Cora's breath fogged and lifted and hung, she thought, to the rhythm of her pulse, I am strong, I am alone, I am strong, I am alone.

Until she heard the boots slowing, then stopping, then a door pulled shut and then a truck starting up and then pulling away and then gone. She counted up to a hundred and back and then to a hundred again and back and up and back again, and again, breathing through the weeds up to the road, then up to the black and star sky.

She was in Alberta now, she must be. She was almost there. She got up, brushed the snow and grass off, and waited for another car to come by.

Finn's parents sang less now. Before going back over to work, his father still hummed sometimes, but more quiet, more slow. And Finn's mother never sang; she slept late into the afternoon and then sat silent by the phone; Finn would tiptoe past her as he came and went, even though it was day, even though it was his own house. Sometimes she would reach out and catch him as he went past and would pull him to her, her breath warm and wet in his hair.

Mom?

Yes? Martha had Finn tight to her again, caught as he went to get a carrot out of the fridge. Her voice muffled by his hair.

There are still fish, right? Like at all, like in the oceans somewhere?

I don't know.

There must be.

Maybe.

Like in Mexico, maybe.

Yes, maybe in Mexico.

And they could swim from there to here, or from Ireland, or Italy, if they really wanted to, right? Like the whales swimming from Hawaii.

Yes, they could.

And, if I got them to, if I got them to swim back, the newspapers and things would report on it, wouldn't they? It would be a famous thing?

If you got them back, Finn, they would talk about it around the world, I'm sure.

And, so, wherever she is, Cora would hear.

Cora might hear, yes.

She'd hear and come home, probably, come and see if it was true?

Martha pulled away from Finn a bit. One of his hairs stuck to her cheek. She might, she said. She might.

Finn found a pail with a lid and a folding chair in the garage at The Philippines! He found an auger, ice chisel and skimmer in South Africa!, and some rubber lures from home. Live would be better, but the ground was too frozen to dig anything up. He found the things he needed in The Philippines!, in South Africa!, at home and, finally, in the downstairs deep freeze in Italy! And then he was ready. He put everything in their backyard shed. The lock that didn't actually lock had ice crystals along its arch like a frozen rainbow.

Back inside, he tiptoed past the kitchen. He was starving, but had a bag of frozen peas from Italy! that he could eat in his room.

Finn? said his mother when he was almost but not quite at the stairs.

Yeah?

Did you see anyone out there?

No.

Did you ask them if they'd seen Cora?

No.

No you didn't ask them or no they hadn't seen her?

No they hadn't seen her, Mom. But they were looking. They said they were looking.

OK.

The next day was a Monday, the second Monday of the month. Which meant, or used to mean, school-field-trip day. Finn was up and out by six, preparing everything. He was back outside his parents' bedroom door by seven. Good morning, Mom. He knocked the rhythm out on the door frame at the same time as he said it. Good! Morning! Mom!

Finn?

He opened the door a crack. Enough to see and reach through. Yes?

What time is it?

It's school-field-trip time, Mom! Second Monday of the month! I brought you juice. Finn reached his arm out, into the room. He'd made orange juice from concentrate, specially borrowed from the Italy! freezer and had poured his mother the biggest glass they had, the glass so big they sometimes used it as a vase. There's more downstairs, he said. There's a whole jug.

Martha ran a hand over her face. Is it me? she said. Am I the parent volunteer this month?

Yes, said Finn. You are, but it's OK. I know the way.

Was there a letter?

Yeah, last month. When Dad was here.

OK. She got up. She was already in her robe, must have slept in it. She went to the door, took the juice and smoothed Finn's hair to the side like she did a lot these days. Give me five minutes, OK?

OK, said Finn. He started back, away downstairs.

Is it the plant? The door fell closed again.

What?

It's the old fish plant, yes? Should I wear my overalls?

Nope, this time it's ice-fishing.

But . . . there aren't any fish.

Still, that's what it said. We can learn about augers, it said.

You want to learn about augers?

Yes.

OK. Extra layers, then. OK. Downstairs in ten minutes.

Even though they knew no other students would come, that there were no other students left, they walked down through the snow to the official meeting point in front of the Anglican Reform Church. They waited from eight until eight thirty. Then Martha took a clipboard with a pen attached to it with string out of her bag and wrote:

1. Finn Connor

on a school-board form to mail back. She did it without taking off her mittens, so the lettering was clumsy and over-big. Then she put the clipboard back in her bag and said, OK, Finn Connor, field-trip time has officially begun.

All the equipment was there, as usual, at the meeting point. Finn picked up the covered pail in one mittened hand and the lures and skimmer in the other. His mother put the chisel in her bag and took the auger and chair in a hand each. They marched together through the snow out to the water, then out onto it, the ice solid and silent beneath them.

•   •   •

All right, said Martha. Her cheeks and nose were red from the wind. You want me to show you how to drill down?

Yes please, said Finn.

OK, said Martha. All right. She put down her bag and the chair and took up the auger. She kicked away some loose snow, clearing a small patch of ice, dark and green and clouded. You have the skimmer?

Yes, said Finn, let me just . . .

Good, said Martha. She was already kneeling down on the ice. Look, she said. Both hands up, here and here, see? Ready?

Yes, said Finn, skimmer out, ready.

His mother dug the drill down a bit, then started to turn the handle like she'd done before, hundreds of times, out with Meredith, out with Molly, out with Aidan. Easy, she said. It's easy, Finn, once you get started. She stopped, looked up at him and, even though she didn't smile, she did something more like smiling, her mouth relaxing, her eyes actually looking at Finn. It's actually even fun, kind of, she said. It's pretty fun, Finn. You want a go?

Yes, said Finn. Yes please.

Mom . . . ? Mom?

They'd been watching their line for about two and a half hours, Finn sitting on the bucket with the lid, Martha on the chair.

Mom!

Martha had gone off behind some snowdrifts to deal with her juice-full bladder. She was walking back.

Mom! Mom!

From that distance, she couldn't see the details of her son's face. Couldn't see why he was shouting.

Mom!

She waved her arms and tried to run, but her boots and the snow and the ice meant she was in slow motion.

Finn?

Mom!

Finn!

Mom!

And then she was back and there was no blood, no danger, just Finn, breathing fast, up on one knee, braced against a ridge of snow, pulling, releasing, pulling.

Oh, said Martha.

It's something, Mom, said Finn. I think I've got something.

Oh, said Martha, oh, oh, oh.

Finn pulled and released and pulled and released and Martha stood by and waited and watched and waited until, finally, they both, at the same time, saw a flick of gray, not the gray of the sky or the rocks or the days, but a shining silver gray, new and real and so, so bright in the water.

A fish, whispered Martha.

Finn got it out and onto the ice and clubbed it with the skimmer all in one motion, all at once.

A half-sleeping winter fish, after the knock on its head it didn't fight, it didn't flip. It lay still, there on the ice between them, bright and silver and new. A fish. A codfish. Another.

Finn sat down beside it, exhausted. He looked up at his mother, who looked down at him and, with one mittened hand half-covering it, smiled.

Oh, she said. Oh, Finn.

I knew it, said Finn.

Me too, said Martha. Me too.

Finn put the fish in the bucket and put the lid back on and they picked up their things and walked home, and the sun shone through the mist in spots and flecks so everything looked new, looked magic.

They called Aidan first. Before even taking the fish out of the bucket, before even taking off their boots. He's done it, he's done it, said Martha, to the woman who took messages when phones rang through, when people were busy on-shift.

Done what? she said.

Just say he's done it. Write that. Write Finn has done it. With an exclamation mark. Write: Finn! Has! Done! It!

With all the exclamation marks?

Yes.

OK.

Then the O'Learys, but there was no answer. Finn knew they'd gone, they'd left the morning after the meeting, but he didn't say anything.

Then Molly, out west, in the middle of a violin lesson, then Meredith, in St. John's, mashing garlic for a bourguignon, then Sheila McNabe, in the ferry office, in the middle of module 2B of her correspondence IT course, and then, when they finally put the phone down to take off their boots and coats, puddles of melted snow and ice around them, faces and hands hot, it rang back at them. Martha picked it up.

Hello?

. . .

Yes . . .

. . .

Yes!

. . .

Yes he is, yes you can, here, here.

Martha held the phone out to Finn, It's the paper, she said, and then, covering the mouthpiece, from the city! From St. John's!

Finn took the phone, and Martha went, at last, to get the bucket from the front step.

Hello? said Finn. Yes, yes that's me.

A wash of cold air from the front door, opened, closed, as Martha carried it into the kitchen and up, onto the counter.

I did. Again, yes, again.

She pulled at the lid, it was on tight, a good rubber seal.

Well, the first time was with a rod, from my dad, and now, just now, was on the ice, with my mom.

When it opened, a spray of water, of salt, splashed up against Martha's cheek, a few drops flying further, onto Finn's arm.

No, nobody else has. Nobody else has been able to.

She poured the rest of the seawater out, into the sink.

Oh yes, oh yes, they tried. But then they gave up.

She lifted the fish up onto their chopping board, worn smooth from years and years.

Well, they said it had to be me, that if anyone could, it would be me, they said.

The fish hung over the edge of the board, long and beautiful-smooth.

If there are fish, Finn can find them, they said. They said it was me or nothing.

Martha ran her hand along the fish, smooth.

Well yes, I guess they were. I guess they were right.

She carefully flipped it over, felt the other side, smooth.

I do, I do think they're coming back, yes. Yes, yes.

She took a knife and split the fish right up the middle of its belly, one clean motion, like she'd done a thousand times, like she'd seen Meredith do ten thousand times, then slid her fingers in and along to scoop out the guts, out and down in one clean motion, but there was nothing. Nothing there, just her fingers again, mostly dry.

So we're going to be OK, yes. We're going to be OK again. Yes, you can print that, yes, it's Finn. Finn Connor. F-I-N-N C-O-N-N-O-R.

Martha tried again, got nothing again. She cut up the neck and up the tail and opened up the fish all the way, exposing the pink and white flesh, smooth like ice, empty like the sea.

And, can you put a note in for Cora, my sister, Cora Connor? Tell her she can come back now, she should come back home.

There were no guts. Nothing but flesh.

OK. Yep, any time, OK.

Martha leaned in, so close she could feel the cold off the fish when she breathed. It was obvious. It was easy.

Any time, any time at all.

She could see where it had been cut before. One clean motion, a beautiful cut, more perfect than hers, more practiced. It was obvious.

Finn put the phone down. Wow, he said.

I need to go outside for a minute, said Martha. Her voice quiet. The fish still lying there, head and tail over the sides of the board.

Outside? OK. Do you want me to finish that? Set it cooking?

I don't know.

And keep the head and bones to show people? For proof?

I don't know. Martha left, went out. She didn't put on her boots, she didn't close the door after her. Finn went to the fish, looked at its glass-cold eye looking at him. Wind from the open door was blowing old crumbs around on the floor. His mother didn't come back. He covered the fish's head with his hand, but could still sense the eye through his fingers, still looking. They never blink, fish never blink. Bits of snow blew in too, chased the crumbs. His mother still didn't come back. He bent down, into the under-sink cupboard, got a rag, and put it over the fish's head, over its eye.

Mom? he said.

She was outside. She was too far away.

Mom? he said again, louder, not moving, still there by the fish. Mom?

Where did the fish come from, Finn? Her voice, around the corner, out the door, had wind all around it.

What?

Where did it come from, Finn? Where did you get it?

From the water, Mom, the sea, you were there, you saw me get it, you—

Before that, Finn, from where?

I . . .

Finn.

The wetness of the fish was soaking through the rag, spreading out in dark splotches. I— said Finn. He stared at the rag, at the dark. I— he said again.

It's somebody else's fish, said Martha.

Finn stared at the rag, at the dark. I— he said.

Already scaled, already gutted, said Martha. Somebody else's fish. Gutted fish don't bite hooks, don't swim free.

I caught it, Finn could have said, I caught it before, when you were away. I caught it and gutted it and scaled it and saved it for you, for when you were home, Finn could have said. He said it in his head, fast, maybe, maybe.

Where did it come from, Finn? Again. Before the water, before I was there.

The bucket, said Finn.

The wind blew and it was like his mother sighing.

And the Beggs', he said. Before that. The freezer in the Beggs' basement. There are ten there, still. Ten more.

And the wind blew.

Mom?

The Beggs. She was beautiful with a gutting knife. He was beautiful with a net. One of her nets, one of Martha's.

Mom? said Finn.

Just wind. And the all-wet-now rag, and the eye underneath, and the crumbs and the snow and the cold.

Mom?

The door was still open, but she was gone. The wind blew sparks of snow into his eyes and up his nose with each inhale. Finn left the door open and went back to the kitchen. He got out the plastic wrap and wrapped up the fish, with the rag still on its head, and put it in the freezer. He put soap on another rag and wiped down the chopping board and propped it against the faucet to dry. The house was cold and getting colder, but Finn's face and chest and stomach were uncomfortable hot, pulsing hot. He filled the sink with water and soap, washed and dried the gutting knife, and put it away in its drawer. The door was still open. His mother still wasn't back. He gathered up the other dirty dishes from around the house, cups from his bedroom, mugs from his parents', plates from the front room, nothing from Cora's, and washed those all up too. He wiped the table, and the counters.

He swept the crumbs and the snow off the floor and out the door. He sat. He waited. He was so hot, he was burning hot. He filled one of the now-clean glasses with cold water and drank it, then washed it and put it away again. He sat. He waited. He should probably have dinner but he wasn't hungry for dinner. He sat. In one of the hard, non-cushioned kitchen chairs. He could have moved to the sofa in the living room, or a cushioned chair at least, but he didn't. He waited.

When the microwave clock showed that his mother had been gone for an hour, he filled the kettle and put it on the stove, and, when the water was ready, Finn poured it out into one of the now-clean mugs, stirring in bits of an old chocolate bar he'd found in his parents' room. It would be better with milk, it should have been with milk, but they didn't have any milk. Then he put on his boots and, even though he was too hot for it, knew that he would sweat right through, a coat. He took the hot chocolate, and went out to find his mother.

He followed her sock prints in the snow, down, out, along the road, and then up again, to the Italy! house. The Beggs'. He rang the doorbell. No answer. He went around to the window, breathed on the glass to warm up a circle to see through. His mother was there, in the living room. She was sitting on the floor beside the Leaning Tower of Pisa lamp, fiddling with the gray paper at its base, ripping it off in thin strips. There were little gray bits of paper all around her. Finn knocked on the window, she looked up. He waved. She hesitated, didn't smile, but did wave back, a little. Finn pointed at the hot chocolate, now mostly cold, and set it on the windowsill. Then he took a folded note out of his pocket and left it there too, under the side of the mug so it wouldn't blow away. Then he turned around and walked back home. He would come back again in an hour. And again after that and again after that and again after that.

Martha waited for him to go. She counted to thirty, then got up and went to the window and opened it and took the mug of cold chocolate and the note:

I'm sorry.

F

In the distance, through swirls of snow, she could see his dark outline. He was in his sister's coat. He looked tiny. When she squinted she couldn't see him at all.

One hour later Finn went back to Italy! His mother was asleep on the flag-couch. He knocked quietly, just twice, on the window, left a note and as much of a wool blanket as he could fit on the sill, the rest dangling over the edge but not quite touching the snow, and went home again.

> *Don't be mad,*
> *I'll fix this. I promise.*

F

Martha heard the steps, the knocks and then steps again. She counted to thirty, then got up off the couch. It was covered in red and white and green paper, noisy and uncomfortable. But it looked nice. She opened the window and saw her faraway son, halfway home. She took the note and read it and smoothed it between both hands and put it in her pocket with the other one. She took the blanket and shook the snow off and wrapped it around herself like a cape. She had to phone Aidan and her sisters and the paper and tell them the truth about the fish. She had to collect herself and be an adult, be a parent, and go back to Finn. But this house was so cold. The fireplace had pictures of horses and muscular men taped all along and inside it instead of wood or coal. So cold and so strange. Martha pulled the blanket up to her mouth and lay back down on the paper couch. Just once more. A count up to thirty and down again. Just once more.

Finn didn't go home. He kept walking past his house, all the way out to the library boat. There was no librarian on the library boat anymore, just a key that was kept in a lockbox on the door that everyone knew the code to, 3145, that was also written on the underside of the box in case you forgot. It was freezing inside, and the ice had pushed it up so the floor was uneven in a way that made him dizzy. Finn collected *Clams, Crabs, Fish and Other Animals That Aren't Quite like Us* and *101 Fail-Proof Lures and Techniques* and *The Intermediate Undergraduate's Guide to Marine Biology: Ecology and Economy* and *Can You Hear What I Hear? Animals and ESP.* He wrote the name of each book, his name and the date in the self-serve checkout notebook in the TITLE, NAME, and DATE OUT columns. The previous entries in the NAME column, going all the way up to the top of the page, were:

Cora Connor
Cora Connor
Cora Connor

and

Cora Connor

There was nothing in the DATE BACK IN column for any of these.

Finn locked the library behind him again and walked home with the books. The wind blew snow sparks into his eyes and he thought of Mrs. Callaghan and the Spanish ships. He took heavy steps through deep snow and thought of all the fish in the world, of how there must be fish still, somewhere, in the world. Things can't just end. Not forever.

He had an idea, a plan. No more faking. He was Finn Connor and he was the only one who could get the fish back, which meant he was the one who had to, so he would make a real plan and he would start tonight, and when his mother came home he'd make her real hot chocolate and he would, yes he would, yes, he, Finn Connor, would bring the fish back, he would bring them all, everything, everyone, back home again, for real, for good.

He had to and he could. He would start like the Spanish, he would start with a fleet.

The Beggs' phone still worked. Martha dialed and Aidan picked up the other end on the first ring.

I've been calling! he said. And calling! But there's no answer at home . . . Martha! Martha, Finn, he! . . .

He didn't, said Martha.

But, you—

I know, I know, but, Aidan, the Beggs' freezer is full of old cod. Totally full.

And . . .

And, Aidan, and . . .

And as Martha told him she listened to his breath, to hear if it got faster or shallower or if he held it, but Aidan's breathing stayed steady, stayed just the same. It always stayed the same with him.

OK, said Aidan. OK.

And now we need to tell everyone, tell the paper.

An extra breath, an extra beat, and then Aidan said . . . Do we?

What?

Do we need to tell them?

Aidan, if they think— said Martha.

Maybe that's OK for now.

But, Aidan, they'll expect something, something more.

Maybe that's OK for now.

Do you really—

Maybe. It could be. OK to let people expect something. To let them hope.

Hope? False hope?

It doesn't have to be false. Unless it's dead, unless there's nothing, hope is just hope, isn't it? It's just something to warm you a bit, and—

And, said Martha, the idea opening inside her like drinking cold water, the papers and the people will keep talking about Cora, keep asking.

Yes, said Aidan. Yes, exactly.

Another breath, another beat. OK, said Martha. Yes.

Another breath, another beat. Where's Finn? asked Aidan. How's Finn?

He's OK, said Martha. He's wearing Cora's coat. He's sorry.

And . . .

And I'm not angry at him, Aidan. I should be, but I'm not angry at all. I had to leave because I didn't want him to know I wasn't.

Wasn't angry?

Yes. I'm tired. I'm too tired to be angry.

Me too.

You too?

Me too.

Finn left a note on the front door:

Just out for one minute. Back soon.

and left the house unlocked, just in case. He put his boots back on, then Cora's sweater over his own, then her coat over that, and went out back into the snow, the wind, the storm. Of course there were plenty of boats, old, unused, all along the rock shore, lots and lots of boats, probably more than a fleet, but Finn needed something he could bring out across the ice to the deeper water, out, further out than he could drag a boat, further out than he could drag anything. That's why, instead of going straight down to the water, Finn walked two lots upwind, to the Darcy house, to Finland!, and around the side of the property, to the garage.

Their truck was in rough shape, with a low tire and mouse holes in the upholstery. Like everyone, Geraldine Darcy had left the keys in the ignition. She'd also left the windows rolled down and there was four inches of snow on the driver's seat. Finn got in, sat on the snow, and turned the key in the ignition. The truck coughed through its freezing motor once, twice, three times, and then rumbled into life for the first time in ten months.

It was easy. Finn assumed an act so strictly for adults would somehow prove impossible to him, but it wasn't, it was simple, it was just like he'd watched his mother and father do a thousand times. No secret word or knowledge required. He was a little relieved and a little disappointed.

He stretched his foot down to the accelerator and rolled, slow and careful, down the driveway and track to the bay's launch point, now frozen up the pier. He drove along it, careful, slow, and then off it, out onto the ice. He drove out further and further to where everything was white, nothing but white. He listened for cracking, for breaking. He felt like an explorer. Like a Spaniard, seeking the edge of the world. Like he could drive forever and ever.

But he didn't. Because he couldn't fall off the edge of the world, he had to be a survivor and strong and have a plan. He listened for cracks and looked for patches of black ahead instead of white. After what he assumed was about half a mile of white on white on white he stopped and got out of the truck, back into the wind, and left it there, the truck, all by itself. He followed the tracks he had just made back to land.

Finn did this six times. Two trucks, three cars and one van. Of the ten vehicles he tried, those were the ones that would start. From the pier, he drove each in a different direction, a scallop shell of tracks, out and out, through windshields of white, and then left them, lonely metal-bodied cairns, on the ice and followed the tire trails, carefully, slowly, back. In a month or so when the ice broke and thaw came, the vehicles would all sink. And, although they weren't Spanish, weren't ships, they would be something. Something that could be safe, could be home. In the underwater cold, they would be ready, would be waiting.

Back at the shore, before going home, Finn climbed up and lay on top of one of the abandoned fish flakes like he and Cora used to do when they were much smaller. If he balanced his body weight just right, spread it out so that every bit of him was the same amount of heavy and none of him was any more than that, he could lie on there and not break it and not fall through. The wooden struts and beams pushed into his back through the sweaters and coat and the wind squashed his hair flat against his head.

Windy weather boys

he sang,

Oh stormy weather, boys

just as loud as he could,

When the wind blows
Oh we're all together, boys

and the wind was as loud as his voice and pushed it out over the ice to the open water, the words dropping in like pebbles one at a time,

Wind
Oh
Storm
Oh
Oh
Oh

and all the lights of all the houses all around were just as dark as the night he sang into.

Martha sat on the paper couch with the blanket around her and the phone next to her. She wasn't going to use it again. She wasn't going to phone anyone else. It was full dark now, outside and in. The Beggs had left a lot there, in their strangely decorated house, but had taken their clocks and VCR, so she couldn't tell exactly what time it was, only that it was in-between sunset and late. Without clocks or people to pace it out, the darkness spread out and out like the sea, like she could sink into it, away.

But she couldn't. She had to go home. She got up, found a pair of boots close enough to her size in the front closet, and, keeping the blanket wrapped around her, she went back out, into the night, and the dark wasn't so dark once she was in it.

She walked the empty road. She leaned into the wind and it leaned into her and, there, there at the edge of it, she heard something, a song. A mermaid. She put her hands to her face, blanket corners against her eyes, and took them away again. It was still there. A song in the wind, coming off the water. Cora. It had Cora's voice. She sat down on the roadside, blanket wet beneath her, and closed her eyes.

When the song finished she waited, she strained, but there was no more. She opened her eyes, got up and kept walking, back to her house, back to Finn.

The tips of Finn's hair and his eyebrows and eyelashes were still frozen, still crusted with bits of ice when his mother got home. It melted and ran cold down his face and her jacket while she helped him take his coat and sweaters off, even though she still had her own on.

I'm sorry, she said, even though everything was his fault.

Me too, said Finn. I was stupid.

I know.

And mean.

I know.

I didn't want to be, I didn't mean to be.

I know, said Martha.

His outside clothes were off; hers were still on. They were stand-ing in the entranceway with all the boots and the coats and no chairs; they were just standing.

Sometimes, said Martha, we're all stupid, we're all mean.

Even mothers?

Even mothers.

And even though his legs were still stinging from going from cold to warm too fast, and even though he'd led his mother to Cora's Italy! house and he didn't know if he was allowed, and even though he had lied to the newspaper and, then, maybe, to all of Newfound-land because of that, and to his mother, who had been more angry at him than ever before, and even though Big Running was hollow, was barely breathing, even though he hadn't seen anyone his own age for almost a year, Finn felt OK, Finn was OK.

His mother finally took off her borrowed boots and took and squeezed his hand and they breathed and they breathed in together and they breathed and they breathed out together.

Cora was dropped off in Edmonton by a family from Manitoba on their way to the mountains for a lessons-for-the-kids, wine-for-the-parents ski trip. Before driving away, the mother had beckoned Cora back to the window and, at an awkward angle so the kids in the back-seats couldn't see, handed her a juice box and twenty dollars. Just . . . be careful, she said. Then her three-year-old noticed the reflection of the juice box in the window and screamed, and her five-year-old brother started kicking the seat backs as hard as he could and the mother had to wind up the window and drive away before Cora could say, Thank you. And, I know, I will. And, Wait. And, Maybe, I changed my mind. Can I come with you? And, I've never been skiing. I've never even seen a mountain. And climbing back in between the kids and reading them stories from chewed cardboard books and riding over and up and into the mountains with this family, who would jokingly call her theirs until they forgot she wasn't, and she became their actual daughter and sister and went skiing up high in the mountains in the winter, every winter.

But instead, they drove away and she walked into the first still-open place she could find, the Buffalo HOT Times Bar and Grill. Not very nice or clean, but open.

You want some food, or you looking for the bar? 'Cause it's over there. The waiter pointed to his left, where a wooden screen, the kind normally used for growing vines in gardens, separated the building's two halves. Behind it there was a light that flashed blue and green and purple with shadows of bodies moving across it. Cora was the only customer on this side of the screen.

Food, thanks, said Cora.

Oh, OK. In that case, sit wherever you want. Most of the food's gross though. Except maybe the Vegetarian Option Pasta. If I had to eat something here, I'd probably be able to stomach that.

Cora sat at a corner table, as far away from the bar barrier as she could, her paper tablecloth changing color every two seconds, blue, green, purple, blue, green, purple. She spread her hands out on it, watching them change too. She could be anyone, she could be anywhere.

OK, here you go, good luck with it, said the waiter, putting a plate of over-boiled spiral pasta in thin red sauce in front of her. And I forgot to ask, before, if you wanted a drink. Do you?

No thanks, I've got a water bottle.

I don't think that's allowed.

Oh.

But I don't care. It's smart of you. Important. Staying hydrated on the road. I have an idea for an invention for that, you know.

Yeah?

Yeah. Here, move over. The waiter shunted Cora along the bench and sat down beside her. He took a crayon out of the kids' activity cup in the middle of the table and drew out a shape on the tablecloth in front of them. A sort of oval with a rectangle coming off the back of it.

See? he said.

Kind of, said Cora.

It's a water bottle with a belt strap. So it just hooks onto your belt or your jeans. Because it's too big to fit into a pocket, isn't it, a water bottle? But you don't want to have to carry a whole separate bag just for that . . .

No, good point.

I'm working on what to do about dresses now. I'm sure I'll think of something.

I'm sure you will too.

Thanks . . .

Claudia-Anne.

Thanks, Claudia-Anne. I'm Stuart.

It's nice to meet you, Stuart. I've never met a real inventor before.

Well, I still work here to get by, you know, but, thanks. I'm trying. I have thirty-two different inventions so far. One of them will go big, I'm sure.

I'm sure too.

They were quiet for a while; Cora eating pasta one spiral at a time and Stuart coloring in the shading for his bottle drawing. When he was done he gave a little nod, satisfied, and put the crayon back in its cup.

You from around here, Claudia-Anne?

No, just passing through. On my way up north. To work.

At the camps?

Yep.

Which one? Blue Horn? White Prairie? Deep Wood?

Deep Wood. That's the one.

Nice. Not too rough, that one, I've heard. Still too much for me, you know, that's why I'm down here, but I've heard it's not the worst, that one. And plenty of money.

And mountains?

Mountains? I don't think so. I could be wrong. I mean, I've never been up there, but I'm pretty sure those are all over the other way. West. You know?

Yeah, of course. I know. She ate a spiral. Red sauce dripped thin as water back onto the plate.

You know, said Stuart. I've got an idea for a compass that you can read by sounds, that gives a nice ding when you face directly north.

That could be helpful in the dark.

That's what I was thinking. And it's dark up there a lot in the winter months, like now. Hey, Claudia-Anne?

Yeah?

Do you need to go right away? Because if not, if you don't mind waiting around until I'm off at eleven, I could run home and get you a prototype. And maybe people up there would see you use it and would see what a good idea it is . . .

Sure, I don't mind.

I'll get you some free buns for while you wait. They're basically rocks, but there's unlimited butter.

Stuart slipped out of the booth and walked back into the kitchen. Once he was gone, Cora took a red crayon from the kids' cup and wrote *Deep Wood* on a napkin, then put the napkin into her pocket.

She waited with her suitcase outside the apartment building. There were snowdrifts pushed up between the sidewalk she was on and the road, the snow gray-brown with street grit. She had never seen it that color before.

Next time it snows it'll get all covered and look nice again, said Stuart, back down from his apartment, standing in the fluorescent light of the building's entrance. Cora turned toward him. He had a plastic grocery store bag in his hand; he held it out to her. The sound-compass.

So, I just follow it north from here and that'll get me to the Deep Wood site? she said.

Basically. You gonna drive through the night? Want me to walk you to your car?

No, that's fine. I don't have one. I was going to walk.

Walk?

Yeah.

Walk.

Yeah. North of Edmonton, follow the sound-compass . . .

Claudia-Anne, it's more than a five-hour drive to the sites from here.

I . . . I know. I know that. Walking to the bus, I mean. I was gonna walk to the bus from here.

Is there a bus this late?

Yeah.

Oh, OK. Still. It's minus fifteen out. Probably at least twenty with wind chill . . . Wait here. Stuart ran back into the building, up the stairs. Cora put her hands into her armpits to keep them warm. She would take one out, she told herself, and stick up her thumb as soon as a car passed. But none did.

When Stuart came back there was another man with him. He was in pajamas, lightweight pants like from the *Thailand!* book, with a robe on top. He squinted at the cold air. This is Luke, said Stuart. My boyfriend. He's going to drive you to the bus station. I can't because I failed my test.

Twice, said Luke.

Twice, said Stuart.

Hi, Luke, said Cora.

Hi, said Luke.

OK, said Stuart. Let's go. I'm fucking freezing.

• • •

The bus station was empty but unlocked, with the lights on.

You'll be OK? said Stuart.

I'll be fine.

He handed her the bag with the sound-compass in it. I also put a card in there with my name and phone number on it. In case you need it. Or in case anyone wants to get in touch about the compass. It's from the restaurant, but ignore that part.

OK. Thank you, Stuart.

You're welcome, Claudia-Anne. Any time.

Luke stayed in the car, but waved before they drove away again.

There was a handwritten sign on the ticket desk that said:

Back at 5 a.m. First bus at 5:30.

Cora opened up her suitcase and took out her towel. It was faded orange with tassels. Back home, Finn had the same one in green. Lying along the plastic bench seats, she used her suitcase like a pillow and pulled the towel over her like a blanket, covering her from the neck to just below her waist. I am strong, I am alone. She watched the headlights of cars as they reflected off the snow and through the windows like slow-motion lightning until she fell asleep.

The next day another newspaper called. And then another. Two in the morning and three in the afternoon. Martha told them all the same things: Yes, Finn did catch the fish. No, he could not talk right now. Yes, he would try for more. No, nothing yet. Not yet. Yes, yes, she was proud. And each time, before she let them go, she'd have them promise, swear, to add a picture, and a line for Cora, We miss you, come home. We miss you, come home.

Sheila McNabe called from the ferry office to say she had some tourists who wanted to come visit the house, see the fish, see Finn, was that OK?

No cameras, said Martha. And Finn might not be home, but OK. And how's your course, Sheila?

Module 4, said Sheila. Chugging along. I've got a cousin with connections in Vancouver, once I finish, if I finish.

Finn snuck out the back door, inland across the rocks to Italy!, just before Sheila and the tourists arrived. They brought cameras. They took pictures of the fish, of Martha holding it, just out of the freezer, the small green rag still covering its head.

Why the cloth? asked a man who, back home, taught art history.

It's traditional, said Martha. For us. Around here.

The man nodded, took a closer-up picture of the fish, the cloth. It's beautiful, he said.

Martha made them coffee and they sat together in the kitchen.

A lovely table, said a woman, an accountant. Homemade? Family heirloom?

Yes, said Martha, even though she couldn't actually remember where it came from.

The art historian nodded and took a photo.

When they stood to go, Martha took a picture out of her pocket. Cora, last Christmas, standing with Finn outside the ferry-port cafeteria, smiling. The tourists passed it around. No, we haven't, they said, I'm sorry, no, no, but we will look. We will try.

Before they all went, Sheila quietly put fifty dollars into Martha's hand. Don't say no, she said. They paid me. They wanted to.

Oh, said Martha. But before she could say anything else, they were gone again, climbing into the bed of Sheila's truck like a hay ride, bumping off down the frozen track.

At the Beggs', Finn had two lists pinned up on the Trevi Fountain fireplace:

THINGS TAKEN
For his conscience. For if people asked.

and:

THINGS BACK
To contrast with Mrs. Callaghan's list. To balance it.

He had just a few weeks left of the ice, probably. Before it started to break up and pull back again. Until he could start the next part of his plan. And until he could row back over to Mrs. Callaghan's. He wondered about her with her telescope. If she had seen him with the trucks and cars. If she had seen him with the fish. His accordion was totally dry now and not ruined; he played at least two songs a day to keep the bellows from going stiff. He had the book of tunes from Cora memorized now. He played those. Again and again and again.

He had five months until the notices took effect. Until they were supposed to leave.

He had a plan. He had a plan. He thought and read and circled and underlined and wrote and played and sang.

He was circling the words "still not strictly illegal" when an envelope, then the mittened hand pushing it, poked through the Beggs' mail flap. The hand dropped the letter and pulled back and out and was gone. It wasn't his mother's. The mittens were black and sleek and not wool. Not homemade. Finn slipped down off the couch and crawled on his hands and knees to the window so as to be invisible from outside, then slowly and carefully raised himself up until he could just see out. There, walking away, was a Consolidated Outports and Villages of Eastern Newfoundland Postal Service worker. Finn recognized the jacket and the bag. Annie Pike, the oldest sister of his friend Mattie, used to do that job, but they had moved away months ago, and he didn't recognize this worker at all. Finn stood all the way up now and went over to the letter. It wasn't a support check. The delivery address was written by hand, not by computer. The envelope was used, the official kind that had a clear section in the middle, and the address was written around it.

Finnigan Connor
Beggs' House
Big Running
Nfld
Canada

There was no return address. Because it was already used, the envelope had been sealed with one long piece of Scotch tape. Finn dug under the edge with his fingernail and pulled it all up in one go.

Inside was a single piece of paper with the top bit ripped off.

Caro Finn,

it said,

Non preoccuparti di me. Sto bene.
Ho un piano. Ti dirò più presto.
Per favore non mostrare questo a mamma e papà, non ancora.

Con affetto,
Cora

Even though he couldn't understand it, Finn read the letter twice. Finn...Cora. Finn...Cora. The rest in code. The rest a mystery. While he read, a little piece of the Leaning Tower peeled and drooped further, toward him. Finn pushed it back into place. Then he stopped. Blinked once hard at the letter. Of course, of course. He stuffed the paper into his pocket and ran out the door, out toward the postal worker.

Do you know Italian? he asked. Finn said it quickly, through fast breath; he had had to run as fast as he could, lifting his feet up and out of snow with each step, to catch the postal worker before she got back into her truck. She had stopped to look out at the ice, out to sea, when Finn caught her.

Oh! she said. Her hood was up and she didn't have the peripheral vision to have seen him coming. She turned to him, away from the water. Finn didn't recognize her face, maybe it was a little Italian. Maybe could be.

Italian, said Finn. Do you know it, at all? Even a little bit?

Oh, she said, um, no . . . I know a little bit of Gaelic . . .

I need Italian, said Finn.

Sorry, said the worker. She held her black mitten-hands out toward him, empty. I don't. I'm sorry. Do you?

No, said Finn. Not at all.

Well, said the worker.

It's OK, said Finn. Never mind.

Well, said the postal worker again. Guess I better go before the ferry leaves.

OK, said Finn.

I'm sure someone around here will know Italian.

Finn didn't say, There is no one around here. Just you. He didn't say, You should miss the ferry. You should miss the ferry and teach me Gaelic and have coffee with my mom and wrap your hands around hot coffee mugs together and look out at the ice, at the sea, whenever you want. He didn't look up from her hands, still open, still empty.

OK, he said. Thanks anyway.

See you later, OK? she said.

OK, said Finn.

She walked the rest of the way over to her truck, got in and drove away.

Finn pulled his sleeves up over his hands, fabric held in place by his squeezed fingers, and ran down to the docks.

The Italian–English dictionary was missing from the library boat. It had been signed out more than two months ago under the name:

Cora Connor

It was overdue. There was still an Italian–French dictionary there, though, and Finn knew some French from school, back when school had been normal. Finn took the dictionary and went back to the Italy! house.

There was a bowl of dry cornflakes and a cup of frozen-on-the-top juice on the windowsill. He brought them in with him and ate the cereal dry, like a horse, while he looked up words one at a time, first from Italian to French using the dictionary, then from French to English using what he remembered from school, until he got:

Beloved Finn,

Do not fret about me, I'm fine.
I have a strategy I'll tell you sooner.
Please do not show this to Mom and Dad, not yet.

With affection,
Cora

A strategy, whispered Finn. He unballed a fist. He put the letter back into its envelope and slid it down the front of his shirt, tucked into his pants so it was hidden but also wouldn't fall out. Then he pulled the two sweaters on top, took his accordion and his notebook, and went home.

The tourists were gone, the house was quiet. His mother was in the kitchen, by the phone, as usual. Finn felt the envelope's corners cutting into his stomach as he walked past, but he didn't stop. He practiced his accordion songs with his bedroom door open so his mother could hear.

There were some tourists again the next day, and the day after that. There were some tourists, not a lot, but some, all week, and two more newspaper calls.

The next week was the same, though fewer on Thursday, on Friday.

And then fewer again on the weekend, even though it was the weekend.

The next Monday there were just two tourists, one of whom was the art historian again.

Tuesday there were none, and Wednesday there was just one, the art historian's mother. He said this place was beautiful, she said. He said you made wonderful coffee.

On Thursday morning, again, no one came. Thursday afternoon Martha phoned the paper in St. John's.

Have you caught anything else?

Not yet, but—

Has anyone else caught anything?

Not yet, but—

So, nothing to report . . .

Yes, but—

We're sorry, but—

But—

Look, um . . .

Martha.

Martha, look, we've heard things. People calling, people telling us this isn't the first time this miracle has happened with this same boy. Telling us that no one else can ever find any other fish. Angry people, Martha, some of them are angry.

But, he—

We're dedicated to the truth, it's our motto, Solummodo—

But he's just—

In Veritatis. We can't print anything we don't—

a boy.

We're sorry.

And my daughter, and Cora—

We're sorry, Martha. I'm sorry, I really am.

On Friday Sheila came on her own, sat with Martha, had coffee. She brought some of the sandwich cookies they sold on the ferry.

I've only got one module left on the IT course, she said.

Finn has a plan, said Martha. For the fish.

Oh, said Sheila. She lifted her mug but didn't drink. Set it back down again. I'm gonna look for Cora in Vancouver, Martha, she said. After I go, I'll keep looking.

Who will direct the ferries?

Ottawa will send someone. They always have, so far.

So far, said Martha. The cookie in her mouth was too soft, too sweet. She had to force herself to swallow. Cora might have changed her name, cut her hair, she said.

I know, said Sheila.

Finn has a plan, said Martha.

I know.

Cora rolled her suitcase up to the security booth at the entrance to the Deep Wood Energy and Industry site. I'm here for a job, she said.

The man in the booth lifted his sunglasses off his face onto his hard hat. He looked at her and raised his eyebrows and said, Huh. We only do prearranged. You prearranged?

Yes, said Cora. Of course.

He ran his finger down a piece of paper on the desk in front of him. Sorry, no, he said. I don't see any . . . I don't . . . unless you're . . . Don?

Yes, said Cora.

Don Coffin . . . the new bear-scarer?

Yes, said Cora.

Spelled like that?

What's it say?

Don. D-O-N.

That's it.

Not D-A—

No. Just like it is. Don. That's me.

Huh. Where you from, Don?

East.

Huh. Well, that's what it says here. Same as me. He looked up from the paper, at her. Then back down again, then back up. He sighed. Don, he said.

Yeah?

If I call the office, if I call HR, and tell them you're here, give them a quick description of you, girl, about so-tall, about so-old, are they gonna be happy? Are they gonna be expecting you, as such?

Yes, said Cora, looking straight ahead. Straight at the man. The rhythm of his voice was just like her father's.

Yes?

Yes.

The man looked at her and then away, back down, and then back up again. I got two kids you know, he said. A boy and a girl. Boy about your age, probably, girl a bit younger.

Yeah?

Yeah.

What are they called?

Steven and Jen. I figure another few months up here, maybe a year, and Steven can go to college. Another couple years and Jen too. University, even, if that's what they want.

I bet they will.

I hope so. I think so. You gonna go to college, Don? College or university, one day?

Yeah, yes I am.

Good, said the man. You should. Maybe even at the same time as Steven, be in a class with him. English lit, is what he's thinking of. He bought me *Wuthering Heights* for Christmas.

Did you read it?

Twice.

Kind of scary, hey?

Terrifying.

The man didn't call the office. Instead he picked up a pencil and made a tick mark on his paper. OK, Don, he said. OK. You go in there, work hard, get out and go to college, OK?

OK.

Promise?

Promise.

OK. OK. Good. The man reached up and took his sunglasses off his hat, smoothed his thin gray-brown hair. Now, he said. Down to business. You got your own dogs or using ours?

Yours.

OK. Another tick. And you got good boots, Don? Good steel boots? For the dogs if they get out of line, and the bears. And the boys.

I've got good boots.

Good. OK, then. OK. I'll radio you through. He smoothed his hair once more, picked up his sunglasses and put them back on. Lenses all scratched. Someone'll be here in five with a truck to bring you in, get you started, he said. Welcome to Deep Wood Energy and Industry, Don. Good luck with those bears. Don't be afraid to shoot, OK?

No, said Cora. Never.

Here are your dogs, said the assistant site foreman.

He didn't tell Cora what their names were. He seemed uncomfortable. Thanks, said Cora. What are—

OK, said the man. He thrust the leads out toward her. She took them.

Thanks, she said, but—

OK, said the man, and turned and left, getting back into his truck and driving away.

Since nobody told her the dogs' names, Cora gave them new ones: Giancarlo and Giannina. They stood up to her waist, one on either side of her. They were like German shepherds but with lighter, whiter fur. Like wolves. They stood perfectly still there, next to her; Cora could feel their tension through their leashes, like they could just go, at any minute, just go.

How do you want to be paid, Don? asked Cheryl, the financial affairs foreperson, one of the only other women on-site. Looks like I haven't got your forms through yet.

Cash, please, said Cora.

OK, said Cheryl. I understand. She patted Cora's shoulder.

Well, said Cora, I'd better go. Better get back to Giannina and Giancarlo.

OK, said Cheryl. But you know you can always come around here for a break when you want. Come around my office. To talk or just sit or whatever. The dogs'll be OK in back.

Cheryl's office was her truck. A mobile office, she called it. She had nameplates on the doors.

Thanks, said Cora. I know.

OK, said Cheryl. She looked like she was going to cry.

Cape Breton, Cora decided. That's where Cheryl's accent was from. Familiar, but not too. Cora listened to each new person she met on-site carefully, mapping the pull or push of the vowels, the *R*s, the gaps between words. If they pulled too far east she shut up and left them alone as soon as possible. She practiced shaping her mouth along with the neutral-flat Ontario tones of the Canadian Broadcasting Corporation radio on break and at night.

Even though it was winter, when the bears should all be sleeping, Cora's job was to walk with Giancarlo and Giannina, along with a big stick, a can of pepper spray, a silver handbell and a small gun, all the way around the borders of the camp, from an hour before sunrise until an hour after sunset, shouting to keep them away, just in case. When her voice got tired she could ring the bell. Mostly she did both. She'd shout-sing to keep herself entertained and play along on the bell. The only songs she knew all the words to were ones from home or Christmas songs, so she'd sing:

She's like the swallow
That flies on high

or:

I saw three ships come sailing in
On Christmas day, on Christmas day

or:

The water is wide
I can't cross o'er

Giancarlo and Giannina didn't mind the noise, trotting along at her sides, always half-tense, always silent and ready.

Apart from the dogs, Cora worked alone.

Every morning now, Finn would check each of Cora's international houses, the mailboxes of the ones that had mailboxes and the floor under the mail slot of the ones that just had mail slots, and then he would walk up and down surveying the water and shoreline for changes, counting the dark spots on the horizon, the vehicles, one two three four five six, and waiting. He watched and waited for the ice to go.

And then, just before the month was out, just before it was his mother's turn to go meet the ferry and leave the car running in the parking lot with Finn in it and for his father to pick it up and take them home again, just before the month was out, the ice cracked and creaked and started to break. Finn heard it from his bedroom. He got up and walked across the hall to Cora's room and looked out her window. He didn't see any boat lights, of course, but there, there across the heavy dark, he could see movement, he was sure he could.

Dad?

Yes?

They were eating dinner. Mostly potatoes again. His first night back, Aidan had asked Finn what his favorite thing for supper would be, and Finn had said, Potatoes, so they'd had potatoes almost every night since.

Do you think it's wrong to steal something that nobody's using?

Hm. Something nobody's using today, or for a week, or ever again? Tonight's potatoes were pan-fried.

For a long time. Maybe not forever, but for months. Maybe even a year. Or more.

Well, I guess it's probably not too bad if you, say, used the thing carefully, gently, and then were able to return it or replace it if they ever wanted it back. Still, probably best to ask them, if in any doubt.

And if they're not around? Finn's hair was sticking up and sideways with static from his toque. Aidan reached across the table to smooth it.

Finn, he said, don't worry. Your sister won't mind you wearing her sweater, I'm sure. And besides, we know she'll be back before a year, right? Long before.

Finn reached up and felt his hair, smoothed it himself. I wasn't thinking of her, he said. Of her things, I mean.

Well, if you were, in case you were, I'd say it's OK. She'd probably want someone to be using it, and probably want that someone to be you.

And, otherwise, for things that aren't Cora's sweater?

Otherwise, think of what you'd like done with your own things, in the same situation.

OK, said Finn. That makes sense, OK.

And, Finn? All the potatoes were eaten off his father's plate, and all the sauce, too, but still Aidan kept running his fork along and around, in case one last bit was left somewhere, hidden.

Yeah?

You have permission to use any of my things when I'm in Alberta. Any of my sweaters or boots or anything. To save you trouble of asking.

OK, Dad, thanks.

Anything, any time.

OK, Dad, thanks.

After dinner Finn took his accordion back to the Italy! house and practiced "The Bog Flower Waltz" until the sun went down. He watched it through the window, sinking like a slow-motion stone until there was nothing left. Then he stopped playing, took off his accordion and went out into the Beggs' yard. They'd left two old bicycles out there, both with flat tires and one with no chain; and one old, small, wooden dory with the hull rotting through where the rain had gathered and stayed. Finn started with the smaller of the two bikes. He rolled it, bumpily, flatly, down and around the front of the house, then down the short track to the shore. It was too dark to properly see where the dips and splits were as he maneuvered the bike up onto and across the rocks. They jutted far enough out that the water around them was black, but Finn could sense it moving. He got a good, firm footing, toes curling in and out in the cold, lifted the bike and threw it out into the water as far as he could.

Its splash startled no one because there was no one around to startle. It sank straightaway, handlebars first, and, just like that, was gone.

Sorry, Finn said to himself, to the night.

Then he scrambled back across the rocks and back up the track to get the next bike.

With the boat it was slightly different. When he got it down to the rocks, he hefted it around so it was upside down and found a rock just bigger than his fist with a rounded point at one end. He remembered his father's words, Gently and Carefully. Sorry, sorry, he said, and brought down the rock in the middle of the weak bit of hull. Sorry, sorry, as he did it again and again, until the wood gave way and a hole opened up, first small, then bigger and bigger until the rock could fit right through.

Still, the boat took longer to sink than the bikes, trying to do its job, do its best, even though it was upside down with a gap in its very middle. It sank slow like the sun. Sorry, sorry, said Finn. Before going back to the Beggs', he built up a small cairn on the rock, a memorial for his growing sunken fleet, a marker for the new homes he was making.

Back in the house, Finn filled in more of his list:

THINGS TAKEN

Truck one (red)

Car one (gray)

Car two (blue)

Truck two (black)

Car three (red)

Van

Bike one (smaller)

Bike two (no chain)

Dory

And the pack ice pushed in and out and in, and every few nights the thaw spread and his fleet got closer and closer to shore and Finn would go to another house and take what had been left, drag or carry or roll it across the rocks and ice as far as liquid water and push or drop or throw it in and watch it sink. He filled in his list: Stroller, Lawn mower, Toboggan, Kitchen Chairs (4), Dories/Punts/Other small boats (25). He built cairns and apologized to them, Sorry, sorry, sorry.

And then, one warmer day when there was sun behind and between the bouts of frozen rain and clear water almost all the way up to the shore, behind and between the bits of moving ice, there, in the green and rusted mailbox of South Africa!, was another reused envelope. Inside, there was another piece of paper with the top ripped off. It said:

Liewe Finn,

Moet nie oor my bekommerd wees nie.
Ek het nou twee honde. Ek dink jy sal van hulle hou.

Groete,

Cora

It definitely wasn't Italian. And not English. Finn looked up to the stuffed lion Cora had stapled to the sofa. South African? he asked it. The lion said nothing. Finn folded the letter, put it back into its envelope, then slipped it down his shirt with the other, Italian one. He pulled on his sweaters and ran back home.

Aidan was in the kitchen, had all the Tupperware out in various piles, big, small, lids, orphans.

Dad, said Finn, what's the South African language?

What? said Aidan. He had two lids in his hands. Neither of them fit anything.

The South African language, said Finn again. Do you know what it is?

Um, he said. I'm not sure. I think there are a few. More than one. Dutch, maybe? I think one is Dutch . . . or, like Dutch.

Dutch? said Finn.

Like Dutch, said his father.

• • •

The Dutch–English dictionary was still there, in the library boat. Some of the words in the letter weren't in it so Finn had to guess and allow for changes in spelling.

Lovely Finn,

Do not worry about me.
I have two dogs now. You will enjoy them.

Regards,
Cora

Two dogs, whispered Finn. Wow. If Cora had two dogs she would be OK, she must be OK.

And then, a week later, another letter, in what was probably Finnish:

Dear Finn,

I have not seen a bear yet, but I think I will soon.

And, little by little, the snow and ice melted off the boulders and soaked back into the bogs and marshes and trickled down into the bay and the ice pans broke and cracked and floated back and away and back and away, smaller and smaller.

And little by little, Finn emptied the houses and filled the sea.

There was a big, main cafeteria in the middle of camp, but Cora never went there. She got her own food from the Camp West Off-Base Supplies and Snack Van, run by a thin and quiet man with DARWIISH embroidered on the breast pocket of all his shirts. He served buns with hamburger, buns with egg or buns with tomatoes, as well as the Deal of the Day!, which was always a Styrofoam bowl of brown-red beans mixed with sugar and butter. Cora got an egg bun for breakfast and a hamburger bun with tomato for lunch and the Deal of the Day! for dinner. Darwiish never said anything, just nodded at her when she arrived, and took her order and money and nodded when she took her food. Behind him, stuck to the sides of the minifridge and microwave and freezer, were photos of children. Children smiling, somewhere hot. Darwiish was in a couple of them too, but mostly he wasn't.

Breakfast and lunch she ate as she walked, half-worried, half-hoping the scent would attract a bear. At night she'd take her Deal of the Day! back to her room and eat it there, watching reflective vests and helmets move across the dark of her window like fish in water.

One day, after buying her Deal of the Day!, Cora asked Darwiish, Do you have any paper? She had used up the half pad she'd found in her room, and the idea of not having any, of not writing to Finn, scared her more than the thought of a bear.

Darwiish stopped, still holding her money in his hand, thought for a few seconds, then nodded and turned around, back into his van.

When he returned he had a brand-new Deep Wood Energy and Industry notepad. It said WHERE WORK AND SAFETY MEET along the top.

How much? said Cora.

Darwiish made his hand into an O and handed her the pad.

There was never anyone else at the Camp West Off-Base Supplies and Snack Van. Cora wondered if anyone else even knew it was there.

All the deep ice, all the real ice, was gone now. All the vehicles were melted under, sunk down. Vehicles and chairs and bicycles and strollers and boats and everything else. Finn imagined them all, waiting, ready, as he paddled his way through the ice back to Mrs. Callaghan's at last. She was standing at her door, waiting for him.

Inside, Finn unlatched and opened up his accordion and Mrs. Callaghan looked it over closely, ran her fingers up and down its creases, sniffed the air between them, had him hold it on its side and let half drop.

Ah good, she said. Won't have to build you a new one after all.

It's OK? said Finn.

It's probably OK, said Mrs. Callaghan. Now, play.

Finn played "The Ballad of the Newfoundland Black Bear" and "The Bog Flower Waltz" and "The Northern Long-Eared Bat Reel" and Mrs. Callaghan listened and shook her head and moved his fingers and listened and shook her head and tapped her finger on his shoulder, one two, one two, and had him sing along to the tunes even though most of them didn't have words. If you can sing it you can play it, she said and listened and shook her head. Good, good, good, she said, and sang along too.

Don't come next week if it's storming or looking like storming or if your dad says it might be storming later, said Mrs. Callaghan as Finn latched his accordion back up. Or if there's ice back.

OK, said Finn.

But do come otherwise.

OK.

Now, do you want some kind of bun before you go? You look half-starved.

They ate Chelsea buns and drank purple Kool-Aid sitting on Mrs. Callaghan's front steps, facing the water, their fingers sticky and flecked with cinnamon. They watched a white bird circling out toward Big Running.

Mrs. Callaghan, said Finn, the sunk boats, the Spanish wrecks, they worked, didn't they? For the fish, to have a place to live and stay?

Oh, did they, said Mrs. Callaghan. Did they ever. When the fish arrived they liked it so much they all stayed and had babies, hundreds of them, thousands of them, and they all stayed too and they all had babies and they all stayed and on and on. So much so that word of it spread and all the countries started sending boats. England and France and Spain again—

And Ireland?

And Ireland. Yes, yes, they came, they all came, and some of them sank too, but some didn't. Many didn't. The ships would come and they'd get help from the people living here, the ones who had always lived here, to bring in as many fish as they could and then they'd go back, back across the ocean to where they'd come from, ten feet lower in the water with the weight of the fish they'd caught. The sailors, they couldn't believe it, they'd look down and see a moving silver sea within the sea. They couldn't believe it.

So they stayed?

No. They weren't allowed to stay. It was strictly forbidden, illegal, upon punishment of the worst punishment they could imagine. Their queens and kings wanted them back so they could keep sending them off, back and forth, keep bringing the fish in. But the sailors, they were so tempted, so very tempted. This place was so wild, so new, so full, full to bursting with things other than themselves.

So they stayed?

No. Not at first. At first they just wanted to. Went back to their ships with heavy hearts on fear of the worst punishment they could imagine, and of the wildness here too. They all went back. For a time. Until this one sailor, this one new, young sailor named Jesús showed up.

Jesus?

No, not Jesus, Jesús. Jesús wasn't Jesus but was named after him by a Catholic mother hoping to make up for his bad start in life, for his nothing-but-some-sailor father. He was a good boy if fairly unremarkable, mostly dull-to-average except for the fact that he was an extraordinary sleepwalker. He'd get up and head toward light, like a moth, like a fish, more confident and strong in sleep than awake. And it was worse still on boats, something to do with the turn of the waves, probably. So, when sleeping at sea, he would take a length of sail rope and loop it around to fix himself to his bunk.

Every night?

Almost every night. There was one night, not long after they'd arrived on these shores and had taken in yet another miracle-like abundance of fish, when all the crew, men and boys, took to whiskey in celebration. They drank and sang and drank and danced and drank and one by one passed out in various places, sometimes their beds and sometimes not. A small fat one passed out draped over the soft wood of the stern railing, and a deeply romantic one who was always sad passed out among a pile of anchor chains, and Jesús, he passed out in one of the little runner dories that was fastened to the big ship, bobbing alongside. He curled up there like a baby in a cradle, his own blond and curly hair the only pillow he needed. And not he nor anyone else tied him safe with a rope when he did. And the moon, that night, the moon over Little Running was big and bright.

So he sleepwalked?

You bet he did. The waves rocked and his muscles twitched, and, finding no restraint, they stood him up and started him walking, up, toward the moonlight on the sea, still fast asleep. There wasn't far to walk, though, in that little boat, so before no time Jesús was at the edge and just stepped over and out, out to the water.

And then?

And then he kept walking. Just kept walking. The fish, the capelin, the cod, were so thick in the water that he could step on and over them just like solid ground. He didn't even get ankle-wet. And that would have been that, except that the noise of it woke Gabriel, the short fat sailor, who then went to relieve his whiskey-full bladder over the side of the boat and saw, there, out on the water, Jesús walking, walking right on top of it. He slapped his own face and still saw it, so he ran to wake up Cecil, the sad romantic in the nest of anchor chains, who came to see what Gabriel was raving about, and together they watched him. Watched Jesús walking on the water, the moonlight glowing through his hair like rapture. Gabriel crossed himself one two three times and Cecil cried slow, heavy tears and they both felt their hearts swell because there, right there, was a miracle, right there, right in this place wild and cold and holy, undoubtedly, terrifyingly holy. A miracle. A sign. How could they go home after that?

They couldn't?

They couldn't.

So they stayed?

So they stayed. They watched Jesús walk all the way to shore and curl up and go back to normal sleep there, on some moonlit rocks, and decided then and there and forever that they would stay. Them and everyone else on that ship. And then more, and more and more. Even though it wasn't easy. Even though it was illegal, remember. They were deserters, they were punishable with the worst things they could imagine. So they had to hide out, in cracks between boulders, or inland with the caribou, or off with me.

With you?

Yes, with me.

How did you find them?

I didn't. They found me. I painted a big pale green circle on my door that would catch and shine in the night and the day, like the moon on the sea. That was a symbol, then, so they knew they could come and be safe with me. And when the captains came knocking on my door, asking after their men and asking to have a look around, I hid the deserters in my bed, because that was the one place a decent captain would never dare to look, inside a strange woman's bed. They were good men, those captains. I don't blame them for trying to do their jobs, to keep a hold on order. Every now and then one would turn up for refuge himself and I'd have to hide him in my bed when the other captains came around. They were rough and wild and terrified and bewitched, all of them, the men and the captains. I did what I could. I painted the circle.

That must have been a really long time ago.

Oh, it was. Ages. Years and years and years and years.

And then what? They couldn't stay with you or out with the boulders and caribou forever . . .

No, no, of course not. After a while, a few weeks or months or a year, their crews and their homes would forget them and move on. Then they'd find a place they could call their own and paint a green-white circle on the door and exhale and feel at home again, finally. They would fade out of belonging to one place and into another.

They must have been lonely.

Yes, of course. Lonely and afraid, but alive, Finn, so alive.

Finn stopped at the Beggs' on his way home. He had all his library books there, held open to important passages by one of the many Italian things Cora had scattered around for ambience. *101 Fail-Proof Lures and Techniques* was propped open with two very small coffee cups, one red and one green, to page 117. Finn crouched over it and circled, twice, in heavy pencil:

Chapter 11

Swimming Toward the Light: Illuminate Your Situation!

(With full glossary of applicable laws and by-laws by state and province)

At home he found his father painting detail work onto the kitchen cabinets, some kind of leaves and vines. He watched him trace the curve of a vine, thin at first, then over again, thicker.

Dad?

Yes?

You know how some ways of catching or attracting fish are OK, but some are illegal?

Do I.

Well, would they still be illegal if someone used them to attract the fish but not to catch them? Just to attract them and then leave them alone?

Huh. Aidan put his paintbrush into a plastic bag, twisted the cap back onto the special art paint he was using and turned toward Finn. That's a good question. I don't suppose they would be then. No, I don't suppose so.

OK, said Finn. Good. Great. Also, Dad?

Yeah?

Do we have any batteries?

Most of the empty houses had at least one flashlight, and Finn also found headlamps and bike lights and some fake candles. But they didn't all have working batteries; most of them didn't. So Finn scavenged. From remote controls and radios, from alarm clocks and toys. He needed as many as he could find, enough for all the flashlights and headlamps and bike lights and candles six or seven times over, he figured, maybe more. As many as he could possibly get.

It was time for part two of his plan. Out in the rain, from house to house, he gathered batteries like berry-picking in summer.

Faallll
On your kneeees
Oh heeear
The angel voi–ces

Cora was making her rounds. Giannina and Giancarlo trotted a little bit ahead, taut but not tight on their leads. She didn't see any bears. She never did. Though she was sure they saw her. Bears, and mountain lions too, probably. In the thickness of trees that surrounded them, watching her watching for them.

But give me a boat
Big enough for two

She thought about how one could run out at her and Giannina and Giancarlo suddenly, at any moment, and then she'd have to do something, would have to act and save the day and that maybe one of the dogs, Giancarlo maybe, since he was a little bit smaller, would be injured, a bite to his rear haunch, and the bear, a grizzly, huge, the one the men whispered about over night shifts, huge and bloodthirsty, ever since it lost a cub, a beloved albino cub that had slipped through the fence and fallen into one of the tailing ponds, where the mother could do nothing but watch it slip down and away, her humongous grizzly heart breaking and freezing over, cold and hard and broken, and they knew, the men knew, that nothing was stronger, nothing was fiercer, than something broken, prowling the area, waiting, waiting for its chance to break in and get revenge, blood for blood, until, at last, through the trees and the snow and the dark and the grief it sees Cora. It sees Cora and the dogs and its moment for revenge and so it bursts out, through the pathetic orange plastic fence, right at Giancarlo, teeth deep into his rear haunch, blood for blood, and Cora and Giannina have to work together, think fast, move fast, Giannina's mouth open, teeth showing, making and not breaking eye contact with the bear while Cora prepares her gun and aims at the sky, to scare it off, just scare it off, to do no harm, like it says in her Official Practice book, but then the grizzly lunges again, breaks the dog's eye contact and lunges fast, too fast for something so big, this time at Giannina, at her throat, and Cora, startled, turns suddenly and shoots, and the sound of the gun and the sound of the bear's cry are one and the same, she's shot, in the heart, right there, in her broken heart, right in the very middle, and she collapses back, dead, free at last from her sad life. Cora takes a minute and closes the bear's eyes and says, I'm sorry, Grizzly. And then she and the dogs drag it back to camp and everyone, all the men, gather around and say, Wow, Don. Wow. We didn't think you had it in you, it's true. We teased, we made fun, because you're a girl! we said. Because you're Newfie! we said. I can think of better uses for a Newfie girl! we said. But no, no, no, we were wrong. We were so wrong. You've done it, Cora, you've saved us all. Thank you, Cora. Thank you thank you thank you thank you. Come, they'd say, come, eat dinner with us in the hall, in the real, main cafeteria, where there's at least two different hot-food options every day, but Cora would just shake her head and say, No, I'll eat with Darwiish and my dogs, as always. And she'd leave the bear there with them, just there, on the floor, and would walk back to the Camp West Off-Base Supplies and Snack Van alone.

But no bear came. Just her and the dogs and the songs.

Cora turned the corner at the southeast edge of her route, the bit where she met up with the road for a mile. She'd been working, doing her rounds for weeks now already. There were still no bears. Or mountain lions. But, just then, just as she turned, she heard something. Not a growl or a footfall, but something. The dogs' ears bristled, turned, and she followed them, looking back, along the road. And there was something. Not an animal, but a truck, coming toward her. It was slowing down, wheels crunching gravel and snow, until it pulled up right beside her, on the Giancarlo side, and stopped. It was a civilian truck, no Deep Wood site logo.

The frosted-over window rolled down in clunky, manual jerks and, from inside, a man said, Hey, you work here?

And Cora said, Yes.

And the man said, Fuck, I'm so late.

Yeah? said Cora.

Yeah, said the man. I always am. Fuck. And then, Hey, where are you from?

East, said Cora. East of here.

Hey, said the man. Me too! Newfoundland?

No, Manitoba.

Oh, said the man. I see. And what's your name?

Don, said Cora.

Well, how about that, said the man. Me too.

Oh, said Cora, oh no.

234 ~ Emma Hooper

Don invited her into his truck to warm up. She made sure it would unlock from the inside and then said, Sure, thanks. They put the dogs in the back. Don had two dogs of his own back there too, in kennels. They sniffed each other quietly through the grilles. Don had coffee mixed with rum in an orange thermos. He offered the lid-cup to Cora.

Thanks, she said, and took it. Drank. She'd never had rum before. It cut through the coffee like color. She coughed and said, Thanks again.

No problem, no problem, said Don.

And then she took a breath and said, I need you to go back, Don.

Go back?

To where you've come from. I need you to turn around and go back there. Or somewhere else, maybe. Just not here. Please.

Well, said the man. I—

I'm not called Don, said Cora. You are.

I am? I mean, I am. You're not?

No, I'm not. Don, I'm you. They think I'm you. Because I told them I was. And if you show up and are you, for real, they'll know I'm not. And they'll laugh and say they were right, they knew it all along, and then you'll take your job and they'll send Giannina and Giancarlo away and send me home. Where there is no money and no future. Where there are no people, no kids, no friends. Not even a dog. Not even one stupid dog for my brother, she said. Where there is nothing. They'll send me home, Don.

Don didn't reply. Sat and thought. Took a drink from his thermos. Blinked. Took another drink. Then said, To Newfoundland.

To Manitoba, said Cora. To Flin-Flon.

Hm. And what's so bad about Flin-Flon?

Please, said Cora.

OK now, said Don. He went to drink again, but the thermos was empty. What's your name, then? Your real name.

Esther, said Cora. It's Esther.

Esther, said the man. That's a nice name.

Just normal, said Cora.

Esther, said the man. We gotta stick together, you know, us from Flin-Flon.

I thought you said you were from Newfoundland?

Same thing. Thing is, we're orphans, us.

Well, said Cora, not really, but—

We are, said Don. And we come out here looking for new families, new lives, now our old ones are dead, and there are lives here to be had. He stopped, gestured behind them, out the back of the truck, the snow, the road, the flashing lights of the site. There are plenty of lives to be had here, but we know, we always know, we already know, really, that they're not ours. They won't be. They can't be. That's why I'm so late. I couldn't bring myself to leave my real, dead life.

My parents are OK, said Cora. I think . . .

Anyway, there's work along this whole highway. Camps and sites and work and work and work. A body can build a pretend life anywhere. That's the thing. If it's pretend you want, Esther, it can be anywhere.

In the back Giannina started whining, which started Giancarlo, which started Don's dogs.

Don, said Cora.

What I'm getting at, Esther, said Don, is that I'll go. Won't lose me anything to go. We gotta stick together, we from Flin-Flon.

Cora let out a breath she didn't know she was holding. Oh, she said.

Anyway, they probably got the better Don here, said Don. Ha. Ha! Now finish your coffee if you want it.

Thanks, said Cora. Thank you, Don. She drank. And then, Did you fish, Don?

Of course, said Don.

Me too, said Cora.

Of course, said Don.

After Cora got out and got her dogs from the back, Don did a U-turn in the gravel and drove back the way he had come. He flicked his lights on and off, just once, as he went, driving east.

Cora and her dogs finished their round as usual,

> *But give me a boat,*
> *Big enough for two*

and there were no bears or lions or anything else except crew noise and light and dirt and snow.

Finn carried pockets full of batteries and other supplies back to Italy! from Ethiopia! and Texas! and China! and Spain!, from Russia! and Thailand!, Yugoslavia! and England!, and sometimes the ice pans were in, a jostling mosaic of white, and sometimes they were out, the water cold and clear. Today they were in. After dropping another load at the Beggs', Finn walked down to the shore to survey them. There were birds out on the rocks, presunset birds that flew away as he approached. Terns, petrels, gulls, guillemots. Birds Finn hadn't seen in months, maybe years. Seabirds. Fish-birds. His heart double-beat. The pans were clean and flat and close. He started to run.

Finn didn't stop running when he hit the water, his legs and head and heart fizzing, he kept going, out, onto the pans, out ice-hopping. He jumped to a pan floating close. Then to another, further out. Then another and another, the jumps bigger and bigger as he went further and further out, the ice pans smaller and smaller. The trick was to not stop moving, ever.

He was good. This year, he was the best he'd been. It felt like flying, like the birds he'd seen had given him their flight. He imagined white, feathered wings unfurling as he raised his arms for each jump, further and further and further, so easy, just like that. Like he was made for it, like breathing. The ice was soft and giving and his foot would stick to it for grip on the jumping side and stick into it again to land on the landing side, it was all about speed and weight and timing, everything was speed and height and flight.

And then, suddenly, it wasn't. And then there was a little bit of ice that looked just the same as the rest, still white and waiting, but that, this time, wasn't soft, was polished slick, from wind or waves or stones or just from time. It looked just the same as all the others. But this time, his foot didn't stick, and this time, instead, instead of gripping and landing, his foot slid back when it hit, and, instead of taking his weight up and on, Finn was knocked back and off like a punch in the stomach, and control was gone and flight was gone and he fell back and hit the water in a shock of cold fierce like a slap, and then he was underneath.

And he couldn't breathe, he couldn't swim, it was so cold it was solid even though it wasn't anymore, now he was down in it, it was all around him and it was in him, it was everywhere and he spat and gasped, sinking down as he pushed his arms up, his wings, up, up, his sweaters heavier than anything, colder than anything, he pushed again and again, and kicked and kicked, his boots clumsy like cartoon feet, until his head was out, almost, almost, then pulled back down again, so heavy, his boots full, his wings gone, his arms tangled in sweaters, in themselves. He could hear his heartbeat through the water, amazing, could feel it all around him. He stopped pushing, stopped kicking and just listened, amazing, amazing.

And then his wings were back. His arms up, lifted. The light rushed back toward him, up and up and then out. He was on his side, coughing, coughing, salt water body-warm out of his mouth, down his face. And then there was no more water and, instead, there was breath, cold and new, and he was turned onto his back, faceup, on a wide, flat pan. A woman was standing over him, looking impossible-tall, her mittens dripping.

Can you breathe? she said.

Finn breathed. He coughed. He tried again. Yes, he said. Yes, I can.

Can you stand?

Finn tried. He couldn't. No, he said. Not right now.

That's OK, said the giant lady, you're heavy with water. Give it a minute. She took off her coat and put it over him, even though she was wet too, was shivering. But not too long, else you might freeze to the pan, she said. She put one leg out in front of her. Started doing some stretches.

Who are you? asked Finn. His words had the taste of seawater around them. The woman's voice was familiar, but he didn't recognize her.

I'm Sophie McKinley, said the woman. I used to live here. She reached down, pulled one knee up to her chest. A long time ago, she said.

Before I was born?

Probably. How old are you?

Eleven.

Yep. Long before you. I left for the Olympics in Germany.

Oh wow. You were in them?

Nope, didn't make it. But made it to the ones after, in Montreal, and then Moscow, and then Los Angeles, but then I was getting too old to be fast anymore, and the Australians noticed and scooped me up to be a coach, so I did that instead.

Fast at what?

What?

You weren't fast anymore at what?

Running, of course. The only real sport. The purest sport. Though swimming's pretty pure too. I did mid-distance. Five and ten kilometers. Once they put me in for a half marathon but I didn't do well. Just got bored.

Wow, said Finn. He was feeling less heavy now. He sat up. Did you win any medals?

Three, said Sophie. All bronze. Canada always gets bronze. My Australians got a gold once though.

Wow, said Finn. That's amazing. That really is.

Do you want to see?

See what?

The medals. Here. Sophie undid the top button of her shirt, reached her hand down and pulled up three medallions by their necklace ribbons. They can get a little cold so I have to wear an undershirt too, she said.

Finn stood, walked over to her. Without taking it off her neck, Sophie held a medal out to him. It had a waving woman on it and was the color of October. It was beautiful. I think bronze is the most beautiful one, he said.

Thanks, said Sophie. Me too.

They carefully hopped back together until they reached shore. Sophie went first, then waited, arms out, to help when Finn lost his nerve. She walked back home with him along the road.

You left twenty years ago?

About that, yeah.

When did you come back?

Not long ago. Few weeks. Got a job no one else wanted, delivering post.

Finn stopped. The Consolidated Outports and Villages of Eastern Newfoundland Postal Service worker. You don't speak Italian, he said.

Nope, she said.

They walked a few steps, a trail of dark wet spots on the rocks behind them.

Why did you want the job nobody wanted? Finn asked.

I don't know, said Sophie. I just figured it was time to come home. I wanted to. I missed it.

You did?

I did.

Do you think everybody does, or would? Miss their homes enough to come back?

If there are enough postal service jobs, then sure, I guess. The problem is, you have to have something to do, like that, like delivering welfare checks. No matter how much you want to be somewhere, there's no point if you don't have something to do.

Even though Finn was freezing, was shaking through his shirt and both sweaters and Sophie's coat, his face got hot, his heart faster. Will you stay? he asked.

I don't know. I guess we'll see. I'm not sure what there is here for me to do beyond post, not many races, and someone's turned my parents' house into a sort of beach . . .

You could coach me. You could teach me to run for the Olympics.

Maybe, said Sophie. She smiled. Maybe.

They came to Finn's house and he invited Sophie in for coffee and cake, even though he knew they didn't have any cake.

Sure, said Sophie, so long as you go change into dry clothes before making me anything.

OK, said Finn. Deal. He left her on the living-room sofa with an *Absolute Angling* magazine. It's a few years old, but still pretty good, he said, then ran upstairs.

Sophie McKinley was there, reading about "Effective and Noneffective Homemade Lures" on the couch in the living room when Aidan came in from the backyard through the kitchen. He'd been washing paintbrushes in white spirit, had the smell in his fingers and on his hair. He stopped when he saw someone new in the house.

Hello? he said.

Sophie looked up from the magazine. Oh, Aidan, hello, she said. She smiled and stood and the medals under her shirt clanged softly against each other.

Oh my God, said Aidan. Sophie McKinley.

What? said Sophie, because he'd been too quiet, because he was whispering.

Sophie McKinley, the crab runner, said Aidan, louder. Oh my God. Welcome home.

Sophie stayed for dinner. Aidan made a new recipe, a sort of layered thing with lots of very thin potato slices one on top of the other, and then, afterward, because they had no cake, took out a bottle of whiskey from the cupboard over the stove and poured some out for Sophie and himself while Finn made himself hot chocolate in the microwave.

I don't normally drink, said Sophie, not while training.

But this is your homecoming celebration, said Aidan. He didn't really need to say anything, though, because Sophie had already pulled her glass toward her, was already taking a deep drink. A drip made its way down the outside of the glass, onto her finger. She brought her hand to her mouth.

• • •

Sophie McKinley stayed past Finn's bedtime, not that anyone told him when to go to bed anymore, but past when he could stay awake, could follow their conversation about years and years and years ago and events and things and people he'd never heard of. She stayed late into the night, so that when Finn half woke, every now and then, her conversation with his father would float up to him like steam and he'd nestle into it and sleep warm.

Sophie came over lots after that. My own house has sand all over it, she explained. Somebody filled it with sand. I've vacuumed and dusted and picked at it grain by grain by hand and I just can't get it all. It sticks to me when I sit and when I sleep. So she spent most days either out running along the roads and shore, or jumping from one boulder to another inland, or over at Finn's drinking and laughing and talking with Aidan, late into the night. Finn would get back from Italy! and creep past them, unseen, up to bed.

Martha was fresh off-shift, just on a break, only an hour until she was back on. There was a knock on her door as soon as she got her boots off. Like someone had been waiting. Yes? she said.

Can I come in?

Of course, John. Of course.

He closed the door after him. Was in off-shift clothes. Corduroy trousers and a red and blue and white plaid shirt buttoned all the way up. Soft flannel. No one else on-site wore corduroys, just jeans or work pants, work pants or jeans. In his hand was a plastic bag with knitting needles poking out of it. Inside were both of their projects, her sweater with two standing caribou on it for Cora, his green mittens with white four-leaf clover shapes over the hands for his sister. He had warned Martha, back when they'd begun, when she was just learning, that a sweater was much too complex, too difficult for a beginner, that a scarf, maybe, would be better. But she wanted to do a sweater, had insisted. Twenty-five years of making nets, she said. Let me do the sweater, John, let me try. She had her hand over his on the needles. OK, he'd said. As you wish.

I brought our things, he said. I thought you might want to work on it a bit before your shift, get your hands back busy. He set the bag down on the bed.

She picked it up, back off the bed, and put it on the floor. Here, she said. You can sit down, John.

OK, he said. He sat down. Laughed a little.

She sat next to him. Despite his clothes, he smelled like work, like here. How's your sister?

Not speaking right now. Still. Mom has to dress and undress her. Each morning and each night. Else she'd just wear the same thing forever.

I'm sorry, said Martha. I bet she'll wear these mittens.

Anything from Cora?

No.

She'll be all right, Martha. She's young, she's strong.

How do you know? That she's strong?

Like her mother, said John. I mean, I bet she is. Right?

Maybe, said Martha.

You go home tomorrow, don't you? said John.

Yes, said Martha.

It's a long time, a month, isn't it? said John.

Yes, said Martha.

They were both facing the knitting bag on the floor, not each other. She looked up, at his face in profile. His skin impossibly smooth for here, for work. She moved toward it and kissed his cheek. Easy. Just like that.

He turned and kissed her back. Easy. Just like that.

Cora finished her shift. She walked Giancarlo and Giannina back to their kennel, fed them, making sure the portions were exactly equal, said goodnight and good job, and went to get her own dinner from Darwiish.

Deal of the Day!, please, she said.

Darwiish nodded and took her money and handed her a disposable Styrofoam bowl, already prepared and waiting for her. He smiled and she smiled back.

Before going to bed Cora got down on hands and knees and pulled her violin case out from under her bed. She opened it. Inside, there was a brown envelope. She reached in and pulled out little stacks of bills held together with hair elastics, one stack per denomination. She removed the elastics and counted the bills out, adding up each stack with the next until she reached a total. Four thousand eight hundred and sixty-five dollars. She crossed out an old number and wrote this down on the envelope, then put it all back. She was halfway there. Almost halfway.

Before falling asleep she thought about the kind of apartment she'd get in Edmonton, the kind of city job. She thought, like she usually did, about the letter she'd write to Finn, in English, to the England! house, when the time came. To get him to join her, go to school like a normal kid, have friends and groceries and a black-and-white dog before it was too late, too late for them both to be just normal.

And then the month was over and Martha came home and Aidan left. They met in the ferry lot, she coming off, he getting on. They spoke but did not kiss, they leaned in but did not hug, both holding their bags, their things, as Finn watched and waited to the sound of the car idling, the seabirds circling, the ferry engine humming long and low.

When Finn and his mother got home, she went upstairs. For a nap, she said. A quick nap. To reset my dreams, she said, even though that didn't make sense because dreams aren't something you can control, not like that.

It was still light out, still the middle of the afternoon. Because it was easier than negotiating his way back into his own now-too-small boots, Finn slipped into his mother's, pulled on Cora's sweater and went out again. He sang into the wind as he walked.

Oh the bog flower waltz is the waltz of the hungry

And it started to rain,

Yes the bog flower waltz is the waltz of this land

but not heavy.

As the wind blows west and the fog rises lonely

At the Italy! house he updated his lists, added all the batteries and everything else to Things Taken, and added Birds (terns, petrels, gulls, guillemots) and Sophie McKinley to Things Back. He put the lists back up on the Trevi Fountain and surveyed the room. He had everything, everything he needed, sorted and ready. He had:

- five bowls of batteries, sorted by type: double As, triple As, little round watch ones, nine volts and big, heavy Ds;
- twelve flashlights, three headlamps, six bike lights, five fake candles and five little ceramic Mary and Jesus figurines that lit up when you pressed the bottom;
- two plastic Ziploc bags per light, one normal and one colored green all over on the inside with permanent marker (the lights would go inside these, waterproofed);
- thirty-one paper clips, each one hooked through a corner of one of the clear bags, each one attached to a length of fish twine;
- thirty-one floats, tied around and attached to the paper clips with the twine (these were just whatever Finn could find that passed a floating test in the Beggs' bathtub: a beach ball, an octopus bath toy, a plastic bottle, a bundle of corks);
- thirty-one pink, white and green plastic flags from a hundred-pack that Finn found in the Doyles' shed (they were duct-taped upright to each float and stuck up and out about twelve inches).

And that was that. Lights in bags marked by floating flags. Simple. Ready. He counted everything one more time, then turned off the lights and put on his boots and went home, to dinner, to his mother.

Martha put down her things and lay down on the bed she shared with Aidan. She lay on her back, facing straight up at the white-painted beams of the ceiling. Her eyes were open. She didn't sleep, she didn't move, she just lay there, staring up. She heard the front door open, heard Finn go out. Then, after an hour or two, she heard the front door open again and Finn come back, his footsteps moving into the kitchen, so she got up. She looked at herself in the mirror, unclenched her hand and went downstairs.

They had toast with beans for dinner, microwaved so it got soggy and sauce leaked through the middle of the bread. Martha was quiet. Each scrape of their knives against the plates, each gust of wind against the window, was the loudest thing.

Once Finn had eaten half, exactly half, of his portion, he asked, Will we go on a field trip this month, Mom? Field-trip day?

Martha was looking down at her beans, at her fork. A drop of red sauce dripped onto her plate. She let it fall before answering. No, Finn, not tomorrow.

Maybe?

Maybe.

That night the fog pushed in and whited out the sunset, the stars, the moon. It pushed under the door gaps, through cracks in the floors and windows. It rose up and covered the Eiffel Tower in France!, the tea ceremony in Japan!, the piñatas in Mexico!, the mermaids in Atlantis. It flowed up the stairs and rose around Finn where he was sleeping and around Martha who wasn't, pulled through her hair like breath, pressed against her head like memory.

•   •   •

By morning the sky had cleared and the light was yellow and simple on the water. Finn watched it out of Cora's bedroom window in
his pajamas. He slept there most nights now. Then he got dressed
and went downstairs to where his mother was drinking coffee in the
kitchen and said, I'd like to take my boat out today.

Martha took a swallow of coffee and said, OK. And then, Eat
first?

OK, said Finn, even though they were out of cereal again, out of
milk again.

Finn took a mug with a green and red moose on it, probably a Christmas mug though they used it year-round, and, before going to Italy!,
boulder-jumped inland to find and pick bakeapple for Mrs. Callaghan, in case she was as hungry as he was. They were still tricky
to find, still small and red and hard, but after an hour or so he had
enough to look all right, there in the mug. He held one hand over the
top as he hopped back, the berries bumping back and forth against his
palm. At the Beggs', Finn packed two flashlights and one Mary, along
with their bags and floats and flags, in his backpack, all that would fit,
and put the backpack on. Then he closed and latched up his accordion
and put it on his front. It didn't look like rain, or heavy mist or hail,
but he brought an empty garbage bag too, an emergency accordion
raincoat, just in case. Accordion on his front, backpack on his back,
garbage bag in one hand and berries in the other, Finn used the door
instead of the window, walking out and down to his boat as the birds
flew up and around and around.

Oh yes, said Mrs. Callaghan. I thought you'd come today.

You did?

Well, the fog last night told me you might.

It did?

Yes.

Oh. Did it tell you anything else?

I didn't get to be this old by telling other people's secrets, she said. She stepped aside and opened the doorway up to him. Come in, come in anyway. You're loaded down like a potato horse, and we've got plenty of work to do.

They ate the berries sprinkled over with dark brown sugar to ease their early sourness.

After the lesson, on his way back from Mrs. Callaghan's, Finn sank his first three lights. Then he dropped off his accordion in Italy!, got three more lights-in-bags, rowed them out and sank them too. And again and again. He had a map he'd drawn of where the things were, the cars and trucks and bikes and chairs. He dropped lights down and into each, glowing green down and down and down among the strollers and van and broken boats. The color of safety, the color of home.

Snow had fallen
Snow on snow
Snow on snow on snow

Again, Cora made her rounds. One last round for the day.

   She's like the sunshine
   On the lee shore

No bears. She fed Giancarlo and Giannina, put them to bed. Visited Darwiish. Deal of the Day!, ready already.

She read some of a Russian–English dictionary and took a few notes, собаки = dogs, скоро = soon, вот = here, and then went to bed. Tomorrow was another payday. She thought of each like a square forward on a snakes and ladders game. Just keep moving forward, look for ladders, don't be tempted by snakes.

She fell asleep around ten o'clock.

The boys came at midnight, like they sometimes did. They banged on her door. They yelled, D-ON! D-OON! Come out with us! They started Giancarlo and Giannina barking. D-ON! D-OON! Come out, come out with us! They barked along with the dogs. Or let us in with you! We love you, Don! We love you! Shaking the door handle, howling. Cora, though awake, kept her eyes closed and thought about the board game, counted how many squares left. Counted and counted again. They yelled and barked and howled and she counted how many squares left.

Once it was quiet, no voices or footsteps, Cora got up, pulled on her oversized Deep Wood Energy and Industry T-shirt and her coat and her boots with no socks and went out to calm the dogs. Before leaving, she slipped the Russian dictionary into her coat pocket. There was already paper in there, and a pencil. She opened Giancarlo and Giannina's kennel, got in and closed the door after her. She sat between the two dogs and stroked their heads in turn and read out loud to them. Собаки здесь скоро, мама папа брат. When they were breathing regularly again, asleep or almost asleep, Cora flattened out a piece of paper on the cement floor and, with the help of the dictionary, wrote to Finn in slow, careful characters.

When she was finished, both dogs were fully asleep and she had to lift Giancarlo's head from her lap to get up. She locked them both in and walked back toward her own room. The sound of the night work mixed with the sound of the night birds and Cora looked out toward the edge of camp, toward the woods. Bears were just as likely to come at night, she knew, she'd been told, but she saw nothing but the darkness of trees and the darker darkness between them.

Sophie held the letter out in front of her. She turned it over. Sometimes foreign ones had the return address on the back, like the ones she wasn't supposed to deliver to officially off-grid Mrs. Callaghan but did anyway, but there was nothing on the back of this one. She turned it around again. There it was, in cheap ballpoint: her own address, her own house, but not her name, or even her parents'. The letter was addressed to Finn, Finnigan Connor, at her house. Finn was getting letters at all sorts of weird places lately, houses that weren't his, and that was fine, she delivered them as addressed, that was her job as stipulated in her Postal Oath, but this was different. For this one, she would have to wait for Finn to come to her, to her house; she'd have to hold on to the letter herself, and that didn't seem right. The Postal Oath was fuzzy on this, but it didn't seem very ethical, her keeping something that was his. It wasn't far to the Connors', if she treated it as speed training she could run over and back in less than ten minutes. The reposting of the letter would be like the passing of a baton; she probably wouldn't even see Martha, or be seen by her, she would just be doing her job.

Martha drank her coffee slowly, hot to warm to cool, then made another cup and drank that. Then she heard the noise of the mail slot opening and closing, something falling onto the mat.

She finished the second coffee and looked down at the still-dark ring in the bottom of the mug, the always-dark ring. You need to stand up, she whispered, into the ring. Stand up, get the post. She stayed for ten more seconds, then thirty, she scratched at the ring, it stayed dark. She turned the mug upside down onto the table, put her hands on either side of it and pushed herself up, away. She walked the fifteen steps to the mail. The letter had landed facedown. She bent, turned it over.

She dialed without stopping to think, without sitting or putting down the letter.

Hello, Bear Falls Energy where safety is chief and quality is standard, this is the central desk, how can I help you?

It's Martha Connor. I need to speak to Aidan Connor right now. I know he's at work, but I need to speak to him now.

Right now?

Right now.

Martha? Aidan's breath was heavy, like he'd just been running or lifting.

She's alive, said Martha. She's alive, she's alive, she's alive.

She's— said Aidan. His voice was quiet, was barely there at all.

She's alive, said Martha.

She's alive, said Aidan.

Martha told him about the letter. It's her writing, I know it is, she said.

And it's to Finn? asked Aidan.

It's to our Finn and it's our Cora's writing, said Martha.

The address, Finn's name, the McKinley house, it was all Cora. The writing as familiar to Martha as a picture, as a voice.

Did you open it?

Finn's not home. He's at accordion.

You can open it, Martha, said Aidan. It's allowed now. It's OK.

Martha made a small tear, the upper right-hand corner. OK, she said. Yes. She slid her finger along and the cheap glue gave way like nothing, like water. The paper inside was small, was ripped, and was covered over in symbols from somewhere else, a language beautiful and illegible. The envelope fell down, onto the floor. Oh, said Martha. It's not English, Aidan. It's . . . far away. She's far away.

What is it? What language?

I don't know.

You can't read it?

I can't read it.

Trucks crunched gravel behind Aidan, shouting men and machines called back and forth. The postmark, he said. Martha, what about the postmark?

Yes, said Martha. Yes, yes of course. She picked up the envelope again. Oh my God, she said.

The trucks and the shouts and Aidan. What? he said. Where?

Aidan, it's, said Martha. It's a picture of a buffalo. It's the stamp for the camps of Wood Buffalo. For the work sites. For—

For where we are, said Aidan.

For where you are, said Martha.

Oh, said Aidan.

Oh, oh, oh, said Martha.

OK, said Aidan. OK, OK, OK. We know Arthur Begg's at White Bison work camp—

And Clem Dwyer's at Blue Spruce—

And Jeannie O'Neil's at Round Mountain—

And Patrick O'Neil's at Clear Springs—

And Ali Doyle's there too, and there's the local papers too, the *Chronicle* and the *Bugler* and the local constabulary and—

Wait, wait, Aidan, wait. Martha opened drawers until she found a pen with ink and something to write on, an old flyer for a dance six years ago. OK, she said. Say them again. Say them all again. And phone numbers if you know them. I've got all afternoon, I've got all month.

Egyptian, said Finn. Or, what they speak in Egypt. He was still carrying his things, he wasn't even all the way in the door yet.

Egypt? said Martha. How do you know that?

I, said Finn, his neck hot, his fingers slippery around his accordion case's handle. We, we studied it for school.

You did?

Yes.

Can you read it?

No, he said. He stopped, his mind splitting off in all the directions things could go, all the things he could and couldn't say. I, he said. I think I could find books on the library boat, books that could help.

Translate?

Yes.

OK. OK, then, let's go there.

Why did she send it to the McKinleys'? asked Martha. They were walking to the library. She was still holding the letter, hadn't given it to him.

I don't know, said Finn.

No idea?

Maybe Cora knows Sophie's the new postwoman. Maybe she thought that'd be faster, sending it through her.

Or, maybe she didn't want us, me or Aidan, to see?

No, said Finn. No, no. The letters under his sweater and shirt were soft and thin from wear, like cotton, like skin.

Martha didn't ask anything else. She didn't ask if there were more.

They walked in silence for thirty-five steps. Then Finn said, You can tell that, from the cancellation stamp? You can tell where a person is?

You can tell where the letter was sent from, yes, yes you can.

Can you tell anything else?

When it was sent, where and when.

Anything else? Like if they've sent anything else, or . . .

No, said Martha, nothing else. But this is already so much, Finn. This already tells us so much. Alberta, Finn. Where Aidan is.

Alberta, repeated Finn.

It was Egyptian Arabic. They worked, books open on the library desks and their laps, for two hours, until they had:

Dear Finn,

My friend Darwiish boy caught fish at home says, to where you are. Is this true, Finn? It was you? Is this real?

Cora

There was no return address in any language.

Before sleep that night, Finn knelt on Cora's bed and counted the flags he could see out her window, his flags: fifteen without binoculars and thirty-one with. The horizon rippled with them, distant pink and green and white, out and out and out. Alberta, he whispered. Alberta.

Martha was on the phone most of the time now. Finn slipped in and out in the morning and evening, and sometimes in between for food or extra layers, and if she saw him she'd nod and lift her pencil in acknowledgment and keep talking.

Can you repeat those last three numbers again?

How do you spell the surname?

No, not blond, never blond. Maybe blond now?

The next thing Finn had to do was sink traps and nets, and he had to do it fast; he had to get everything done and ready before Cora came home, before they got her home. It was illegal, he knew, if he caught and kept anything, but just traps and nets should be OK. As soon as he caught something, started catching things, he would note it down, maybe take pictures for proof if he could find a camera, and then release them again. He didn't want to be a criminal. And he didn't want to kill anything. He wanted them to stay and have babies, hundreds of them, thousands of them, that would all stay too and have babies and stay alive, all of them alive. He set a trap or a net by each light, and then set five more in random locations in between because he didn't know for sure where the cars and trucks and van were and because, of all the things, old traps and nets were the easiest to get a hold of, were the one thing nobody had taken away with them.

He marked the traps and nets with balloons. They had them saved for birthdays and other celebrations in the kitchen's special occasion drawer, along with birthday candles and regular candles, and they floated pretty well and were different enough at a distance from the flags and the other floats that he could keep things straight. He marked each spot with three balloons, so there would be two back-ups in case of popping or deflating.

• • •

And, John?

...

Just keep asking. Just keep asking everyone, OK?

...

Yes, I—

...

Yes, I do, I do too.

Finn slipped by, up the stairs, unseen, out of the way, up to the other phone.

And, Martha?

Yes?

The melt is happening, finally, here, did you notice? The birds are all coming back.

They weren't yet, not when I was there.

They are now, Martha. If you get far enough out they're all you can hear. I'll take you when you're back. I'll show you.

I'd like that.

You will.

I will.

Now that everything was set and ready, Finn spent his time making the rounds, checking the traps and nets by day, nothing yet, nothing yet, with a spare pack of balloons ready in his raincoat pocket. He checked the lights in the half-dark just before sunrise or just after sunset, the bowl of spare batteries rattling against his legs on the dory floor. He wasn't supposed to be out on-water after dark, but he'd only stay until it was barely night, just enough to check the lights properly, before rowing home. His mother didn't say anything about it and so neither did he. Once a week he rowed all the way back out to Mrs. Callaghan's and she pushed his fingers with her fingers and counted one two one two and they drank Kool-Aid and sang songs that didn't have any words.

And at night, through dark bigger than anything, Mrs. Callaghan kept talking, she kept talking and talking.

(1974)

And in the evenings, after dinner, Martha and Molly would sit in front of the fire and Molly would write letters to Meredith and Minnie, and Martha would work on her project and Molly would say, What are you working on?

And Martha would say, Net, just net.

One morning, after one of those evenings, Molly took the boat out. She knew that Aidan was on-water for the next few days and that Martha would stay home to finish commissions and split wood. It was Molly's first time rowing out to Little Running by herself; she was surprised at how easy, how quick it was.

Mrs. Connor answered the door after just one knock. You must be a Murphy, she said.

How can you tell?

Just look at you.

Molly looked down, looked at herself, but didn't see what Mrs. Connor saw. Mrs. Connor, she said, I'm Molly Murphy, the youngest sister of Martha Murphy, and I've come to talk to you for a minute, if you've got it.

Well, seems I was right, then, said Mrs. Connor. She stood aside, held the door. Come in, come in of course. I've got coffee and biscuits enough to feed an army of Murphys.

They drank coffee and ate biscuits with dark berry jam from last year's crop. They talked about the rain, about the fish. And then Mrs. Connor said, Now. I suppose we should get to it. You want to talk to me about Connors, about Aidan, I suppose.

Well, I, said Molly. She swallowed a biscuit piece without chewing, dry and hard.

It's OK, said Mrs. Connor. You're not the first. There was Sophie last year. There was me thirty years before.

There was?

There was.

And . . . what did you tell her? What did they tell you?

The same thing I'll tell you. That all Connors are cheats.

All?

All. But, Molly, if you're trying to save your sister, you needn't bother. All Connors are cheats, yes, because all people are cheats. All people, Molly, she said. All of us. She stopped to pour some more coffee, refill cups.

Always?

No, said Mrs. Connor. That's just it. That's just the problem. Not always.

They both took a drink of coffee and Molly felt the biscuit piece wash away, down.

That's the problem, said Mrs. Connor.

Before Molly left, Mrs. Connor wrapped up a dozen biscuits in wax paper and handed her this with a new jar of jam. For you, she said, and your sisters.

Sister, said Molly. There are just the two of us now. Just me and Martha.

Oh, said Mrs. Connor. Of the four?

Yes, just two, said Molly.

Oh. Well, all the more for you, then, said Mrs. Connor. All the more. She stepped out the door, toward Molly and her boat. Hey, Molly Murphy?

Yes?

I hear you can play the fiddle. I hear you can play it well.

Well enough to dance to.

That's well enough for me. Molly Murphy, I would like it if you would come again sometime and teach me to play. I've got preserves and cakes enough to pay.

You have a violin?

I have my husband's. He's not coming back for it anytime soon.

You didn't—

I didn't burn everything, Molly Murphy. I burned a lot, but not everything.

OK, then. I'll come back.

Good. Next week?

Yes. Next week.

And sometimes, after they'd said and done everything their bodies and minds needed to, Aidan and Martha would row out, not far, just far enough, and lie across the hard wooden planks and hold hands across the boat and Aidan would close his eyes and Martha would look up to the pink-blue morning and they'd listen and they'd hear the mermaids, they'd hear them for real.

(1993)

Finn was on his way out to check things after dinner as usual. His mom wasn't on the phone as he passed, she was sitting next to it, just sitting there. Coffee cup on the table.

Mom? said Finn.

Yes, Finn?

How many months now, until the relocation?

Two and a bit.

Two months, eight days?

Yes, two months, eight days.

The mist was low on the water, curling around Finn's oars as he pushed through. His lights shone up green and steadfast. All were in working order except one flashlight and one Jesus. He pulled them up, opened their bags, gave them new batteries and sank them down again. He was finished and on his way home, still only some stars, still before full-dark, when he saw the berg.

Icebergs were normal this time of year, were always passing across the horizon like the big boats used to. That, Cora had explained to him when he was eight and she was twelve, is fresh water riding across salt water. I bet you didn't know that.

I did, said Finn. I did know. Even though he didn't. Even though he hadn't ever thought that ice could be salt or not salt.

Liar, said Cora.

The bergs were usually far out, distant moving mountains, though very occasionally they pushed closer in, depending on the tide and the wind and their shape. This one was one of those, was closer. It wasn't close enough to be dangerous, but it was close enough for Finn to see clear through the early night and make out its full shape, to see its packed snow and ice in stripes, and to see that there, on top of it, was something. Was a hulk of snow moving back and forth, pacing, white and solid and sleek as the berg itself. Bear, whispered Finn. Bear! He rowed back home as fast as he could.

Bear! said Martha. There hasn't been a floating bear here in years. Wow, wow! She was putting on her coat and boots. She was opening drawer after drawer, trying to find a flashlight. Oh well, she said, we'll have to trust our instincts down to the water. We know this place, right?

Right, said Finn.

Martha rowed because it was now dark. They took her boat, which had a light built into the front. She followed Finn's instructions, dodging balloons and flags, out toward the iceberg.

Geez, it's like a party out here.

Yes, those are mine.

Yours? said Martha.

Yes, said Finn. Martha didn't ask any more about it.

They got much closer than Finn had been. Got as close as they could, as close as was safe, and turned so that their headlight was facing the iceberg straight on, lighting it up like a movie screen. Up there, way above them on a stage of snow and ice, the polar bear paced back and forth, back and forth. We need to go home and call the animal rescue team, said Martha.

OK, said Finn.

But they didn't, not right away. They stayed there, just watching. Watching the bear. Huge and beautiful and alone, back and forth, back and forth.

The days went by and Finn made his rounds. Changed batteries, righted floats. Checked and rechecked traps and nets, nothing, nothing, nothing. Held his accordion across his chest and felt the bellows pull and shake. The nights went by and he leaned into Cora's quilt, listened to the rhythms in Mrs. Callaghan's voice, held the phone tight and close.

(1974)

And Aidan rowed through the heavy wakes of trawlers and pulled up half-full nets of red-gray fish and thought, for the first time in his life, that he might want to have a child someday.

And Martha worked and worked. Net and net.

And, one day, while practicing bow holds and flexible wrists, Mrs. Connor said, Molly Murphy, I'd like to introduce you to my neighbor, last house up the track. She's lived here forever; she plays beautifully, beautifully.

Fiddle? said Molly.

No, said Mrs. Connor. Accordion.

(1993)

And Cora made her rounds. Shout-sang as loud as she could. Fed her dogs, fed herself. Watched for bears, hoped for bears, nothing, nothing, nothing. Moved forward square by square.

And Aidan made his rounds. Handed out tools, gloves, directions. Spoke to Martha, watched the sky, slept alone on a narrow single cot. Showed Cora's picture to each new hire, nothing, nothing, nothing. Stood on the deck of the ferry, wind over everything.

And Martha made her rounds. Phoning, answering the phone. Another relative, another officer, a friend, a husband, a lover. Waiting, listening, waiting for news.

Nothing,

nothing,

nothing.

Drove to the ferry lot and waited.

There, said Martha. There it is.

They watched the ferry draw up, like slow motion once it got close.

When they pulled out the metal ramp, Finn undid his seat belt and leaned up from the back seat to kiss his mother on the cheek. He wasn't allowed in the front seat until he was twelve, a rule Martha and Aidan sometimes remembered. I'll see you soon, OK? said Martha.

OK, said Finn.

And I love you, OK?

OK. Finn stayed in the car. Redid his seat belt and watched his mother roll her tall, flat suitcase out toward the boat while his father rolled his, a matching one, toward her. Watched them say things he couldn't hear, watched the wind blow his mother's hair in front of her face, his father push it back, away.

Finn went out in his boat while his father stayed in to clean the kitchen. Look at this, Aidan had said. Look at the state of this.

There were no fish in the traps, but some of them had old urchin shells rolled in between their slats. They were like decorated Easter eggs, patterned and fragile and clean. Finn collected them and kept them in rows along Cora's bedroom sill.

He ate dinner with his father in a kitchen that smelled of vinegar. Don't stay out very long tonight, said Aidan. The wind is up.

The flags pulled and whipped on their floats. Finn replaced the batteries in one bike light, one flashlight and two Jesuses. The supply bowl was getting low; maybe enough for another three weeks, maybe less. Come on, whispered Finn, into the wind. Come on, come on, come on.

Sophie McKinley came over that night and was there when Finn got in. She lifted his arms, checking for muscles like she always did. Good, good, she said. And then, God, seems like I haven't seen you for ages. You're looking good, Finn boy, looking strong. Still running?

Sometimes. Mostly rowing.

Both are good. It's all good. Arms and legs and head, right?

And heart, said Aidan, coming in from the kitchen with two cans of beer.

And heart, said Sophie. Of course.

They stayed up talking and laughing past when Finn went to bed. We'll see you tomorrow, said Aidan. Sleep well.

Yes, see you tomorrow, said Sophie. Sleep strong.

·   ·   ·

After the beer, Aidan and Sophie moved on to the whiskey she had brought. They poured it into milk cups and drank side by side on the sofa. Do you remember, said Sophie, that party, that beach party?

At the Berrys'?

Yes, at the Berrys'. God, that feels like a long time ago.

It was a long time ago.

But then again, so does a month.

Feels like a long time ago?

Yes, a month also feels like a very long time, sometimes. She turned to face him and her face was warm with firelight and his body was warm with whiskey.

Yes, it can, he said. It does. And she smelled like home, like something from a long time ago, and he leaned into her and she leaned into him and their bodies and their faces were warm with whiskey and with fire and with each other. They pulled off clothing piece by piece, careful, reaching out to help each other like parents. They drank from each other like liquor, took from each other like it was everything and the only thing that they needed.

The next morning Sophie was up and dressed before sunrise, out before Finn or Aidan or the terns or the gulls or the guillemots. She closed the door as quietly as she could, then took off running, out and on down the track, past her house, past all the other houses, onto the main road, out and on and on and on, the only moving thing for miles.

Aidan woke up, still on the couch, alone now, and went to the bathroom and closed the door and knelt down and retched.

•   •   •

Finn woke up and went to use the bathroom and found the door closed. From inside he could hear his father, hear that he was sick. He hesitated. He should do something or say something, like his father and mother did for him when he wasn't well. But he couldn't lift his father into bed and they didn't have soup mix or ginger ale. He went back to his room and put on some pants, a shirt and Cora's sweater. It was warm enough that he only needed one and his own was too tight in the arms now. He went back and stood in front of the bathroom door. His father was still in there.

OK, Dad? he asked.

OK, Finn. I'm OK, said Aidan. But he didn't come out. Didn't sound OK.

Finn went to the kitchen and got out the coffee and the SQUIDJIG-GINGGROUND! mug and a plate. He put one of the cookies Sophie had brought the night before on it. He arranged it all on the table so it looked ready, easy. Then he put on boots and went to the Beggs', where there was another bathroom he could use, with his accordion. He could practice there until his lesson later.

Once he could hear that Finn had gone out, Aidan wiped his mouth and stood up. He left the bathroom and went to the kitchen and called Martha, even though he knew she would be on-shift. It rang and rang and rang and then cut off. He sat down at the place Finn had set him. He picked up the cookie and then put it back down. He stood up and tried Martha's number again.

I'm tired today, Finn, said Mrs. Callaghan. Only airs and laments today. So Finn played slower, longer tunes and sometimes Mrs. Callaghan told him things to change and sometimes she just listened, eyes closed.

After he finished "The Ballad of the Newfoundland Black Bear," through which she had sat frozen-still, Mrs. Callaghan opened her eyes and said, The flags. The flags and the floats, those are yours, yes?

Yes.

And the traps and lights?

Yes.

I thought so, I thought so. I saw you out there, in your small boat. The lights look wonderful from up here, you know, at night. Thirty-one deep green pools. If I were a codfish I would dive down there. Jump straight off this rock.

But you're not.

No, I'm not.

They sat there for a few minutes more. Mrs. Callaghan closed her eyes again, and Finn wasn't sure whether to play more or pack up and go. Finally, when he was quite sure she was sleeping, hopefully sleeping, he latched his accordion and stood, took it off and went to get Cora's sweater.

Wait, said Mrs. Callaghan. She opened her eyes.

Finn jumped, turned. I thought you were sleeping, he said.

I wasn't sleeping, I was remembering.

Oh, said Finn. OK. Sorry. Anyway, I can just go—

No, said Mrs. Callaghan. You should put your accordion back on and close your eyes.

Me too? Why? said Finn.

It's important, said Mrs. Callaghan.

But why? said Finn. If my eyes are closed I can't see my fingers.

It doesn't count if you can see your fingers.

Why not?

Shh. Close them and play me a low C.

So he did. He picked his accordion back up and put it back on and closed his eyes and felt with his finger until he found the divot button. C.

Just C? he said

Just C, she said.

So he did, and the shaking bass of it and the pulling open of the bellows against his chest felt like . . . something. Not music, but something. He exhaled.

Good, said Mrs. Callaghan. Now you can open your eyes.

Finn did. Mrs. Callaghan was right in front of him. Her eyes were still closed. That was easy, right? she said.

Yes, said Finn.

Right, now play a song that way. Close your eyes again and play a whole song.

Without opening them once?

Without opening them once.

So Finn closed his eyes again and played a song, a whole song, without opening them. He could hear Mrs. Callaghan breathing in the rests. When he finished she sighed and said, Yes, exactly. Then she asked if he'd like a drink before rowing back home again.

Grape Kool-Aid, said Finn, taking the accordion back off again, putting it back in its case, pulling the worn black garbage bag back over the case. Please. Thanks.

She brought it out in mugs, slowly, shakily, one red with small dogs all over it, one orange with PALS written big and white across the front. Finn took PALS. Mrs. Callaghan took the red dogs and, as she carefully, one-handedly, lowered herself back down onto the sofa, said, The thing is, Finn, when you can't see you can hear. You can hear more; you can hear as strong as seeing. Or, even stronger.

Finn balanced his mug on top of his now-waterproofed accordion and sat down on the floor beside it, cross-legged. That's why I played with closed eyes?

That's why. And that's why the sailors and explorers, the ones that came here, that ran and hid and stayed, that's why they sang.

They sang?

Yes.

Because they were blind?

No. Well, maybe some of them were, maybe a couple, but mostly no. Mrs. Callaghan took a drink of Kool-Aid, her lips soft-purple with it. No, she continued, it's because they were homesick. Even though they wanted to be here, needed to be here in this new place, they were still homesick; it couldn't be helped.

I don't—

They didn't have cameras then, so they didn't have photos of home, of where they were from. And most sailors and explorers were rubbish at painting, that's why they were sailors and explorers, not painters, so the only, the best, way for them to remember home was through singing, through the songs and tunes they knew from home. When they were homesick, when they needed to remember where they were from, they could sing to see, to remember. They could close their eyes to block out where they were, and sing and remember where they used to be.

Even if they were hiding? Even if they were trying to be sneaky and quiet to escape their captains, like you said?

Even then, especially then. They'd be most homesick then.

But wouldn't they get caught? Wouldn't the captains hear the singing and follow it to the caves or your house or wherever and catch them? . . . Unless no one could hear because of the wind?

Oh no, they'd hear. They'd hear. The wind would push the singing out to them and they'd hear and they'd sing along. After all, they were homesick too.

They wouldn't go try and catch them?

No. No, they never would. Of course they never would.

But why? Why not?

Because singing together makes you allies. Automatically. Always. Even if you're enemies, normally, or far apart, or both. So they would hear and would sing or hum or play fiddle or accordion or guitar and all remember together. Every new voice would make a bigger, better picture of home, filling in some gaps, bits they might forget alone. So, no, they wouldn't go catch them, they'd sing along, all together, sing and sing until morning.

And then?

And then they'd go back to whatever they were doing, hiding or searching.

Back to eyes open.

Yes, back to eyes open.

Finn blinked. Eyes closed, then open. He looked around the room. Fireplace, sofa, Mrs. Callaghan, mugs, accordions, music books. Mrs. Callaghan? he asked. Would they sing the same songs we play?

Mostly, yes.

So we're learning homesick songs?

All songs are homesick songs, Finn.

Even the happy ones?

Especially the happy ones.

Before he left, sweater on, accordion on his back, Mrs. Callaghan said, Any fish yet, Finn?

Not yet.

OK. Well. Don't forget St. Patrick.

And the snakes?

And the long sound, the low sound.

Finn balled his fists around the ends of his sleeves, of Cora's sweater sleeves, squeezed his hands into them. Mrs. Callaghan?

Yes?

Do you think something like that could work in opposite? Like, instead of driving all of something away, that you could call something back like that, with a long sound, a low sound?

I don't know. Maybe you could.

Maybe we could.

Maybe we could.

Finally, finally, Martha got off-shift. Her first one since coming back, a night shift. The early north Alberta sun was already up as she walked back to her room, to bed. Her arms and legs and head and eyes were heavy for sleep, but the air and sky were light. The light here, she thought, was so clear. Was a whole different kind of light.

There was a note from John on her floor, slipped under her door. She didn't have a chance to unfold it before the phone rang. Who would call, she thought, who would call at this hour? But then she remembered, this hour wasn't any hour. Was just regular morning, she was the one backward, on the wrong side of time.

Hello? she said. She lay down on her bed to answer, on her back, facing the white temporary ceiling; she leaned into the phone like a pillow.

Martha, said the voice on the other end. Said Aidan, Martha. He sounded sick, sounded small.

Aidan?

Six months is too long, Martha. It's too, too long. His voice stopped in a dry, empty cough.

She waited for him.

All Connors are cheats, he said. All of us.

Martha's heart beat up through her chest, her neck, her mouth, the backs of her eyes. All of us, he said.

Oh, Aidan, she said.

All, he said.

No, Aidan, no, she said. Not just Connors. Not just you. All of us, all of us.

They both held the line, not hanging up, not saying anything. On her end he could hear the call of men, the growl and purr of machinery. On his end she could hear the wind and the waves and the wind and the waves and nothing else. They listened together, they breathed together.

I'm going to come home early, said Martha. I'm going to call the last week off sick and come home and you'll be home and Finn will be home and I'll be home and we'll pack up. We'll pack up, all together. And then, we'll all come here, and we'll all look for Cora together and we'll find her and all be here, all of us.

All of us, said Aidan.

All of us, said Martha.

Before falling asleep, Martha pulled the cradle of the phone over to her, dragging the cords out from the wall, up over the small plywood desk, onto the bed. She hung the receiver up and pulled the whole thing close, up against her chest, curling her body toward it.

Finn rowed straight back to the Italy! house. He went to the window and pushed his accordion through, then climbed in himself. He got *Can You Hear What I Hear? Animals and ESP* and turned to page eighty-six:

> *Fish, too, have a number of nonstandard extrasensory abilities.*
> *Enhanced use of sonar is just one example of this. In general, fish-*
> *hearing, as such, is most receptive to what we'd consider low-sounding*
> *pitches, or, beyond, to infrasonic sound. They can then use this to*
> *communicate with one another across often great expanses of seascape.*
> *Messages can vary from Danger!, to Is Anyone Looking for Love*
> *Tonight?, to All Is Well and Safe Here.*

Finn read it again. Took a pencil and underlined *fish-hearing, communicate, great expanses of seascape* and *All Is Well and Safe Here.* Underlined them again, and then again, and again.

When Martha woke again it was midafternoon, Alberta-time. She put the phone back and picked up John's note:

I'm off at 6 p.m. Come eat with me?

The sun was strong and direct through her window. She put one hand over her eyes, pulled the curtains closed.

Finn went through all the international houses looking for instruments, but apart from a recorder in Thailand! and some sleigh bells in Namibia! there weren't any. He knew the Kellys had played guitar and the Brophys pipes and fiddle and the Sullivans accordion, like him, but they were gone, all gone. People had left their cars and clothes and quilts, but they'd taken their instruments, all of them.

Instead, Finn found a letter in Russia!

Finnigan Connor

Sullivans' House

Big Running

Nfld

Canada

The writing was all shapes and backward and beautifully impossible. He went to the library boat. The Russian–English dictionary was gone so he took out Ukrainian instead, the closest-looking language he could find. He also took out *The Intermediate Undergraduate's Guide to Acoustical Physics: Theory and Practice*. He repeated Mrs. Callaghan's phrase to himself on his walk home. Maybe I could. Maybe we could.

John was already seated, already had his pasta and bun and salad and water. He was wearing corduroys and a buttoned shirt. He had dressed up. He waved when he saw Martha enter the cafeteria, then stood and waved again.

I'm sorry, he said. I didn't know if you would come. I would have waited, but I didn't know.

It was fifteen minutes past six.

I'm sorry, said Martha. Let's go outside, let's eat outside.

But you don't have any food.

I'm not hungry yet. Let's go outside, still.

They sat on a bench outside the cafeteria block. All around was noise and work and movement.

Your hand, said John.

Martha looked down at it, didn't unclench. I'm sorry, she said again. John, I'm so sorry.

Sophie ran and ran and ran. She could run for hours when she wanted, could run for days. She stopped and ate tart, early berries. She drank water from the flask she always had on her, a curved silver hip flask she tucked in her high socks. She ran. She ran until she was back where she had started on the one circular island road, then picked up and started again.

There was a different camp where they needed a new site-welder. A camp where John could get work, fifty miles northwest. More forest, more oil, more work, he said. It's all the same, here or there or there or there. It's all the same.

What's it called? asked Martha.

Will you visit, or call, or write?

No.

Deep Wood, he said. It's called Deep Wood.

I could go, she said. I could go instead.

No, he said. I will. I'll go. I want to.

The second time Sophie came around the island, back to the start, she found Aidan there, out standing by the road. She slowed for him, stopped. Breathing hard, hands on her knees.

Not again, Sophie, he said. OK? Not again.

I know, she said. She straightened up. I know. Took a big breath like she was about to jump into water and started again, running.

Dear Finn,

Russian or Ukrainian, that bit was easy, was always the same,

I think I'll be ready, have come soon. Soon.

Love,
Cora sister

John unpacked and showered and read through the Deep Wood Welcome Pack and Safety Guidelines and still had three hours until he was due to start his first shift at the new camp, so he left. He made his way north and west and north and west and north, away from the noise and light, until he came to the camp boundary and woods beyond. He kept walking, over the fence, into the trees, over logs and roots and brush, pushing through branches that slapped back after him, no paths here, away from the site. He was still in his good clothes; his corduroys and the good shirt he had worn to meet his new bosses now had burrs sticking along their edges and little streaks of moisture and dark from branches and sap and dirt. He kept walking and the trees thickened and their shade spread until all signs of the site, all sound and light and vibration, were gone. John turned one way, and then another and another until he was sure, totally sure, that he had no idea how to get back. Good, he said to no one. Good. He found a big rock and sat on it and stared out through the trees and trees and thought, I could stay here, I could just stay here.

I loved my love

sang Cora, through the light, through the trees.

But my love is no more

She was almost at the furthest northwest point of their north-western site.

Nor have I wings

She kicked a rock in front of her, Giannina chased it. Giancarlo didn't,

With which to fly

instead he stopped. Barked once. Pulled the lead the wrong way, into the trees, off-site. Cora and Giannina stopped too. Bear, whispered Cora. They turned and followed where Giancarlo was leading, over the fence, into the forest, over logs and roots and brush, no paths here, away from the site.

John heard something, heard the brush of movement. Bear, he thought.
But he didn't go; he didn't move.

Giancarlo led and Giannina and Cora followed. Burrs on their fur and on her clothes. Branches and sap and dirt.

The bear was getting closer, John could hear it. Could hear animal breathing. He turned his head and willed it on, looked for it in the space between trees. If he made a sound now he could scare it and it could run away. But if he waited until it was closer, was right in front of him, the bear might startle, it might attack. That would be OK, John thought. That would be good. He turned and waited, silent as the trees, the shadow, the stone.

And then he saw it. Saw her. Martha. Walking toward him. He stood up. Brushed the dirt from the front of his trousers. Martha. Martha with dogs to find him. Martha, Martha, Martha. She stepped from the shadow of a spruce into the light and, suddenly, wasn't Martha anymore. She was just a girl. Smaller than Martha, with shorter hair and less time on her face, less certainty in her step. Not Martha, just a girl. Cora, he said, this time out loud. Cora Connor.

Giannina barked, Giancarlo pulled forward and Cora turned toward the voice, toward her name, her real name. She hadn't heard it in months. Cora, she repeated. The man was sitting on a rock in a shirt buttoned all the way up. An ironed shirt, thought Cora, in the middle of the forest.

Sorry, he said, if I startled you, I mean. I mean, I'm John.

John? said Cora.

I knew your mom, said John.

Cora's chest tightened. She made sure the dogs were between them, between her and this man. And . . . she sent you here to find me? Here in the middle of nothing?

No. I work here. I live here. At Deep Wood. Now I do, anyway. And, and I was just out walking.

In that shirt?

Yes, said John. He moved over on the rock a little, careful of the lichen. Want to sit down? he said.

No, said Cora.

Please? said John.

I can talk standing up, said Cora. I can talk from here.

They're terrified, Cora. They have no idea where you are.

I'm fine.

They don't know that.

They should know that.

You should tell them. At least that.

And if I don't, you will?

I will. I have to, Cora.

Because you're a grown-up.

You are too now.

They'll make me come back.

Maybe.

They'll trace my call, they'll come and get me.

Maybe.

Cora's shoulders lifted and then dropped. I've got a plan, John. I'm moving forward, I've got a plan.

To do what?

To just be normal.

John smiled. Pulled a burr from his trousers and threw it at the ground. Nobody's just normal, Cora. Nobody. His hands smoothed the place where the burr had been. Beautiful nails. Impeccable nails. Call them tonight, Cora, he said. After your shift. Promise me you will.

Or else you will.

Yes.

Cora watched her dogs, watched Giancarlo sniffing the ground, watched Giannina watch him. She sighed. OK, she said. I will.

You promise?

I promise.

They used the sound-compass to find their way back to camp, arranging it until it sounded for due north, and then walking in the opposite direction. Your mom told me you play violin, said John, stepping over a fallen tree, then moving aside so the dogs could get over too.

I did, said Cora. But I had to sell it.

You did?

I did.

That's too bad.

I guess.

I have a sister, she used to play guitar. She would play and my mom and I would sing along.

Not anymore?

Not anymore.

They separated at the road. John had to go back and change before his shift and Cora had to finish her rounds. Before they did, Cora asked, John, where are you from?

Here.

Here?

Not far at all, pretty much here.

Wow, lucky you.

You think so?

I think so.

Cora finished her rounds, saw no bears, put the dogs in for dinner and bed, got her own food, went to her room, picked up her phone and dialed home.

Aidan was wiping down kitchen baseboards when the phone rang. He hung the rag over the side of his bucket and wiped his hands on his trousers and reached over to answer it.

Hello?

Dad?

John's new job was driving. Into town and back to the site, into town and back to the site. A trainer came with him on the first run and then left him to it. On his next run he made one extra stop on his way out of town, at the Gently Used Pawn Shop.

She's OK, Martha, she's OK, said Aidan.

I, said Martha. I—

So you don't need to cry, she said she's OK.

So you don't need to cry either.

She's OK.

She's OK, Aidan, she's OK, she's OK, she's OK.

They wanted her home. They wanted her now. She wanted to stay. She wanted more time. So they came up with a plan. A simple plan. At the end of this work cycle, not very long, not very long at all, Cora would take the camp shuttle down to the airport. She would meet Martha there, and they'd fly and ferry home together. Not forever, just for a week or so, to talk and pack and plan and to see Finn, to get Finn. She would call home or her mom at work every night until then. She didn't tell them about the money, not yet.

Cora was leashing up the dogs the next morning when Katya, the post girl, came by. I know you never come to the main site to check your box, she said. She put a package down between them. So I thought I'd bring you this myself. She smiled and her cheeks dimpled, still flushed from her jog over. Cora smiled back.

Thanks, said Cora.

Your dogs are beautiful, said Katya. She held a hand out for Giancarlo to sniff.

You could come back tonight, said Cora, when I feed them, if you want.

I'd like that, said Katya. Her hair was the summer brown of new tree bark.

The package wasn't a proper package. Just a violin case with FOR DON (BEAR-SCARER) written on a piece of masking tape on the outside and a fully strung and ready violin on the inside. A one-line note had been tucked in, under the scroll:

Play for your mother.

Did you tell him?

I did. Right after I got off the phone with you. He was already in bed, in her room, half asleep. I told him and his face changed. He got soft again, Martha, he got young again.

You told him—

That we found Cora. That she's OK. That you're coming home together and that we'll all be here, again. That we won't be broken anymore.

And then? Did you tell him about what happens then? What we're doing next?

He was so relieved, Martha. He cried. He cried and cried and cried.

You didn't tell him.

Not yet.

We have to.

I know. Just not yet.

Soon.

I know, I know.

The camp will give us a family suite for a few weeks, until we can find a place in town. I asked. They said it was no problem. We'll find schools, find real schools. It will be good for him, for everyone.

I'll tell him, Martha. I will tell him.

It will be good, Aidan. We can make it good.

The last letter Finn found was in the Atlantis house. Completely in code, all shapes and numbers, not any language. He showed it to his dad. Didn't tell him about the others, but showed him this one, this last one. He was allowed to now, he figured, now that everyone knew where Cora was.

This, said Aidan. I know this. I've seen this. He lifted his arms, mimed an invisible fiddle, checked the letter, moved his left hand slowly, finger by finger.

The water is wide

he sang,

I can't cross o'er

It's a song, he said. She's sent you this song.

Finn worked in the Atlantis house now. The last stage in the last house. Under shining blue walls and mermaid lamps he underlined phrases and made a list:

Night-time
Directed
Low
Pulses, like a drum
Through the water. For miles. And miles and miles.

He looked at it, tapped it with his pencil. He drew a snake in the margin. A small yellow boot-snake who was blind in one eye. The point of the St. Patrick story, he thought, wasn't St. Patrick. It was him first, but then everyone else too. It wouldn't have worked without that. It wouldn't have worked without everyone.

After finishing dinner, mashed potatoes with cheese and bologna mixed in, Finn laid his fork and knife next to each other and said, Dad, you like singing, right?

More than anything, except my family.

And this place.

Yes, yes, more than anything except my family and this place.

OK, good. I think I'll need you to sing with me soon.

Of course, Finn, of course. After dinner tonight, now? I'm not doing anything; I could do that.

Not yet, said Finn. Soon, though. The first night Mom and Cora are back, I think. OK?

OK.

And then you'll have everything, Dad. You'll have everything on your list. Your family and singing and this place. All together. That'll be pretty good.

I'd be happy with just one, or two.

But you can have three. All three.

I can. Sometimes I can.

The day the support checks were delivered, Finn waited outside, on the road. He saw Sophie before she saw him and ran over to catch her. She was in her summer uniform, navy-blue shorts, no more mittens.

Hi, said Finn.

Finn! she said. Long time.

Sophie, do you play any instruments or sing?

Hm. Well, I'm decent at bodhran, and, well, everyone can sing, can't they?

Sure, sure they can.

And he tended to his nets and traps and lights. There was one Jesus and one bike light that had gone out and that he had no more batteries for. He collected urchin shells from traps, ran his fingers along their patterns and bumps, kept the complete ones and dropped the broken ones back in the water one at a time, empty, sinking moons.

Finn? called Aidan, from the kitchen to the hallway. Are you free to talk? Are you busy right now?

Finn had his arms full of shells. He was taking them up to Cora's room, more of them. All her shelves were covered now, and the windowsill and the small table beside her bed.

A bit, Dad. I've got a bike ride I need to do right after this, now that it's not raining.

OK. We'll talk later. We'll talk when you get back.

Finn biked down the long, empty ring road, riding with no hands whenever it was flat. He saw three caribou and six gulls. He rode with the wind all the way to the ferry port, to the little house that sat just before the parking lot and where Richard Peterson, the newest ferry and gas station manager, lived. The new guy from Ontario. He'd been there just a few weeks, just since Sheila McNabe finished her course and left for Vancouver. Finn had never actually met him, only knew of him through overheard phone calls between Aidan and Martha. He rang the doorbell and waited. He waited a long time. Rang it again. He was getting back on his bike when the door opened. Richard squinted through the screen like he hadn't ever seen sun or sky. YES? he said through the wind. YES WHAT?

HI, said Finn, standing back, words carried forward on wind, I'M FINN CONNOR AND I WAS WONDERING IF, MAYBE, YOU CAN PLAY ANY INSTRUMENTS OR SING AT ALL?

The next time Cora called, Finn got his dad to hold the phone up toward him while he played "The Water Is Wide" on his accordion. He made a few mistakes, but mostly he was doing it right. After the first verse, Cora said, Oh, oh, I get it! Wait, hold on . . .

They heard her leave, move around a bit and then come back. OK, she said, start again. This time she played along. Once they got to the end, Finn and Aidan heard her put the violin down, back in its case. That's it, she said. You got it.

After they hung up the phone, but before Finn had a chance to go, Aidan said, Finn, we might leave.

Finn was crouched down, doing up the buckles on his accordion case. What? he said.

We, this family, might leave. Might leave here. After Martha and Cora come home. We'll talk about it and then we might go. We'll probably go.

Finn stood up. Faced his father. His face pale behind his freckles. We still have a month, he said. The notices said. We still have a month and eight days, we—

It's time, said Aidan. It's time now, Finn.

Finn's right hand clenched. We have a month and eight days, he said. I have a plan and if, if the fish come back, then you wouldn't say we had to leave, then you wouldn't say it was time, then you would—

Finn, said Aidan, I don't think—

But what if? What if they did?

Then, yes, we wouldn't have to leave. We could work here. We could stay. But, Finn—

Then we would stay?

Then we would stay.

Finn rowed over to Mrs. Callaghan's, pushing against the wind. All his flags were straight out, whipping with it. You shouldn't have come, said Mrs. Callaghan. It's too fierce.

Do you know "The Water Is Wide"? asked Finn.

Know it? Boy, I wrote it.

Can we come and get you, in one week and one day? Can we row out and get you? You and your accordion?

Will we go into Big Running or stay on-water?

You can stay on-water.

OK, then. You come get me. I'll come.

It was Katya, finally, who convinced Cora to come out one night, to leave her room. They held hands and walked down toward the main site; Cora brought her violin.

There was a piano in the lodge lounge and a man was playing a waltz. There was beer and there were three other men playing cards and a man and a woman playing Scrabble and four more men just sat around the piano, listening. Some of them hummed along. When the pianist finished he turned around and saw Cora and said, Now you, now you play us something.

And Katya smiled and said, Yeah, go on.

So Cora did. She opened the latches and got out the fiddle and lifted it and played "She's like the Swallow."

The listening men listened and two of the card men stopped and listened too and one of them started singing and then one of the Scrabble players too, the woman. When Cora finished she was warm, warmer than the night should be up there; she put down her violin for a minute and took off her sweater while Katya got them both beers. Then Cora tightened her bow a bit more, rosined it a bit more, counted a beat of four and started up "The Northern Long-Eared Bat Reel" and the card players whooped and stood up and started dancing and Katya and the Scrabble woman danced with them and the piano player figured out the chords and joined in and Cora played every repeat and the piano player laughed and followed until, after four times around, he pulled them off into another tune, a jig, around and around until Cora pulled him off into another, and back and forth, and another and another, as more and more people came and danced and drank and sang and danced and sang and sang.

Cora kept an eye out for John all night, in among all the people coming and going and spinning and dropping, wanted to show him her violin, her playing, but he never came.

The night before Cora and Martha came home was clear. It was dark and light at the same time, it was so clear. No fog, no mist, no rain, Finn could see right out across the water, past his flags and balloons and lights, out and out and out. He went to the hall, dialed the number, pulled the phone back into Cora's room, shut the door, but stayed standing up this time, stayed where he could see out the window.

We might go, he said.

I know, said Mrs. Callaghan.

And then you'll be alone, you'll be all alone here.

I know.

You don't mind?

Someone has to wait for the fish, Finn. For when they come back.

You think they will?

Everything does, eventually.

It does?

It does.

The wind pushed against the window glass and Finn could feel it through his pajamas, against his skin; his flags pulled and pulled on the water.

Do you want the story again? asked Mrs. Callaghan.

Just the end, said Finn. Just tell me the end.

OK:

(1975)

Martha worked and worked and worked and then was done, was ready. The wind bayed outside and the fire glowed inside and she ran her fingers through what she had made and, for the first time since her parents had died, she wanted something. Even though she had heard about his father, and his father, and his father, even though she had heard that all Connors were cheats, she wanted him, as sure and strong and full as her body, she wanted this.

Aidan sat in his boat in the dark of fog and night and followed the blurred glow of moon out onto the sea and thought of Martha and thought, I can be bigger than myself, I can.

He opened the parcel out on the water. It was from Martha and she had told him to open it out there, well and far out, alone. His hands tangled in it as he ripped the brown paper away. It was a net, a new net, made for him by her. He brought it to his face, smelled her fireplace, her hands. He threw it out over the side and the floats she'd sewn in held it up and spread it out and moving across the water and it was more than just net, it was words. He read them by the star- and moon- and mist-light:

MARRY ME AIDAN CONNOR

it said, in a thousand tiny knots.

(1993)

And then? asked Finn, the phone pressed warm into his cheek, his ear.

And then everything, said Mrs. Callaghan.

Martha waited just outside the airport door. It slid open and closed as people walked by, in and out, open and closed. It was a small airport; this was the only door.

Her camp shuttle had dropped her off an hour and forty-five minutes before Cora's would arrive. She knew this, but she still waited outside. Just outside the door, her suitcase propped against an ashtray. White cigarette sand blew onto her case whenever the door opened. In and out, in and out. Her eyes stung from watching the road; she needed to remind herself to close them, to blink.

The Deep Wood shuttle arrived after one hour and fifty-two minutes. Painted green and white, it drove up the road, then into the lot, then into the loading bay, then right up to the door, right up to Martha.

Four passengers got out and off in a ballet of luggage and good-byes and then, from the back, a child. Her child.

Cora's skin was darker and her arms and legs were fuller, stronger. She looked adult; she looked grown-up. But all Martha could think, could say, was,

My Baby,

My Baby,

My Baby.

Cora had a suitcase from the same set as Martha's. She had a violin.

I'm not sorry, she said. But I'm sorry. I'm really, really sorry, Mom.

She didn't want to cry, but she did.

Cora and Martha were arriving on the afternoon ferry. Finn and Aidan got out of the car and watched the boat close the space between the water and the port, between Martha and Cora and Aidan and Finn.

Aidan lifted his daughter like she was a child, like she was a girl. She pushed her face into his shoulder and closed her eyes and let herself be small.

The car was alone in the lot, the pavement all around cracked with rock cress and sweet vetch and barrens willow, all breaking through.

Finn and Cora sat side by side in the back while their parents lifted bags into the trunk, while their mother went to their father and leaned her forehead against his forehead, while her hair fell and blew between them so both their faces were hidden, while he put his arms around her and she put her arms around him.

They drove past boulders, they drove past waterfalls.

There was no one else, said Finn. Quiet, beneath the road noise. Too quiet for their parents, up front, to hear. You left and there was no one else but me.

I was coming back for you, said Cora. I was always coming back.

There was just me and the empty houses and the empty water and nothing else. Nothing else.

I sent you letters, said Cora.

No one, said Finn.

I left you the houses.

No one, said Finn.

They drove past cairns, they drove past lichen blooms big as boats.

I've got dogs, said Cora. I've got dogs for you. Real dogs.

Out west.

Yes.

Finn put his hand up against the window. They drove past terns and gulls and guillemots. You have more freckles, he said. You're different.

Yeah? said Cora.

Yeah.

Dinner was large and long, with meat and bread and chocolate from the ferry and whiskey for the adults and a tiny bit for Cora. The wind picked up against the windows and wove around their voices, the same voices as always and the same wind as always and everything, everything, was the same, perfectly the same as always.

And then the sun began to set and Finn said,

OK, it's time now.

And Aidan and Martha and Cora said,

OK.

Aidan rowed over to Little Running and met Mrs. Callaghan, who was waiting barefoot, ankle-deep in the water, accordion on and hair swept up and back. Ready, she said.

There was a knock on the door; Finn opened it.

I'm ready, said Sophie McKinley. Richard Peterson stood beside her, holding a French horn without a case.

WE'RE READY, he said.

Aidan and Mrs. Callaghan rowed into sight just as the last bit of light left the sky. He rowed them to the shallows, then anchored and helped her out, into the water, accordion on her front like a child. Her skirts were pinned up but the water still reached them, bleeding into her dress. Aidan stood beside her, one arm out to keep her steady.

Wait, said Cora. Wait . . . She handed Sophie her violin and ran back to shore, to the house nearest them, Thailand! She came back with a telephone, dragging its wires out across the stones. They know the song too, she said. They're going to sing too. She dialed the Deep Wood lounge and Katya, ready at the other end, picked up and held the receiver out to a circle of workers, a circle of men. Cora handed the phone to Martha and took back her violin. OK, she said. Ready, I'm ready.

Finn lifted his accordion and stepped into the water, feet cold on wet stone. He walked out through the low waves and the others followed until they were all up to their knees. OK, said Finn,

and he took a deep breath

and Aidan took a deep breath

and Martha held out the phone

and Sophie lifted her beater

and Richard put his mouth to his horn

and Mrs. Callaghan pulled open her bellows

and Cora lifted her bow

and the stars shone down

and the green lights shone up

and the flags pulled and pulled in the wind

and all around them the water,

the water,

the water

was dark and empty and waiting,

ready.

Thank you

Mark, who was making beautiful nets long before
me, and who showed me the island,

and Jeff, who helped me explore it.

Lee and Jim, for a frozen, perfect cottage.

Chiara Braggion for the Italian,
Abel Selaocoe for the Afrikaans.

Iris and Fogo Island Arts for a bit of time
in the Doctor House.

The Macdowell Colony for picnic baskets and
swimming and time, time, time.

Cathryn and Annemarie, for being out there for me.

Kirsty and Jay for being readers, thinkers, helpers.
Nicole and Marysue and Juliet, for guiding, editing,
polishing, waiting.
And Ione
and Rick
and Chris
and Erin
and Charlie
and Aubrey,
my always inspiration.

AUTHOR'S NOTE REGARDING SONGS

Many of the songs referenced in this novel are traditional folk songs of mixed Old and New World lineage. For those interested, I'll take a few words to discuss some of them here.

"She's Like the Swallow" is perhaps one of Newfoundland's best-known and most celebrated songs. It was first collected in 1930 by Maud Karpeles, who described the singer she collected it from as "old and childish." It has scattered English roots (although there are some who dispute this), and is remarkable among the Newfoundland folk-song canon for two reasons. First, the melody is modal, meaning it's based on a scale that's neither major nor minor, a rare thing for songs in this region, lending it a melancholic, ancient feel. Second, it's not a fishing, boating or work song, but instead has the more Old World theme of ill-fated love.

The origins of "The Fish of the Sea" aren't entirely clear (or agreed upon). Though it most likely stems from a Scottish sea shanty, there are a number of versions, including at least one variation distinct to Canada. In traditional shanty format, the verses would be sung solo, by the "shantyman," with all the other sailors joining in together on each chorus. Shanties would often be sung while working, hauling or heaving, to keep the sailors coordinated in time with each other.

"The Water Is Wide" is probably the oldest song mentioned in this book. A folk song of Scottish and English origins, it's based on lyrics that partly date back to the 1600s. Cecil Sharp first officially published the song in his 1906 book *Folk Songs from Somerset*. It's been popular ever since, arranged, performed and recorded by an impressive array of artists, including Benjamin Britten, Bob Dylan, Barbra Streisand, Neil Young, Joan Baez, Enya and the Indigo Girls among many, many others.

ABOUT THE AUTHOR

EMMA HOOPER is an author, musician and academic. She lives in England but comes home to cross-country ski in Canada whenever she can.

Visit her online at emmahooper.ca.

OUR
HOMESICK
SONGS

Emma Hooper

This reading group guide for Our Homesick Songs *includes an introduction, discussion questions, ideas for enhancing your book club, and a Q&A with author Emma Hooper. The suggested questions are intended to help your reading group find new and interesting angles and topics for your discussion. We hope that these ideas will enrich your conversation and increase your enjoyment of the book.*

INTRODUCTION

Meet the Connor family, one of the few households left clinging to a fading way of life on the rocky, windswept shores of Newfoundland, Canada. For generations, their idyllic village sustained itself on the traditional fishing industry, but in recent years the fish have mysteriously disappeared, and with them the locals' livelihoods. Determined to hold on to their home, Connor parents Martha and Aidan alternate months away from home working at an energy plant in faraway Alberta and raising their children.

Surrounded by the wild emptiness and abandoned homes, Finn and Cora Conner spend their days exploring empty houses and holding fast to their parents' songs, histories, and epic love story. As Martha and Aidan's time apart strains their relationship, and the village continues to empty, Finn and Cora decide to take matters into their own hands in separate and unforgettable ways.

TOPICS & QUESTIONS FOR DISCUSSION

1) Newfoundland and Labrador is the easternmost province of the Canadian territory, and so geographically remote that surveyors in 1949 determined much of its residents were living a life not far off from that which they would have been living a century earlier. Have you ever heard of Newfoundland, or spent any time in remote locations such as Little Running (described in *Our Homesick Songs*)? How do you think placing characters in an isolated area shaped the story?

2) Finn and Cora are homeschooled, but take much of their curiosity into their own hands. How did being homeschooled affect their personalities? Would they have been as committed to their home and family if they had more of a structured educational system or were surrounded by other students? Do you know anyone who was homeschooled?

3) Cora creates fantastical learning environments for Finn in the abandoned houses. Did you have a favorite country or house as a child? Discuss how Finn and Cora entertained themselves and each other using the resources at their disposal. How did Martha and Aidan impact their children's education?

4) Music weaves throughout *Our Homesick Songs*—the children play instruments, Aidan's singing calls Martha to him as young lovers, and Finn especially understands how the rhythms of their folk

music is as necessary and natural to the landscape as the rising tides. How does listening to and creating music have meaning for the members of the Connor family?

5) Why does Finn believe music will call the fish back to their coast? Do you believe it worked?

6) Emma Hooper's debut novel, *Etta and Otto and Russell and James*, also follows the power of love and familial bonds across space and time. In it, octogenarian Etta sets out one day from the home she's shared with husband, Otto, in rural Saskatchewan, walking toward the coast, determined to see the ocean during her lifetime. Etta's journey and Otto's yearning at home are interlaced with the memories of their early love, wartime, and friends. If you've read *Etta and Otto And Russell and James*, do you see comparable themes in the two novels? In what ways are they similar and what ways do they differ?

7) When Martha's parents pass away, she and her sisters each inherit an item that leads them down a different path. What did each of these objects signify, and how important were they to the choices each sister made as they grew older?

8) How did the journey to see Meredith in St. John influence the relationship between Martha and Aidan? Discuss the stages of the trip. Were you ever worried they wouldn't make it?

9) Why do so many characters repeat the phrase, "All Connors are cheats"? Do you think those who voice it believe what they're saying? Why or why not? How does the saying affect Aidan?

10) Why did Mrs. Callaghan tell Finn the story of St. Patrick and the snakes? How did her storytelling impact the Connor family, and what subsequently happens in Little Running?

11) How did Martha and Aidan fare when they were working and living far from each other, their children, and their home? Where did they look for comfort, and do you think it was healthy or necessary? Have you ever been separated from your home and loved ones in a similar way? How did you cope?

12) Why do you think Cora left home? Consider all the people she encounters after doing so, including the "real" Don, who tells her "We're orphans, us . . . We gotta stick together" (page 236). Does her purpose change after being away from home and meeting new people? In what ways does Cora grow, or remain the same, during her time away from home?

13) Consider what Mrs. Callaghan means when she says, ". . . the only, the best, way for [the sailors and explorers] to remember home was through singing, through the songs and tunes they knew from home. When they were homesick, when they needed to remember where they were from, they could sing to see, to remember" (page 281). In what ways do the characters in *Our Homesick Songs* sing, or use other senses, to feel close to memories? Can you relate to this phenomenon? What helps you remember what you love?

ENHANCE YOUR BOOK CLUB

1. Music plays a large role in the lives of the Connor family, especially the traditional folk sounds of their home in Newfoundland. The folk music heritage of the Newfoundland and Labrador province is based on the Irish, English, and Cornish traditions brought to its shores by settlers centuries ago. Many of the songs are influenced by its Celtic origins and the area's strong seafaring tradition. Listen to traditional and modern Newfoundland music from artists such as Great Big Sea, Tickle Harbour, or Shanneyganock.

2. Pick your favorite destination Cora builds for Finn inspired by travel guides, or pick a city you've never been to and create your own travel spot. Look up traditional recipes, pin up pictures of landmarks, and use a translation dictionary to learn how to introduce yourself in the local language.

3. Newfoundland became the center of attention when, in the aftermath of the September 11 attacks, all commercial airlines were forced to immediately ground their planes. As a result, thirty-eight passenger planes landed at the seldom-used airport in the small town of Gander, Newfoundland and Labrador. The unexpected seven thousand stranded passengers instantly doubled the town's population, and Gander's residents shocked the world with their hospitality and kindness as they housed, fed,

clothed, and comforted the travelers for six days. The story of this small community's resilience and generosity inspired a Tony Award–winning musical *Come From Away*. Read more about the show at comefromaway.com and watch the cast perform at the Tony's here: https://www.billboard.com/video/2017-tony -awards-the-cast-of-come-from-away-performs-welcome-to -the-rock-7825787.

4. Learn to play like Finn! If you don't have an accordion of your own, download the music app on a smart device (appcordions.com) and try playing "The Water is Wide."

A CONVERSATION WITH EMMA HOOPER

Our Homesick Songs is set on the edge of the world, in a remote and quiet community. How were you inspired to set the story in Big Running? Have you spent any time in Newfoundland?

Yes, I have. My first trip was to Fogo Island, which is a small island off the bigger island of Newfoundland itself, just like the setting of the book. I went to visit a friend and to finish up a draft of the novel I was working on then, *Etta and Otto and Russell and James*.

A year later I still couldn't get the unique, beautiful, lonely, breathtaking place out of my head. My writing process always begins with setting, with a place. *Etta and Otto* began with the idea of the long, dry openness of Saskatchewan, and it was clear to me that my next book project, *A Long Sound A Low Sound*, would be inspired by the distinct, windy, foggy, bouldered, and berried setting of Fogo Island.

I went back again a year later for a longer time to undertake research, gathering all sorts of stories and songs from my wanderings around the landscape and from my newfound friends and neighbors there (including joining the Fogo Island Accordion Group for a couple festival gigs in my "other" capacity as musician).

You grew up in Alberta, on the other side of the country from where Our Homesick Songs begins, but also where Martha and Aidan journey for work. How did the geography of Canada shape your story? Do you know people who came to Alberta to find work?

I remember lots of people, workers, coming pretty much all at once, over the course of just a few years, back when I was a kid. At the time it was framed for me as a story of exciting Albertan growth; it wasn't until later that I learned the other side of the story, that all these workers coming to support our boom in industry were doing so due to the bust of their own. I had lots of friends who went "up north" to work at the camps, including a cousin who first introduced me to the real-life job of "bear scarer."

Is there one character in the novel who you identify with the most? Why or why not?

Of course there are little bits of each character that I relate to: Aidan's singing to himself for entertainment and solace, Finn's optimism, Cora's tendency to bend the rules to fit her, Martha's particular type of shy melancholy . . . but, if I was choosing just one, it might be Sophie. Although not a primary character, exactly, I really love her and definitely relate to her need to run . . . not just [as] a physical outlet; Sophie runs to process her emotional traumas. She feels most "herself" while moving. I can relate to that a lot! (I also love the Olympics.)

How was your experience writing *Our Homesick Songs* different from writing your first novel, *Etta and Otto and Russell and James*?

Longer! For two big reasons. First, with *EORJ* I was writing about places I already knew well; I didn't need to take nearly as much time for research as I did with *OHS*, which involved multiple trips to Newfoundland outports, interviews about net-making, books on codfish, etc.

Second, my first son was born in between drafts of this book, so, for a few months there, writing (and sleep) time dwindled significantly.

Where did your inspiration for Cora's crafty travel destinations come from? Do you like to travel? Are there any destinations that you wish Cora could have built for Finn?

I think Cora would have liked to build "NORTHERN ALBERTA!" for Finn after her experiences there. Talking openly with siblings, especially at that age, can be difficult; these "travel" houses are one way that Cora has found to comfortably share with her brother.

Myself, I LOVE travel. If I haven't been anywhere in about a month I start to feel very itchy-footed . . . It doesn't have to be hugely far away or exotic, but I do definitely crave the newness of travel an awful lot. I think that, for me at least, the way it makes you pay attention to detail (buildings, smells, flowers, different kinds of grocery stores) stops you from slipping into the sort of automatic living that scares me. It makes my life (seem) longer!

At one point in the novel, young Aidan thinks, "Time on land is different than time on-water." How does Aidan's experience at sea, both his livelihood and the early near-death storm, determine the kind of man he becomes?

Being at sea is a certain kind of being "in between." Though "at work" with others in sight (or their boats at least), it affords Aidan long stretches of time alone and away. I think this both scares him a little (so he sings to comfort himself and keep himself company) and calms him. It's where Aidan can go to find himself, like Sophie and her running.

In addition to being an accomplished writer, you are a musician, singer, and songwriter. How does being an artist in many fields influence your creative process?

It means I have more excuses to take breaks! As in, if I'm sick of writing I can take a break and practice some music without the guilt I'd feel if I just stopped to, say, eat some cereal.

My musical background, I think, also makes me overly sensitive to things like rhythm and white space in my writing. I can spend a long, long time staring at a sentence that's perfectly grammatically correct, but doesn't sound quite right. It certainly explains all the repetition, all the repetition.

Can you tell us a little about the kind of music in the novel? Were you drawn to the folk music of Newfoundland? Why did you have Finn and Cora play the accordion and violin?

Instead of asking why Finn and Cora play music, you might as well ask why they brush their teeth, or eat breakfast . . . I wanted to portray this culture in which music-making is as natural as conversation, just a basic part of life for everyone.

As for the music itself, originally I wanted the book to feature "authentic" Newfoundland folk music. But then, while researching, I found that there really didn't seem to be such thing as a pure "Canadian" folk song, as pretty much every tune I studied took me back, eventually, to somewhere else: Ireland, Scotland, Germany, etc. (Unfortunately, and not without controversy, little to nothing remains in our national canon of any aboriginal music.) Music, I realized, and musical identity, isn't a static thing, isn't solid, but is, like us, a hodgepodge of what, and where, came before.

There's a point in my book where one character tells another, "All songs are homesick songs," spelling out, in essence, this lesson I came to learn about sound, music, history, and heritage. Canada may only be 150 years old, but our heritage is much, much older than that. It has been sung and shared across oceans and generations over and over and over again. I am Canadian, but really that means I am Irish. I am Scottish. I am German and Aboriginal and Romanian. My self, my music, pulls out and back forever, to other, older times and places. All my songs are homesick songs. All everyone's songs are.

The fish disappear, Cora has Giancarlo and Giannina, Martha and Finn see the floating polar bear. What role did you mean animals to play in *Our Homesick Songs*?

Looking back, I realize that animals function as signalers a lot in this story, whether quite literally, like Cora's dogs listening for and signaling the presence of bears, of danger, or more metaphorically, like the loss of fish signaling the loss of a way of life, or the polar bear as a suggestion of a larger ecologically problem.

We see the characters in *Our Homesick Songs* through many stages of their lives: from Martha as a sister, orphan, wife, and mother, to Aidan as a fisherman and father, and the children growing older—Cora "becoming" Don, and more. What was important about capturing these various identities in the Connor family, and how did they evolve?

One of the things Aidan eventually, and crucially discovers, is that "who you are," some core, unchangeable essence, isn't coded unchangeably into a person, and that, yes, while there is the possibility of all Connors being cheats, it's no more or less than that of anyone. He has more control over his identity and "fate" than he thought. This fluidity and malleability of identity is a core theme I wanted to explore. (Both in the book and in life in general.)

Did you grow up with a storytelling tradition? Are there any traditions present in the novel which take inspiration from your own childhood?

Well, as a child just starting lessons, I did have a cardboard violin with strings drawn on it before given the chance to graduate to a real one! The tradition of shared and community music was definitely something I grew up with (and am grateful for).

I think the tradition of family-lore storytelling is something we almost all have experience with, though maybe not something we think of in those terms very often. We humans are natural and really good storytellers. The stories your parents tell you about when you were a baby, or when they met, or the story of your grandparents lives as you understand them . . . they all contain little bits of fiction, of rounding off of rough edges and blurring of details over time as little by little they turn from lived experience into narrative, into better stories.

Are you working on anything new you can share with readers?

I am! I just gave birth to a second son, so there's that. And also, I've recently started on a novel not set in Canada (!) that features things like fight scenes and lots of running around. It's all pretty scary and exciting.